oxygen

oxygen

Andrew Miller

HARCOURT, INC.
New York   San Diego   London

www.HarcourtBooks.com

All characters in this novel are fictitious and any resemblance
to real persons, living or dead, is purely coincidental.

First published in England by Hodder and Stoughton.

From *Duino Elegies* by Rainer Maria Rilke, translated by David Young.
Copyright © 1978 by W. W. Norton & Inc.
Used by permission of W. W. Norton & Company, Inc.

Library of Congress Cataloging-in-Publication Data
Miller, Andrew, 1961–
Oxygen/Andrew Miller.—1st ed.
p.   cm.
ISBN 0-15-100721-7
1. Terminally ill parents—Fiction. 2. Hungarians—France—Fiction. 3. Mothers
and sons—Fiction. 4. Paris (France)—Fiction. 5. Translators—Fiction.
6. Dramatists—Fiction. 7. England—Fiction. 8. Actors—Fiction. I. Title.
PR6063.I3564 O99 2002
823'.914—dc21   2001051459

First U.S. edition
A C E G I K J H F D B

Printed in the United States of America

This book is dedicated to the memory of my old teachers, Malcolm Bradbury and Lorna Sage.

oxygen

The Dream Catcher, an artifact made on the reservations of Native Americans and sold in the souvenir shops there for little money, was a circle the size of a man's palm, formed from some pliant wood and then banded with a leather thong. Across the centre of the circle was a weave of plastic thread like a spider's web, and at the heart, like the spider itself, a single green bead. Larry Valentine had bought one for his daughter Ella at a place called the Indian Bear Meat Den while filming in North Carolina on what turned out to be one of his last shows with *Sun Valley General*. It hung now at the window of her bedroom where, according to the explanatory leaflet, it would snag the bad dreams in its web, while the good ones, dreams of cloudless mornings, of days out at Muir beach, of friendly doctors and loving fathers, would reach the bed where she slept.

He gazed down at her, feeling enormous in this room of little things. She had a single cotton sheet over her and lay beneath it in a hot sprawl, her mouth partly open, pulling the summer-night air in a hiss over her tongue. Wisps of hair were scattered like cuttings around her face, and her eyes were shut tight as though sleep were something to be concentrated on, like colouring and not going over the black lines, or the sums she did with an unwieldy pencil in her school book.

He started the search without much expectation of success, though his record of finds was still superior to Kirsty's, a fact that subtly needled her, as though it somehow implied he knew their daughter better than she did, that he had insights she didn't share. He began with the jeans Ella had been wearing that afternoon, turning out the pockets but finding only scraps of tissue paper, a silver nickel, a Gummy Bear. Then he eased off the head of a chubby-limbed doll, one of those which, when squeezed, complained that she was wet, or pleaded hunger, or said 'I love you'. Ella had once hidden an old-world silver chain here, one that Kirsty had inherited from Grandma Friebergs, but tonight the head contained only air and a whiff of something feebly toxic, some humid residue of its manufacture adhering to the inverted features of the skull. Next, he investigated her collection of seashells, picking up each in turn and shaking it in the hope that one would rattle. None did. The music box, which he had bought for her in London, was another old hiding place, all the more cunning in that it could not be searched without sounding its own alarm. He flipped open the lid and shook it out, spilling a half-dozen pinlike notes of 'Oranges and Lemons', but nothing fell into his waiting hand. He slid open the drawers in the dresser and probed the neatly ordered knickers and vests, the bundled socks and tights, then lifted the front wall from the doll's house and used his key-ring torch to check beneath beds the size of Amex cards, and the delicate spidery dining table where he had once located his ITF cuff links, but where now there was only a wooden family in felt suits, mama, papa and two stiff children, sat before a porcelain ham like people under a spell.

He retired to the window, rubbed at the stiffness in his neck, and gazed through the weave of the Dream Catcher to where the bay lights were heaped up against the night. She was undoubtedly getting better at this. In the beginning she had not understood the necessary feints and anticipations good hiding required, but she had learned. Her hiding places had become increasingly sophisticated, even possessing a certain teasing quality that gave weight to Professor Hoffmann's theory that the 'borrowed' items were always intended to be found. This was not pilfering, a simple case of childhood kleptomania. Hoffmann had not decided on a name for it yet. He was still collecting the evidence.

He heard her turning under the sheet, and whispered, 'You awake, El?'

He padded to the bed and studied her, as though her physical form were a kind of clue: a warm, shadowy hieroglyphic. She lay now on her left side, her right arm trailing over the edge of the bed, where Rosa, the impossibly good-tempered maid from Chihuahua, had lined up the child's shoes, quaintly, according to season. He paused, looked from the girl to the shoes, then crouched down, his knees ratcheting from old cartilage problems acquired after years of pounding and twisting on the courts. He ignored the summer sandals and started with her trainers, then her school shoes, then the glossy red boots that he called wellingtons and Kirsty called galoshes. Last of all were the winter booties lined with lamb's-wool which Alice, her thoughts full of English winters, had sent for Ella's sixth birthday, but which she would have outgrown by the fall. He upended them, shook them out, then burrowed his fingers into the wool. In the pointed toe of the left boot he touched something smooth about the size of a Deroxat capsule, and with his fingertips working like pincers he disentangled it from the fleece and held it up, squinting at it against the orange glow of the window, though he knew already it was the missing ear stud, one of the pair

Kirsty had left unattended for an hour on the ledge of the bathroom sink.

It meant, of course, there would have to be another talk, one of those gently reproachful interviews of which there had been so many since the first ring had gone missing eighteen months ago; Ella perched on a chair, her feet swinging over the carpet, just the faintest hint of insolence in her eyes, as if her parents' failure to comprehend the secret purpose of the game excited in her a childish contempt. Hoffmann, $150 an hour, had cautioned Larry and Kirsty not to make these discussions in any way traumatic. 'It's a delicate matter,' he had warned them, smiling from the far side of an expanse of burnished desk, 'like pruning bonsai,' and he had gestured to his collection of tiny mutant willows that clearly thrived in the dimmed and filtered air of his office.

On the clock beside the bed, Mickey Mouse's white-gloved hand flicked to the hour. Two a.m. Ten a.m. in the UK. But despite his promise, he was too weary to call Alec now, too bone tired to deal with what he might hear. He would call tomorrow, from LA perhaps. Tomorrow would be soon enough. He picked up Ella's inhaler and shook it to check the reserves of salbutamol in the canister. Apparently there was a new and better inhaler on the market, a device called a SmartMist with a microprocessor to measure the drug intake and some other novelty that let you test the peak air flow. The researchers at UC had endorsed it. Kirsty wanted Ella to have it. Some of Ella's school-friends already had it.

One last time, before leaving to spend the remains of the night in the spare bedroom, he gazed at her. Her expression had softened. If – however distantly – she had been aware of him before, now she was gone, borne away into the labyrinth

4

of sleep, her spirit unlaced, her face astonishingly still and perfect, so that for an instant he had the panicky urge to wake her, to bring her back into the world of solid things. He leaned down, almost touching her. Then, like some tender ogre from the type of fairytale children were not supposed to read any more, he gently inhaled her breath.

NIGHTWATCH

'Thou wouldst not think how ill all's here
about my heart . . .'

Hamlet (Act v, scene ii)

1

Inside the house his father's clocks were striking the hour. Faintly, the chimes carried to where he stood in the garden, a lank young man in a summer sweater and shapeless blue trousers, wiping the lenses of his glasses with the corner of a crumpled handkerchief. He had spent the last hour with the hose watering the flower-beds and giving the ground around the younger trees a good soaking, as he had been instructed to. Now, having carefully coiled the hose, he made his way back towards the house, his progress shadowed by a cat that pushed through the stems of delphiniums and peonies and oriental poppies. At the top of the house, the light in Alice's room shone dully from between half-open curtains.

It was the dusk of his third day back at Brooklands, the house in the West Country with its grey stone walls, brown-tiled roof and rotting summerhouse, where he had spent the first eighteen years of his life. His own small flat in London was shut and locked, and his neighbour, Mr Bequa, whose clothes carried their own atmosphere of black tobacco and failed cooking, had agreed to forward the mail, though there would not be much. Bequa had even come down into the street to wave him off, and knowing where he was going and why, had done so with gestures of extravagant melancholy, – 'Goodbye, Alec friend! Good heart! Goodbye!'

Wandsworth Bridge, Parsons Green, Hammersmith. Then

west along the M4 past out-of-town superstores and fields of rape. A journey he had made so many times since Alice was first diagnosed he often completed the entire trip in a daze of inattention, startled to find himself rounding the last corner by the poultry farm, the sky ahead of him falling in luminous sheets towards the estuary and Wales. But this time, as each familiar landmark had dwindled in the rear-view mirror, then passed out of sight, it had seemed irretrievable, and carrying his suitcase into the hallway at Brooklands he had known with utter certainty that it was his last true homecoming, and that one half of his life was about to slough off like tons of earth in a landslide. For fifteen minutes he stood there surrounded by the soft weight of coats and hats, old boots, old tennis pumps, staring at the over-vivid snap on the wall by the door into the house – himself, Larry and Alice; Stephen must have taken it – arm in arm in the snowy orchard twenty years ago. And he had bowed his head, hearing from upstairs the chatter of his mother's radio and the rasping of her cough, and had wondered to himself what could possibly comfort him. Where on earth he might look for consolation or ease.

Coming from the garden, the house was entered by descending a short flight of mossy steps from the lawn to the terrace, and opening the glass doors into the kitchen. Here, by the worn mat, Alec slipped off his shoes and went through the house to the stairs, hoping that Alice would already have fallen asleep and would not need him. She had refused to have a room made up for her on the ground floor, despite everyone – Dr Brando, the visiting nurse Una O'Connell, and even Mrs Samson, the woman who for as long as Alec could remember had come in one morning a week to clean the house – saying how much better it would be, how much easier on good days to get into the garden. Wasn't there a perfectly suitable room downstairs, undisturbed for years other than by the daily swipe of sunlight across the mirror? But Alice had smiled at them all like a child made special and irreproachable by illness, and said that she was too used to the view, to the potato field, the church, the line of hills in the distance (like a boy, she once said, lying on his belly in the grass). And anyway, her bedroom had always been upstairs. It was too late to start 'rearranging the entire house'. So the subject was dropped, though for an angry moment Alec had wanted to tell her what it was like to watch her, that twenty-minute ordeal, hauling herself a step at a time towards the landing, her fingers clutching at the banister like talons.

Some measures she had agreed to. She took sit-down showers instead of baths, had a raised plastic seat on the toilet, and on Alec's last visit he had rigged up a bell, running the wire down the stairs from the bedroom and screwing the bell-housing to a beam by the kitchen door. There had even been some laughter when they tested it, Alice pressing the white knob by her bed (complaining that it sounded like the dive klaxon on a submarine) while Alec moved around the house to check the bell's range, and then went out to the garden, giving the thumbs-up to Una, who leaned dashingly from the bedroom window. But by evening, Alice had decided that the bell was 'a silly thing', and 'quite unnecessary', and she had looked at Alec as if its installation had been tactless, yet another item among the paraphernalia

11

of her sickness. More inescapable proof of her inescapable condition.

She was not asleep when he went in. She lay propped against the pillows in her nightgown and quilted robe, reading a book. The room was very warm. The heat of the sun was in the timbers of the roof, and the radiator was on high, so that everything sweated its particular smell, a stuffiness half intimate, half medical, that hung in the air like a sediment. Vases of cut flowers, some from the garden, some from friends, added a note of hothouse sweetness, and there was a perfume she sprayed as a kind of luxurious air-freshener, which masked very little, but which Alec could always taste in his mouth for an hour after leaving the room.

Cleanliness – even the illusion of it – was an obsession with her now, as though the sickness were something, some lapse in hygiene, that might be hidden behind veils of scent. For an hour each morning and evening she washed herself with catlike attention in the en-suite bathroom, the only real physical work she still did. But no soaps or night creams or lavender shower gel could entirely hide what filtered out from the disasters inside of her, though nothing would ever be quite as disturbing as that first course of chemotherapy the winter of two years ago, when she had sat wrapped in picnic rugs on the sofa in the living room, alien and wretched and smelling like a child's chemistry set. When her hair had grown again, it had sprouted brilliant white, and was now a weight of frost-coloured locks that reached to the mid-point of her back. This, she said – the one thing remaining to her she could still be vain about – was the reason she had refused more treatment when she came out of remission, and of all the people who attended on her now, it was her long-time hairdresser, Toni Cuskic, who had the greatest power to soothe. They had a new arrangement: there was no question of Alice making the twenty-minute trip into Nailsea, so once a week Toni drove out from the salon to pull her heavy brush the length of Alice's hair, while Alice tilted her face to the light, eyes shut, smiling as she listened to the gossip from the shop. Sometimes Toni brought her poodle, Miss Sissy, a show bitch with tight black curls, and Alice would stroke the animal's narrow skull and let it lick her wrists, until it grew bored of her and wondered off to sniff at some stain or savoury relic around the fringes of the bed.

'Everything all right, Mum?' He was standing just inside the door, hands in pockets, very slightly rocking on the balls of his feet.

'Fine, dear.'

'Need anything?'

She shook her head.

'Sure?'

'Thank you, dear.'

'Cup of tea?'

'No, thank you.'

'I've done the garden.'

'Good.'

'How about some hot milk?'

'No, thank you.'

'You haven't forgotten your Zopiclone?'

'No, dear, I haven't. Do try not to fuss.'

She frowned at him, the old headmistress again, bothered by some wittering pupil. A go-away look.

'I'll let you read,' he said. 'Look in later.'

She nodded, the movement triggering off a fit of coughing, but as he moved towards her (what was he going to *do*?) she waved him away and he went out, listening from the landing until she was quiet, then going slowly down the stairs, blushing from an emotion he could not quite identify.

On the wall at the bottom of the stairs, where it could not be avoided, hung the Perspex-framed double-page profile of Larry, from the US celebrity magazine *PLEASE!*. Made up mostly of photographs, the feature was entitled 'America's Favorite Valentine' (heart-shaped point over the final *i*), and showed, on the first page, an old Press Association shot of the nineteen-year-old Larry holding up his racquet to the stands after beating world number seven Eric Moberg at the French Open in 1980. Below appeared a heavier, browner Larry, leaning against a silver Jaguar in front of the Manhattan Flatiron building, dressed in the type of clothes a successful young bonds dealer might wear to the golf club, this from the time he worked for Nathan Slater's advertising circus in New York. Then there was the inevitable still from an episode of *Sun Valley*, in which Larry, white-coated and waxy-faced, was plunging defibrillators on to the chest of an attractive cardiac victim. But the largest of the photographs – filling the greater part of the right-hand page – was a family portrait of Larry and Kirsty and the three-year-old Ella gathered on a couch in their 'beautiful home in San Francisco's North Beach district'. Larry has his arm around Kirsty, who looks cute and excited, the lucky girl who landed *Sun Valley*'s 'perfect gentleman', while Ella is wedged between them, though with an expression so determinedly mournful it was not difficult to hear the pleas of the photographer (bylined as Bob Medici) – 'Can we get the little lady to smile too? How about it, huh?' But even at three, Ella had been a tough child to plead with, and ever since the picture had gone up, Mrs Samson, adjusting the angle of the frame or wiping the Perspex with her yellow duster, could not keep herself from muttering, 'Bless . . .' or 'Shame . . .', and furrowing her brow, as though the child's displeasure somehow amounted to a judgment on them all.

In the kitchen Alec took from his back pocket the piece of folded paper with columns in Una's handwriting that detailed the drugs Alice was to take, together with the times and the dosages. Antidepressants, anti-emetics, analgesics, laxatives, steroids. She had a plastic box beside the bed, its inside divided into segments – blue for the morning, orange for the afternoon and evening – but illness, fatigue, the pills themselves perhaps, had begun to create lapses, lacunae in her concentration, and on Alec's first day down, Una, sitting beside him on the not-quite-even bench outside the summer-house, had suggested that he discreetly oversee the filling and emptying of the box, and he had agreed immediately, eager for a chore that would not make him feel incompetent. Now he made a small tick on the list, picked up his leather satchel from the kitchen table, and went on to the terrace.

A pale half-moon hung in the blue of the twilight, and in some quarter of the sky the comet Hale-Bop, that vast event of ice and dust, was making its passage back towards the celestial equator. In the early spring he had often watched it from among the TV aerials on the roof of his flat, and had found it hard to believe that its great ellipse would not provoke some happening in the world, or many happenings – countless individual fates falling in an astral rain from the comet's wake – but for the moment at least the sky was unexceptional, the usual faultless machine with nothing extraordinary or dangerous happening in it.

He lit the storm lantern and looped the wire handle over a metal bracket beside the kitchen doors, for though it would not be quite dark for another hour, he liked the tang of the paraffin and the companionable hiss of the filament. He intended to work. Alcohol did not agree with him and he had never learned how to smoke. Work was his refuge, and sitting in one of the old canvas chairs he tugged the manuscript, dictionaries and marker pens from the satchel and began to read, holding the script close to his glasses, struggling at first to concentrate, his mind still snared in the room above his head where his mother lay. But at last the work drew him down into the orderly double-spaced world of the text, and under his breath he sounded the words of a language he had made half his own.

2

In the narrow kitchen of his fourth-floor apartment on rue Delambre, László Lázár was preparing a dinner of veal escalopes '*en papillote*'. It was a recipe that called both for delicacy and good timing, so he was more irritated than alarmed when one of his dinner guests, Laurence Wylie, informed him that her husband, the painter Franklin Wylie, had brought a gun with him and was waving it about in the dining room. The escalopes, tender pink, almost translucent, were laid out on the slab of the chopping board. He was about to hit them with a mallet.

'A gun? Where the hell does he get a gun from?'

'From some cop he drinks with at Le Robinet. For God's sake, László, tell him to put it away before there's an accident. He'll listen to you.'

She was standing in the doorway of the kitchen, wide-eyed, straight as a dancer, her hair held back from her face by a silver clasp. She was smoking: one of those cigarettes that come in white or almost white packets, and which to László seemed completely pointless.

'Franklin listens to nobody,' he said.

'But what if it goes off?'

'It won't.' He began to beat the first escalope. 'It's a fake. Or one of those old guns they neutralize and sell to collectors and nuts. There's a place by the Bourse that has a windowful.'

'It looks real,' she said. 'It's black.'

'Black?' He smiled. 'He's just showing off, Laurence. Trying to impress Kurt. Do you want to help me in here? I need the mushrooms sliced. And four of those shallots.'

She came into the kitchen, shrugging and pouting, then lined up her rings on the worktop and took one of the big black-handled Sabatier knives, topping and tailing the first shallot with two clean strokes.

'He's impossible now,' she said, beginning the familiar lament. 'Sits in the studio all day. Does nothing. Takes tablets but won't show me what they are. Lies to me. I don't even know if he loves me.'

'Of course he loves you. He couldn't get through a single day without you. And what do you mean he's impossible *now*? He was impossible before.'

She shook her head; a teardrop broke from her skin and splashed among the onion rings. 'I keep thinking something terrible's going to happen. Really terrible.'

László stopped his work and hugged her, the mallet in his hand still, the knife in hers.

'It's so tiring,' she said, speaking into the side of his neck. 'I always thought that when we got older things would be easier. Clearer. But it just gets more confusing.'

'Mother of Christ!' cried Franklin, shuffling into the kitchen so that the room was suddenly crowded. 'My wife is being seduced by a Hungarian invert. Unhand her, you bastard.'

László glanced at the American's hands. 'What have you done with it?' he asked.

'The Gat? Gave it to that beautiful young Aryan of yours. Any danger of a decent drink, you pinch-ass?'

'A decent drink comes with conditions,' said László, attempting to sound stern. 'You know that Karol is coming tonight. Let's just have a nice, quiet evening.'

'Karol *likes* me,' said Franklin. He opened the freezer compartment of the fridge and pulled out a bottle of Zytnia vodka. In the warm air of the kitchen the glass quickly frosted. 'Russian hooch!'

'Polish,' said László. 'Russians drink gasoline. Diesel oil.'

'Nothing wrong with diesel oil,' said Franklin, stowing the bottle in one of the pockets of his jacket. 'You can go on with my wife now. I'll shoot you later.'

'You'd miss,' said László, turning back to the chopping board. 'You'd miss for sure.'

Long-time resident of the sixth arrondissement, author of *Saying Yes, Saying No* (1962), of *Flicker* (1966), of *Sisyphus Rex* (1969, his first play in French), and thirteen other productions all well received other than by those critics of the far left or far right who found his work maddeningly uncommitted; one-time artistic director of the Théâtre Artaud in San Francisco, now part-time lecturer in Dramaturgy and Eastern European literature at the Sorbonne (Monday and Thursday afternoons), László Lázár struck the veal and recalled his first encounter with the Wylies, a night in '61 in a jazz cellar on rue St Benoît, when the woman who now sliced vegetables at his side, telling him about her insomnia and her trouble with doctors, emerged from a cloud of tobacco smoke, her hair cut short like Jean Seberg's in *A Bout de Souffle*, smiling at him as he sat at a table with a half-dozen other émigrés, pale young men with bad teeth smoking maize-paper cigarettes and drinking slowly in a doomed attempt to save money. Her smile then had told him everything important he needed to know about her: that she was kind, and as much without darkness as any human being he would ever encounter. István invited her to sit and found a chair for her, but it was László she talked to, leaning forward under the bray of the saxophones to laugh with him and listen to his thickly accented French. Fate, of course, if you believed in such things – kismet. And later that evening came a second such moment when she introduced him to a crop-haired American, a tall, loose-limbed athletic type with the steady blue stare of a Hollywood farm boy. Franklin Sherman Wylie – only five years older than László, and yet as he stood behind Laurence, his hand across the shoulder strap of her dress, his old GI shirt spattered with paint stains that he wore like medals, he seemed gifted with that same glamorous and manly confidence Péter had possessed, and which László found so lamentably absent in his own life.

As they came out into the starlit oxygen of St Germain and said their goodbyes in the narrow street, László's heart, always inflammable, ignited; but though he desired them both, it was Franklin he kissed in his dreams, a truth that Franklin soon discerned and then tolerated with an amused grace. The following week they went together to see *Krapp's Last Tape* sung by Michael Dooley at the Sarah Bernhardt Theatre, then sealed the friendship, always a delicate thing of three, in an epic night walk to Sacré Coeur, ending at first light in a bar beside Les Halles, breakfasting on pig's trotters and Alsace beer.

Such was the template. He had no idea how many other nights there had been. A hundred? Five hundred? But of all the things that happened to László in those years – and much else *did* happen: lovers of both sexes, trips to Italy, Spain and America, winters in ateliers dangerously heated with paraffin stoves, working on draft after draft of play script – those rambles with Franklin and Laurence, the mood a mix of high seriousness and high foolery, were the reason why '61 to '69, the Algerian crises to the Apollo moon landing, had for him now, looking down from the height of his fifty-ninth summer, an almost intolerable glow of nostalgia. The years before belonged to another world entirely. Cold schoolrooms. Youth parades. Speeches on the radio. His grandparents' stories of Admiral Horthy on his white horse. The seamed and weary faces of his parents, both of them doctors at the Peterffy Sandor hospital. And the revolution, of course. Sweet Budapest.

Then, as though they had been swimming farther out than they had realized, the three friends were caught up in the grim business of success. Franklin's big aerosoled canvases were bought by image-conscious banks and dealers in New York like the Wildenstein family, while László's plays, with their insistence on the futility of action, began to seem prophetic, and drew first-night crowds of the chic and famous. Laurence became a darling of the lifestyle magazines on both sides of the Atlantic ('AT HOME WITH MRS FRANKLIN WYLIE', 'LA BELLE MUSE FRANÇAISE DE FRANKLIN WYLIE'), but she exited her thirties childless and with many anxious lines on her face. That charm which had made men of all ages want to be her friend, but also to put a hand on her thigh, showed itself more fitfully as each of her husband's feebly concealed infidelities left its mark. Franklin became a specialist in rage. On his fortieth birthday, inspired by demons whose names László could only guess at, he rammed his car into the side of a tour coach full of startled though miraculously unhurt elderly Americans on the rue des Ecoles, and was only saved from the consequences by the US ambassador, who persuaded the police to view the incident as essentially artistic rather than essentially criminal. Two years later, he beat up, with no obvious provocation, the owner of a Lebanese restaurant in Belleville with whom he had long been on friendly terms. Most recently he had been fined five thousand francs for throwing his chair at a waiter in the Brasserie Lipp (a fellow with a moustache like a hussar). But for László, nothing in this catalogue had been more dismaying, more sad and perplexing, than the day he called at the apartment on rue du Deguerry to find Laurence carefully scraping dried food off the wall of the studio, the floor brilliant with smashed glass and china. It was the moment he had given up trying to understand them, for unless you had grown up beside a person from the beginning, had breathed the same air, there was too much about that life you would never be able to explain. You had to love, if you loved at all, as an act of faith, uncomprehendingly.

He seasoned the escalopes with salt and pepper and lemon juice. The big Creuset frying pan was on the gas. The butter, a creamy *demi-sel* from the butcher's where he had bought the meat, was beginning to bubble. He fried the escalopes lightly on both sides then took them out and placed them on a side dish of thick white china that had fine blue lines like little veins running beneath the glaze. He took the chopping board from Laurence, kissing her hair lightly, then sautéed the shallots and mushrooms and threw in a handful of chopped parsley. Finally, he wrapped the veal, mushrooms, parsley and onions, together with slices of ham and thinly cut Parmesan, in heart-shaped pieces of greaseproof paper that he had carefully buttered with his fingertips. When he opened the oven door the heat broke over his face in a gentle wave. He placed the parcels on the middle shelf and shut the door, leaving butter prints on the steel handle.

'Twenty minutes,' he said.

'I'm OK now,' said Laurence, brushing a lock of hair from her brow with the heel of her palm.

'Good,' said László. 'We're too old to be miserable.'

Just then, the gun went off.

3

Alice lay with her head propped on a nest of pillows, dabbing at her eyes with a little ball of pink tissue paper. She did not know why she was crying, why now, specifically, though she had felt obscurely upset after her little conversation with Alec. He had been interfering, of course, standing at the end of her bed, peering through his glasses, his 'specs', pretending to be some kind of doctor perhaps. But she had been rude to him and now she was sorry. Unless the drugs were to blame. How could she tell? How could she know what was her, the old Alice, and what was some kind of toxic side effect? Is this me? she thought. What am I now?

She pushed the tissue into the sleeve of her nightgown and felt around on the eiderdown for her book, an old 'Library of Classics' edition of *The Black Tulip*. It was hard now to find something that didn't immediately wear her out or just seem too frivolous to spend time on. *Livre: quel qu'il soit, toujours trop long.* And people were forever giving her books, as though cancer were a sort of dull cruise for which she needed some distraction. A pastime. She chose the short books and the books she knew from years ago, and they helped a bit, if only because they made her tired in a more interesting way than most things did.

Una had offered to get some of those talking books. Derek Jacobi reading *Great Expectations*, that sort of thing. But listening wasn't the same as reading. Not as intimate. And there was nothing wrong with her eyes. Her *eyes* were among the few things left to her that worked perfectly. Like her hair, which went on growing as if it hadn't the slightest suspicion of what was happening in the rest of her body. She needed to speak to Una about the medication. The painkillers were not killing any more, and the stuff she was on now just constipated her, something she detested. She wanted the next level. Nepenthe? Or there was Oromorph, which she had been told tasted like whisky. That might do. But perhaps it would be wiser to speak directly to Brando. He was the power and the glory, the last word in it all. And he had promised to look in before the end of the week. Sit on the bed and chat. Then an odd minute or two of staring at the ceiling while he touched her chest and neck, saying how he hoped his hands weren't cold, which they never were. Secret confab with Una downstairs. Milligrams of this, millilitres of that. Update the prognosis. Leave.

How had they managed it in the old days? In Dumas' time? A maid tiptoeing out of the door with a chamber pot. Pomanders to cover the stinks. The doctors and apothecaries bringing their rubbish. Numbing people was an art form now. There were pain specialists in pain laboratories, and the World Health people had created an analgesic 'ladder' so that you were never just in pain, plain and simple. She had to keep a record for Una in a little red 'Silverstone' notebook. Sharp. A dull ache. Jabs. Waves. She had awarded herself seven once. Ten meant the worst you could imagine. You had to keep ten in reserve. Then, if you were lucky, they did for you, like Cousin Rose at Bransgore, a tumour the size of a football in her stomach, taking a syrup called Brompton's cocktail and dying like a seventeen-year-old dope fiend, Lord knows what gurning at her from the shadows. But that was years ago. It would be much neater now. Some harmless-looking tablet you could swallow with a sip of tea. Something they kept in a special container, like a monstrance, in a cupboard to which Brando had the key.

Or would they force her to go on? Make her live until she was an utter stranger to herself? She glanced across at the pillbox on the bedside table, its segments like the chambers of a gun. If she were to take a whole week's pills in one go, with, say, a large Scotch, would that do for her? Could she be sure of it? Nights were the worst, of course. Days she could still endure, despite the occasional snap of temper, those moments when she thought why bother, why go on if going on just meant more of *this*. She knew now what turning your face to the wall meant, and it tempted her, saying no to the fag-end of life, yes to oblivion. If that's what it was. Oblivion. But not quite yet. There were still good times. Little unexpected pleasures. A card from an old friend. The *greenness* of grass. Some nonsense on the radio that made her laugh. Even the sound of Mrs Samson singing to herself in the kitchen, a fifty-year-old woman singing like a girl. You couldn't explain it to people without sounding gaga. But when the light began to fail, however lovely the evening, she became nervous and plucked at herself. Drawing the curtains didn't help. Night thickened behind them, pressing at the glass like floodwater.

*   *   *

She opened the book, wondering if another page might tempt her to sleep. It was such a delicate little book, hardly bigger than her hand. Dark blue binding coming unstuck at the spine. Very fine paper – wartime paper – that tore if you turned the page too quickly. Her father had given it to her. Desmond Wilcox. Captain. And because he had not written an inscription she had done it herself, in black ink, on the page opposite a picture of Rosa showing Cornelius the precious tulip at his prison door.

For Alice from Daddy. April 29 1953.

He had bought it on one of his business trips. In Bath perhaps, or Wells, or Salisbury. There *were* businesses once. Gravel. Irrigation pumps. Even some scheme to do with growing mushrooms in an old barracks near Chard. But she was not very old before she understood that 'business' was mostly a euphemism for taking off on the motorbike, a machine like the skeleton of a greyhound, oily black, impossibly loud, pouring smoke like a bonfire when he started it. She had a memory of him – though in fact it was the memory of a photograph – sitting astride the motorbike on the drive, leather jacket, old parachute boots, goggles that made him look like the Baron von Richthofen. Never said when he was coming back. Hours. Days. Just her and her mother in the house, listening. On a still day you could hear the engine all the way to West Lavington.

Had he ever come home without something for her? Some little parcel thrust into one of the pockets of his jacket, a peek of brown paper, the loop of a white string bow? Then handing it to her as though it were worthless, something picked up on the way. Never waited to be thanked. Hated fussing. Just gave her the present and went out to pull weeds, or mend the seed boxes, or put creosote on the fencing, or any of those numberless, endless little jobs that went on, painstakingly, year after year, until suddenly, one day, they didn't.

'*Well, then, on the 20th of August, 1672, as we have already stated at the beginning of this chapter, the whole town was crowding towards the Buitenhof, to witness the departure of Cornelius De Witte from prison, as he was going to exile . . .*'

She was four when he went to the war and she saw him twice before it was over. A man in khaki who gave her bars of Cadbury's chocolate in wax-paper wrappers. When he came back for good he was a hero. Tunisia, Sicily, Arnhem. Especially Arnhem. Above all, Arnhem. Second Battalion the Parachute Regiment. One of the sixteen who got out. Won his DSO there rescuing his sergeant. Desmond Wilcox, Captain. DSO. The one who stepped forward when the others were too frightened or weary or confused. Wouldn't that be enough? Knowing it was you? Remembering it? But when the street parties were over and the flags were back in the attics, he didn't seem to believe in much. Not in God or King George or the Welfare State. Something had been lost. In the Rhine perhaps. All that gallant slaughter. And truly, she had tried to understand, but how could she, girl that she was? Though now that she was older, much older than he'd ever been, she thought she did understand. The blankness. The way sense can unravel so completely you never quite recover it. What was the word for when nothing made sense any more? The one time she asked him about the war he'd made a face as though tasting something unpleasant on his tongue, and said, 'Oh, that.' Didn't have the language for it, any more than she had the words now to tell the others what it was like, every night a stepping-stone and always wondering if there would be another, or if the next step would take her into the water.

The last summer of his life he sat hours together on the old chintz-covered swing-bed in front of the willow tree, chain-smoking Woodbines and watching the shadows flood the lawn until they swallowed him and only the tip of his cigarette still showed, a faint red pulse. How she had longed to bring him in, to rescue *him* as he had rescued his sergeant. Her mother wasn't up to it, sitting all day in the kitchen listening to Alma Cogan and Ronnie Hilton on the wireless, biting her nails until they bled. So it was she who had gone, crossing the lawn at dusk to stand in front of him, waiting for the right words to come into her head, for a dove that would bring her the gift of speech. But nothing came, and he had gazed up at her through the smoke of his cigarette as though from the far side of a pane of glass. He felt sorry for her perhaps, knowing why she had come out, knowing the impossibility of it. But instead of saying sit down beside me Alice, sit down, daughter, and we will try to understand together the unbearable truth that love is not always enough, that people cannot always be brought back in, he had said, very conversationally, as though in reference to a discussion he had been having with her in his head for weeks, 'They used flame-throwers, you know.' And she had nodded, yes, Daddy, and left him, and gone to her room, and pushed her face into the pillow and bawled. Because she should have done it, *should have*, and she had failed.

The summer ended, the doctors came, the first frosts. Suez.

The day he passed over she was in the parlour with Samuel and heard from the bedroom overhead a noise like something dropped, an ornament, a small vase or something, and then her mother calling, 'Desmond! Desmond! Desmond!'

After dark, Miss Bernard came to lay him out. BerNARD, dear, not BERnad. Put her umbrella in the elephant's foot by the door. Shook hands like a man. Got Daddy's parting wrong. The old people were afraid of her because she seemed to know where she would be needed next. To have an instinct for it. Samuel paid her – a guinea? – and all night they sat up listening to the water spill off the gutters because no one had cleared out the dead leaves. What a muddle it was! The hissing of the rain. Her father in his astonishing stillness. Samuel's breath like feathers on her cheek.

Ting!

The mahogany balloon clock in the living room chimed the half-hour; always five minutes fast, just as the grandmother clock in the hall was five minutes slow and would strike with a soft double note, and the little silver moon with the dreamy face that Stephen had worked on for days would slide a quarter-inch higher on its rail. Tick tock tick tock tick tock. Like drops of water through the sieve of her bones.

It was lunch-time in America. Larry and Kirsty and Ella would be sitting round the table eating one of Kirsty's curious 'health' meals, though there was nothing wrong with any of them other than Ella's asthma, and the less fuss made over that the better. Wasn't Kirsty some manner of Buddhist now? Before that it was veganism, Scientology, God knows. Restless people, the Americans. Everyone wanting to be Peter Pan or Tinkerbell. Foolish to found a country for the pursuit of

31

happiness. People just got into a panic when they hadn't got it. But good-hearted people. Generous. And Larry had been very happy there, though she had never stopped hoping he would come home. She had every episode of *Sun Valley General* on videocassettes in the living room. Still didn't understand why it all had to stop. Artistic differences, he said. But what did that mean? It wasn't a particularly artistic show. And last Christmas, when she was in San Francisco, he had spent hours sprawled on the big couch watching television and drinking ('It's just beer, Mum. Relax!'), which had immediately brought back horrible memories of Stephen.

She closed the book, a feather for a bookmark, and turned off the reading light. For a moment the room disappeared, then returned, slowly, in familiar grey outlines. It was like being sent to bed as a child before it was properly dark, lying there wondering what the grown-ups were doing, somewhat amazed that the world went on without you, that after all you were not necessary to it.

Below her window she heard Alec moving one of the chairs on the terrace. She knew that he liked to work out there, losing himself in work as though stopping his ears with paper. Poor love. And now that he had the play – some gloomy Russian who wrote in French – he had the perfect excuse. She hadn't asked him to come back! Mooching around the place like a reproach. It wore her out. What did he want from her? And why didn't he have any proper clothes? At thirty-four he was still dressing like a student. Why didn't he buy some *nice* shirts?

In her chest, high on the left side, the pain dug drowsily with a single claw and she shut her eyes. Around her, the boards of the house, the old beams and joists, cooling now, creakcd and whispered. It made the air seem talkative. Well inhabited. Full of presences not quite apparent.

4

In San Francisco, the late morning southbound traffic moved at walking speed towards Market Street. Larry Valentine drummed his fingers on the steering wheel of his dark green Thunderbird 'Town Landau', and watched, through green-tinted windows, a huddle of elderly Chinese playing mah-jong in the park, using a bench as a table. Tomorrow evening he would take Ella up to Chinatown for her piano lesson with Mr Yip. The lessons had been Professor Hoffmann's idea and were intended to help the girl express herself, to bring her out of her shell. Hoffmann had recommended Yip, who was almost as expensive as Hoffmann, but after eight months of classes, during which Ella had learned the first fifteen bars of 'Clair de Lune' and a piece called 'Mr Xao's Magic Garden', she remained the same determinedly introverted child she had always been. The thought of flying to England with her was not comfortable. Ten hours in the cigar tube and who knew what they might find at the other end.

On 4th the traffic eased, and by the time he was on 101 he was travelling south at a steady 60 mph (a good speed for an old car), the sun breaking off the waters of the bay to his left. He felt for a cigarette from the pack on the passenger seat, lit it, and turned the radio from the talk on KPFA to KYCY in search of some country-and-western, a type of music he had once thought risible but now found soothing and honest. From here it was a twenty-minute drive to the airport, long enough to preview the day ahead of him and to think seriously of turning the car around and going back into the city. There was a bar below Broadway with a cool, woody interior, and two or three tables outside for the smokers. Or Mario's, where he could eat focaccia and resume his nodding acquaintanceship with Francis Coppola. He could even go home. After all, he would have the place to himself (two six-packs of Red Tail in the fridge), while Kirsty was at the zendo in Japantown, cross-legged on a mat, solving riddles and learning to breathe.

On KYCY Charlie Rich began to sing 'The Most Beautiful Girl'. Larry turned up the volume and sang along at the top of his voice, somewhat frenziedly, so that a woman glancing across as she overtook him in her gun-metal coupé frowned at him – this large man at the wheel apparently in a rage with himself – before leaving him in her wake, dismissing him, no doubt, as one of that shifting population, that five or ten or fifty per cent who, at any give time, were not, mentally speaking, making ends meet. He ground his cigarette out on the butts in the dashboard ashtray. He was thirty-six years old, and though the weepy strains of the slide guitar seemed to invite it, he would not cry. All morning, since waking alone, gasping as though he had spent the last five hours swimming under a surface of thick ice, he had felt the imminence of another episode, one of those ugly downward lurches he had been experiencing since the last days of *Sun Valley*, and which came with their own rich panoply of symptoms. He had, for example, become neurotically conscious of his own heartbeat, the muffled ticking of his life, and the organ itself, a muscle that had encoded among the tangle of its DNA the hour, minute, second when the teasing pause between one beat and the next would extend itself to infinity. In Barnes and Noble he had scanned the home-doctor books (the busiest section of the store) in the hope of identifying the condition, but the books, with their colour plates and flow charts – *Is the coughing accompanied by bleeding? Is there discolouration of the stool?* – had only invited him to diagnose himself with a fresh selection of maladies, until it had seemed incredible he could walk out of the store unaided. Quite what he had done to deserve all this, other than to ride his luck too long, to imagine that what began well would go on in the same way without any special effort on his part, was not apparent to him. Something had failed; the reasons hardly mattered now. What counted was hanging on, toughing it out as though he were two sets down and had just been broken, and as he passed the final exit before the airport he held his breath and gripped the wheel more tightly, leaning forward a little, as though watching the man at the other end of the court toss up the ball for that thunderous first serve.

At SFO he stopped by the British Airways desk to collect the tickets for London. Two tickets for 3 June and one, for Kirsty, on the 10th. Alice's birthday was on the 18th.

The girl at the desk, a honey blonde with a fine peach down on the skin of her face which glowed golden in the light of the hall, enquired whether there were any special dietary requirements.

My wife,' said Larry, 'is presently a Buddhist, so some kind of high-fibre sushi might be suitable. My daughter won't eat anything that looks like food. I eat whatever you can send out for at two in the morning.'

She smiled at him with what seemed her entire being. All

the food was prepared by a team of nutritionists. There were vegetarian meals and special children's meals. Everybody's needs were catered for. Larry smiled back and said that he appreciated it. He wondered if she had recognized him: Americans were not usually shy of saying so. 'Hey, aren't you . . . ?' Being on TV here meant being injected into the bloodstream of the democracy, but in the eighteen months since he had 'parted' from the show – he, incandescent with rage and badly cut cocaine; L. Liverwitz Jnr, the new director, their fourteenth, incandescent with rage and too many exotic vitamins – he had begun to look less like Dr Barry, that suave and effective man who had brought a touch of English class to the high-tech corridors of *Sun Valley*, and more like the doctor's uncle, a heavier man, more florid than tanned.

'How d'ya like California?' she asked.

'I live here,' he said.

'I guess you like it, then.'

She passed over the wallet containing the tickets, her look of professional rapture beginning to fade as their business concluded. Larry wished her a nice day and pocketed the tickets. There were fifteen minutes before the shuttle left. He swallowed, dry, a tab of pink Xanax, and hurried past disciplined queues of elderly tourists (Taiwanese? Korean?), wondering to himself how the BA girl might have reacted if, in some confessional outburst, he had told her the truth about himself, about where he was going and why. He imagined her pressing some secret panic button under her desk and his being led away by airport security, raving as they handcuffed him in some back office with two-way mirrors. Or perhaps he underestimated her. Who was to say what her own private life was like, what dramas *she* went home to at night? At her age, a face betrayed so little. How were you supposed to tell?

The shuttle was on time: a crowded lunch-time flight. Businessmen and businesswomen filed into their seats and switched off their cellphones. Some began impromptu conferences with colleagues, talking what to Larry's ears was a kind of corporate super-babble, a strange fusion of figures and gossip and euphemisms of a vaguely military character. The younger ones looked extremely fit, as if they were all members of expensive gyms, which they probably were. Some wore elegant spectacles; most had laptops. Above all, they were people tense with purpose, decision-makers, movers and shakers, compared with whom he – ex-sportsman and soap star manqué – was a kind of decoration, a baroque squiggle.

The seat next to him, which he had hoped might remain unoccupied, was taken at the last moment by a woman and her infant daughter. The woman wore a large shapeless black dress decorated with various ethnic trimmings, and a kind of cloth bonnet from beneath which a pair of thick chestnut curls straggled over her forehead. Regarding her with sidelong glances as the plane taxied to its place in the queue for take-off, Larry realized she was much younger than he had first thought – mid-twenties perhaps – though dressed as if to make herself appear older and less attractive, bulked out by mysterious pouches and padding, designed perhaps to insulate her from too much direct contact with the world. The child on her lap, three or four years of age, thin, listless, rather sickly looking, possessed the darkest and saddest eyes he had ever seen. He smiled companionably at the mother, who did not smile back but said, 'She's nauseous,' in such a strong New York Jewish accent Larry thought at first it must be the child's name, and was trying to puzzle out which feisty Old Testament heroine she was named after, when the woman snatched the air sickness bag from its slot behind the in-flight magazines.

'Hope's she's not sick on you,' she said, in a voice that suggested it would be his fault if she were. The child wriggled on her lap. 'You wanna chuck up?' asked the mother, and placing a firm hand on the back of the girl's head she thrust the little face into the mouth of the sack, where it remained for some minutes before reappearing, comically distressed, her cheeks puckering with disgust, her great eyes returning Larry's anxious stare with a mixture of hostility and weariness and sly appeal. He felt for her, imagining that he understood her, the character of her disenchantment with the world, and as they flew over the scuffed California desert, the coast to the right of them fringed with blue and pearl, he dedicated himself to making the child smile, a game he had often played with Ella, who shared with this little pale Jewish girl a heaviness, an elfin knowledge of things, which he found disturbing.

All the photographs of himself as a boy, most of them at Brooklands still, displayed him in Kodachrome gardens, or the vivid green of the sports field, or shoulder to shoulder with Alec on a beach in Brittany or Ireland, the same trademark grin on his face. Even in adolescence, when now and then he had slammed doors, and the skin around his mouth had turned raw for a year, his features had never failed to exude the good-tempered optimism of a boy entirely at ease in the world. Unhappy children, even children who *seemed* unhappy, roused in his increasingly suggestible mind the spectre of a darkness from which even innocence gave no immunity, and against this he continued, doggedly, a little desperately even, to do battle.

The child observed him, peeking from behind her mother's black-cloaked bosom, then staring more openly as her mother harried the air hostess to find a packet of crisps on the trolley bearing the little K for Kosher. Larry wrinkled his nose, winked, crossed his eyes, frowned in mimicry of her own expression, all without the least effect. If anything she became more severe, more regally disapproving of him, his antics, and he began again, this time discreetly including his pulling-off-the-thumb routine, one of Ella's favourites, but it was not until they banked over the coast above LA and flew in over acres of neat houses, over freeways and brilliant wires of sunlit traffic, that she consented to be amused, her face lighting up with a smile of such radiance he had to turn away from her. He stared down at his hands (the wedding band on the left; his right hand, his former racquet hand, still puffed with muscle) and spoke to himself, spoke behind the curtain of his face, easing himself away from the fear that he was about to commit, in this cramped and public place, some lavish inappropriacy. Laugh like a hyena, or curl up in the aisle, or caress one of the chestnut loops on the mother's brow – an act that would certainly have startling repercussions. It was part of the new intensity, of course, the new waywardness that forced him to keep checking on himself, taking bearings on normal. But what troubled him most was the sense that something in him was colluding with it all, this unravelling, some impulse whose true character was still hidden from him, but which he suspected might, like his father's, be merely destructive.

From her jump-seat by the emergency exit door, one of the

air hostesses, her face stiff with cosmetics and fatigue, was watching him without much sympathy, and seemed on the verge of putting some procedure into operation, but now they were descending sharply, the plane suddenly on a level with the roofs of the airport buildings, and there was no longer time to do anything but mutter the garbled end of a prayer (Christ, don't let us crash and die here . . .).

The businessmen sat very straight, braced, their fingers on the switches of their phones, ready to power up. Something fell in the galley; someone laughed, grimly. As they touched down, the child had her face in the bag again.

5

Above certain words and in the margins, Alec made notes with the fine point of his pencil. Slowly, under the light of the storm lantern (this least stormy of nights), he was learning the music of the new piece, and how to sing, in a head quieted at last of all other thoughts, the approximate, imitative song of the translation.

He had never met László Lázár, and knew what he looked like only from a photograph he had cut out of the *Sunday Telegraph* magazine which showed a delicately built man with cropped grey hair and large eyes, the pupils unusually prominent and dark. It was winter, and Lázár had been posed beside the boating pond in the Jardin du Luxembourg, a place Alec had often visited on solitary walks during his year abroad at the Cité Universitaire. But what gave the picture its particular character was the package Lázár was carrying, hugged against his grey overcoat. A book perhaps, or something from a local patisserie, a cake for Sunday, but it lent him a vaguely conspiratorial air, like a nineteenth-century anarchist on his way to plant a bomb in the foyer of a reactionary newspaper office. That, together with the somewhat silly caption 'As a young man Lázár knew how to handle a tommy-gun', had helped confirm in Alec's mind the idea of the playwright as a romantic figure with a mysterious and violent past, owner of the kind of history he himself would never have.

Millions had died to produce the world Alec had grown up in. This he had been told at school on every Remembrance Sunday before the bugle sounded and silence fell over the ranks of schoolboys who would not be asked to play their part because others had done it for them, had laid down their lives like so many garments of tissue and silk, so that in England at least, cars did not arrive in the middle of the night to take dissidents to basement torture chambers, and democracy, 'the dear old dog', could go on slumbering in its long after-dinner sleep. And this was a great success, of course, a triumph, because everyone knew, or had been told, that war was hell. He had watched the *World at War* series twice – once on television, once on video – Laurence Olivier reciting the horrors of the Russian front, Hiroshima, the Camps. And there was no shortage of more contemporary evidence. Iran and Iraq. Afghanistan. Chechnya. Endless wars in East and Central Africa. Wars like 'Desert Storm', carried out with textbook brutality, with press briefings and generals from Central Casting. Wars full of astonishing neighbourly murderousness, such as those that had ended uneasily in Croatia and Bosnia. Fighting was still a consuming occupation for large parts of the planet. But Alec was in England, and had only ever witnessed, from a safe distance, the kind of flailing, closing-time violence that all British cities vomited up at the weekend. For this he knew he should be grateful. Road kills upset him. The sight of a fishmonger 'cleaning' a fish made him queasy. He was delicate, prone to colds. His own front line had been four years teaching French at a South London state school, at the end of which (one pitiless Tuesday lunch-time after the Christmas break), he had simply run away. But still, he could not quite free himself from certain naïve and powerful daydreams in which he fought at the barricades with a man like Lázár, or ran under a fiery sky with Grandpa Wilcox to haul some bleeding comrade to safety. It was comically depressing, the realization that there would never be a picture of him standing gravely on Tooting Common with the legend, 'As a young man Valentine knew how to handle a tommy-gun'. That wasn't his kind of life.

Since his appointment as Lázár's translator, there had been a to and fro of e-mails between Paris and Alec's flat in London, queries arising from the text, and replies – precise and businesslike – signed not by Lázár but by a certain 'K. Engelbrecht', presumably Lázár's PA (Katrina? Katya?). Alec was scheduled to meet Lázár at a reception in London in September, together with the director from the Royal Court, and various actors, designers, technicians and management, who would be part of the production. Barring the unforeseen, there would be a first night at the end of January.

For Alec, this was, without question, the most important piece of work he had ever undertaken. Marcie Stoltz, the Court's literary manager, had seen his new translation of *Le Médecin malgré lui* at the Rathaus in Hackney when she was looking for a replacement for Chris Eliard, Lázár's regular translator, who had disappeared from his yacht in mysterious circumstances while sailing single-handed across the Golfo di Genova. Stoltz had called Alec and invited him to lunch at Orso's in Covent Garden, a class of restaurant he had never been into in his life, and after plates of asparagus, and lobster ravioli, she offered him the contract, explaining that the new play was something of a departure for Lázár, not exactly upbeat, but not *gloomy*. 'Certain actions innately graced, etc.', she said, fork in one hand, a Marlboro Light in the other, studying Alec with an amused and soulful gaze. There was, as usual, very little money in it – 'would love to offer you tons more' – but enough, with careful budgeting, to mean he could give up the detested 'technical' work (the latest was a document on braking systems for SNCF). After two large glasses of house white and saying goodbye to Stoltz, almost bowing to her as she squeezed into a taxi on Wellington Street, he had spent the remainder of the afternoon walking around Regent's Park, smiling at dog-walkers and tourists, even at the police, who nodded back warily, suspicious of being liked. At last he was a man of prospects! And though he had long since given up competing with his brother – the futility of which had been apparent to him since primary school – he would not now, with Lázár at his side, be *utterly* overshadowed. He called Alice from a pay-phone somewhere in Marylebone, stumbling over his words, embarrassed at how much he wanted her approval, how relieved he was to hear her full-blooded 'Well *done*, Alec!' But as he made his way home, his feet starting to ache, his head thickening from the drink, a new restlessness and dissatisfaction had replaced the euphoria, as though someone had twitched back the curtain and let light into a room that had been tolerable only in the dark.

The play was called *Oxygène*: sixty-seven pages of card-bound typescript that told, in a clipped, elliptic language, the story of a mining disaster in eastern Europe. It was to be shown on a revolving stage, with two sets, 'above ground' and 'below ground', alternately on view. The action commences with the explosion that traps the miners at the end of a narrow shaft. Above ground, a rescue team and a chorus of relatives attempt to force a way through to them. Hope endures to the end of the first act, but by the beginning of the next it is apparent to everyone that the rescue can only have a single outcome. Underground, the miners struggle to come to terms with their fate. For one, it is nothing but the crude majesty of facts – too much rock, too little force. Another finds peace in a religious quietism, wedding himself to the will of his Creator. A third rages at the mine-owners who have forced them to go on drilling despite warnings about the safety of the tunnel. In the middle of the act a fight breaks out between two men so starved of air they can do no more than slow-dance like drunken lovers. Despair seeps in like a gas. Even those above ground succumb to it, gasping as if they too were under threat of asphyxiation. But at the moment when all further effort seems futile, one of the trapped men, György, a veteran of the mines, rouses himself, rallies the last of his strength, and renews his assault on the rock, while on the surface a young woman, unhinged by grief perhaps, takes one of the abandoned picks and clumsily wields it at the earth. As the house lights are dimmed and the audience sits on in the dark, the air rings with the steady percussion of the tools, a noise that the text insists should be '*a triumphant sound but also a mocking one*'.

The force of the play was apparent to Alec on his first hurried reading of it in the hour after the motorcycle courier – whose presence in the flats had deeply impressed Mr Bequa

– delivered it at the beginning of April. The following day he had taken it with him to Brooklands, where Alice, still officially in remission, had invited him to enjoy the good weather, and he had read it a second and a third time sitting in the orchard under a canopy of apple blossom.

Stoltz was right. The play did not share the bleakness or scepticism of Lázár's earlier work, and much of the reason lay with the character of György, a man who in his youth might have served as a model for a classic Soviet worker-hero, and seen himself sculpted in monumental brass for a public square, but forty years on, unillusioned, free of all dogma, he is merely decent, with the kind of gut courage and gut morality Camus endorsed. With the young woman to keep faith with him above ground, who was to say they did not in the end escape? It was unlikely, of course – highly unlikely – but there was nothing in the text forbidding such a thought.

In the midst of its spring boost, the garden at Brooklands was untrimmed, straggling, almost luxuriant. Bees were at work in the blossom; the earth ticked like a warm car. Alice abandoned the last proscriptions of her elaborate diet and they went shopping at the deli in Coverton to buy her old favourites – Parma ham, apple strudel, Vienetta ice cream, brandy snaps – foods from a golden age before biopsies and staging tests.

As Alec worked, he was aware of his mother glancing up at him from her book, and he had enjoyed that watching, had felt the weight and warmth of it, that regard never quite uncritical but of a quality and intensity he was quite certain no other person would ever have for him, or could have. Three days, three warm days in April which, in retrospect, seemed an entire season, and it amazed him that he had not been more conscious of his happiness then, that it had not somehow *impressed* itself upon him like a mark, whatever the opposite of a scar was.

The following week she called him at the flat early in the morning while he was still in bed. She had sounded slurred and depressed, also angry, and he had travelled down full of dark presentiments. Even the good weather had gone, and on the way to the hospital for the new tests they drove through sopping air on roads silvered with rain. He waited for her in the hospital carpark, listening to the radio and looking out at a landscape of Portakabins and scruffy trees and barrack-like buildings through whose doors harassed people scurried with coats over their heads, or stood outside battling to angle their umbrellas into the wind. There were scans and blood tests, then a ten-day wait to collect the results from her consultant. Even in so brief a time, the change in Alice was observable, measurable. The navy blue dress she put on for her appointment with Brando looked two sizes too big for her, and her make-up, applied more thickly than usual, seemed a clumsy attempt at concealing what was happening to her face, the deflation of her features, the rings beneath her eyes as though sleeplessness had bruised her. He parked the Renault as close to the doors of the oncology department as he could, but when he had hurried around to her side of the car and taken her arm she had shaken him off and walked away on her own, even managing a cheery 'Afternoon!' to a nurse she thought she recognized. She was gone for forty minutes. When she came out, pausing at the step to get her breath, to collect herself, it was as if, somewhere in the recesses of that ugly building, she had been disassembled, then put together again in a hurry, unsuccessfully. Even getting into the car was suddenly an action fraught with difficulty, a pantomime of decrepitude. He saw that her eyes were bloodshot, and one of her cheeks was red, as though she had been pressing something against her face.

She gave him the news as they drove, talking to the windscreen and using many of the technical expressions she had learned over the last years from the doctors. When she had finished, Alec felt like a child who in some bizarre anxiety dream has been given his father's place in the car. How would they get around the next corner? How would they *stop*? Frantically, he had tried to think of what he could say to her (surely the situation could not be as hopeless as she suggested?) but the moment when he needed to speak, when nothing more was required from him than the kind of sincerity peddled by American soap operas five nights a week, the words would not come. And though he had visions of himself pulling over into a lay-by to hug her, making some show of his *own* pain, he did nothing, for fear that whatever he could say or show would be grossly inadequate. For fear too, perhaps, of what might happen if he did manage to express what he felt.

At Brooklands she had politely thanked him for driving her. The rain was over, the clouds had dispersed, and the evening was unexpectedly serene and blue and mild. He went into the house to make tea (he found the cups still full the next day), then spied on Alice from the window on the upstairs landing, watching her in the garden moving from flower-bed to flower-bed, in what, with a great sinking of his heart, he imagined to be an act of leave-taking.

By eight o'clock she was in bed. At the kitchen table he wrote to Larry, a stiff, garbled, furious, self-pitying letter

(*Remember us? Your family?*) which he immediately tore into pieces, hiding the pieces in an old yoghurt pot and hiding the pot deep in the kitchen bin. Later, he spoke to Larry on the telephone, and hearing the shock in his brother's voice, his anger had evaporated, replaced by a desire to put himself entirely into his brother's care, to be carried by him. For half an hour they talked until Larry had said, so tenderly Alec did not trust himself to reply, 'I'll get over there, bro. Can you hold out a bit longer?'

Settling the papers on his lap, Alec took off his glasses, closed his eyes, and massaged the bridge of his nose. He was working now entirely by the imperfect light of the lamp and had strained his sight and given himself a slight headache. When he opened his eyes again his gaze fell upon the tangle of small cream and raspberry roses that hung over the remains of a brick wall that had once divided the terrace from the rest of the garden, but which, in his father's time, had been demolished, leaving just this short section for the flowers. These were Alice's roses, and when he looked at them he saw her – an image, a superimposition, already starting to lose its vividness – dead-heading the discoloured blooms with quick, neat movements of her wrist. Insects hid in the moist hearts of the flowers, and perhaps destroyed them. Sometimes they would crawl under the cuff of her blouse and she shook them out, not quite indifferent to them, but not someone to indulge herself in squeamishness. She had no time for the kind of women who would shriek at the sight of a spider or a mouse. More than once he had seen her face down dogs, mongrel Doberman types that sprang from the end of farm tracks, or appeared suddenly at the bend of a quiet lane. And the story of her squaring up to the drunk who waved a broken wine bottle in her face in a multistorey carpark in Bath was part of family folklore. It was, of course, what one would expect from the daughter of the hero of Arnhem, whose photograph, looking remarkably like a 1940s version of Larry, gazed out from its silver frame among the ancestors on the walnut sideboard in the dining room.

Thus far, her courage had sustained her. From the beginning she had talked of 'getting on with it', which meant behaving properly, not making a fuss. But who could resist the assault of a disease that seemed to possess its own malicious intelligence? That hated life, but fed on it ravenously? The day would come, or the night, a night like this, when she was no longer 'getting on with it', and someone else would have to take the strain. Then what? He glanced down at the manuscript. '*Hammer blows, steel on rock, a triumphant sound but also a mocking one.*'

6

László Lázár stood on the landing outside his apartment looking down over the banisters to where his neighbour, Monsieur Garbarg, was standing outside his own apartment, looking up. Garbarg held a red-and-white chequered napkin in his hand, the little banner of his interrupted dinner. At his shoulder, in the opening of the door, stood Garbarg senior, who was blind, and wore on his face his customary expression of cautious astonishment.

'Something in the oven, messieurs,' called László, cheerfully. 'A little explosion.' He shrugged, hoping to suggest that such happenings were a tiresome but amusing part of the human condition. The younger Garbarg nodded, though without returning László's smile. They had been neighbours for fifteen years, and while knowing almost nothing of the hard facts of each other's lives – László had no idea what Garbarg junior did for a living – they had somehow come to know each other very well, as if by a process of mutual osmosis. As soon as László had heard the shot, so bizarrely loud and like nothing in the world but a pistol shot, he had known that Garbarg would be pushing back his chair and striding to the door to await an explanation. László suspected his neighbours of harbouring dark misgivings about émigrés, even ones who had lived in the country for forty years and knew and loved the country and spoke the language as fluently as their mother tongue, more so perhaps. Of course, the Garbargs may have had other reasons to dislike him. It was hard to tell how much of his life was visible to them.

'I am sorry, messieurs, to have disturbed your meal. *Bon appétit!*'

The neighbours retired to their respective apartments. László shut his door discreetly, careful not to make any noise that sounded like a bang, an explosion, a shot, then walked quickly down the parquet corridor, the spine of his apartment, to the dining room at the far end. Before going out to placate the Garbargs he had established that no one in the dining room was hurt. Now, uncertain whether to be amused or appalled, he entered the room like the detective in a country-house murder mystery, the kind of story, in tatty Hungarian editions, he had sometimes read as a boy.

His secretary, Kurt Engelbrecht, corn-blond hair shaved on to his elegant skull, was loosening Franklin Wylie's collar, while Laurence stood on the other side of the table, tearful again, and dropping ash on to the carpet. Franklin, grey and aghast, but already starting to look pleased with himself, was sprawled along the divan. On the linen, next to a bowl of fresh figs, the gun lay like a piece of expensive tableware.

'What did you hit?' demanded László. Franklin pointed a weebling finger at the bookshelf at the end of the room, and László went to examine the damage. The bullet was embedded in the spine of a book of poetry, head height on the bookshelf. He drew the volume out and showed it to them.

'You have shot Rilke,' he announced. 'The act of a fascist.'

'Didn't think the damn thing was loaded,' said Franklin, lamely. Kurt was on his knees now, fanning the American with the programme notes to *Madame Butterfly*.

'Some fake!' said Laurence.

László shrugged, and carefully filled four small glasses with the Zytnia. 'Idiot,' he said, gently, giving Franklin his glass.

Once they had drunk, then wiped their lips with the backs of their hands – something that seemed unavoidable when drinking vodka – László asked: 'Does anyone know how to take the bullets out?'

But it seemed that no one wished to touch the weapon now, as though it were merely resting, curled on the table next to the figs, a thing with mayhem in it. At last, muttering to himself and feeling that he was the only adult in a room of difficult children, László dropped a napkin over the gun, wrapped it carefully, and crossed the corridor to his study, a room twenty metres square that looked south towards the boulevard Edgar Quinet, and the cemetery where Sartre and de Beauvoir and the glorious Beckett lay. There were two desks in the room: the one nearer to the window was heaped with papers and scrawled-over index cards and a dozen of the black ink fibre-tip Pentels László preferred for writing. The other, a larger desk bought second-hand at a bankruptcy sale, was equipped with a computer, a fax-telephone, and a green-shaded lamp with a solid brass base. On this desk the papers were neatly stacked, and on the corner of the desk a vase of yellow freesias perfumed the room. This was where Kurt worked – typing letters, organizing the diary, fielding the telephone – ensuring the playwright could spend his time on art rather than life.

László switched on the lamp and uncovered the gun. It was a small black Beretta .32 with a snub barrel of the type designed for more covert use, a gun for spies and undercover cops and nervous housewives. He lifted it from its nest in the white damask. It was a long time since he had held a gun – a lifetime – and the thing's mysterious energy intrigued him. It could not have weighed more than an old-fashioned silver cigarette case, or one of the bulkier Livres de Poche – *Les Misérables*, say – but there was no doubting the purity of its purpose, nor the power it conferred on him as he closed his fist around the cross-hatching on the grip. He could go downstairs with it now and shoot the Garbargs, the neat tap-tap of death's index finger on the back of their necks, so that they fell face first into their soup plates. Or if his dinner party should not be a success, if the veal were spoiled or the conversation dull, it would take only a moment to massacre his guests. Then again, if the world offended him so, it might be simpler to shoot himself, as some years ago a friend of his father's had done, a fellow doctor, leaning out of the window so as not to splash his brains on the carpet, and leaving behind no note, no statement other than his own corpse draped over the windowsill. Was it possible that anyone went through life without, for an hour or two, contemplating the thick blue line of suicide? *Se donner la mort.* To give oneself death. And what was the distance you had to travel between the idea and the act? Not far perhaps, not far at all when you had a machine like the Beretta and nothing more wearying to do than squeeze the trigger. As a young man, when, for obvious reasons, the idea had come to him more than once, come in its most seductive guise, as the resolution to an exhausting and insoluble inner debate, he had known he could never go through with it while his mother was still alive. But she had been dead since '89, buried in Vienna where she had spent her final years with Uncle Ernö, and he remembered how it had indeed entered his head as he travelled to Vienna on the train for the last time, that vestigial death wish which suddenly he was free to enact, for there was no one other than her who would not survive it, who could not recover. He raised the gun and brushed his temple with the satiny blunt of the barrel, imagining (with a certain pleasure) the conversations after the funeral, when friends would stare at each other, shake their heads and say: 'He had so much to live for! Do *you* know why he did it?'

The phone rang, twice, stopped, bleeped, and an edge of paper began to slide from the mouth of the fax. László rewrapped the Beretta in the napkin, hurriedly, as though he had been caught striking poses in front of the mirror. In heavy black type the words *Serbian Justice* were curling into view, and then – blurred but quite graphic enough – pictures he did not wish to look at but could not at first look away from. A human back, black and swollen from a beating. A man's body sprawled in a ditch. And the inevitable corollary: a woman in a headscarf, bewildered, terrified, her hands outstretched in wretched supplication – an image that seemed emblematic of the entire century. It was not the first such material he'd received. Since the beginning of March there had been maps, photographs, statistics, horrors. He knew more or less where they came from, and felt again a flare of resentment at being solicited in this way. Political junk mail! Kurt could deal with it in the morning, file it somewhere. Had he known how to, he would have turned the fax off, sabotaged it, perhaps by pulling at the skeins of wire that led to the wall socket, but he had remained fabulously ignorant of what he still called the 'new' technology, and he did not want to run the risk of Kurt sulking for half a day.

On the shelf above his desk the digits of the radio alarm

flicked from 8:59 to 9:00. Karol was due at any moment and there were still a dozen jobs to be done in the kitchen before they could eat. But as he left the study he imagined the fax continuing all night, the paper spreading over the desktop, over the floor, then rising in rustling loops to the ceiling. An inexhaustible complaint. An oracle. A relentless call to arms.

7

With his jacket slung over his shoulder, Larry negotiated the shuttle satellite at LA airport. Ahead of him the young Jewish mother carried the child on her hip until the two of them were met by a party of Jewish men in *Streml* and skullcaps, one of whom, a magnificently built young man, his beard as soft and glossy as a girl's pubic hair, was evidently the child's father, and she climbed into his arms, all nausea forgotten, proud and giggly, reunited with her hero, rescued.

Larry watched them for a while, furtively, from between the gathered suits under the flight information screens. How sweet if he could somehow be included in that little group and share in their happiness! He imagined himself in a crisp white shirt, Uncle Reuben perhaps, with the type of excellent pale skin that comes with certain kinds of righteousness. He would own a dry-goods store downtown, or a kosher delicatessen so that his fingers smelt faintly of pickles. *Vi gay'st du*, Reuben? Come into the circle!

He moved on, entered one of the concourse bars, and ordered a Budweiser, taking it to a stool by the wooden Indian. It was only his third beer of the day – the first two in the kitchen at home before setting out – and this he still considered an acceptable level of consumption. He knew that there were those among his Californian acquaintances who considered him an alcoholic because it was nothing to him to drink a bottle, a bottle and a half of Napa Valley wine at a sitting, or half a dozen cans during a TV show, but they had not seen a real alcoholic at work, and he had and he knew the difference.

His father, Stephen Valentine, for the last six months of his life, had lived uninhibitedly as a drunkard, no longer troubling to top up his morning tumbler of vodka with an inch of orange juice, or have a spoonful of coffee with his whisky at eleven. He had drunk the stuff raw and with a certain sad bravado, revealing at last the full measure and tyranny of his thirst. And there had been a certain slewed dignity to it that had made things easier, freeing them from that wearying and shaming pretence, the sorry fiction that 'Daddy's just a bit tired'. Though, of course, in a sense it was true; he *had* been tired, fatigued to the point of madness from trying to live a life he considered, with that secret insider view no wife or therapist could ever share, an irreversible failure.

Early on, the brothers had learned how to survive his rages, those evenings when he moved around the house like an electric storm, bawling accusations and hunting down the lost first cause of it all, the wrong turning that had led to his ruin. More difficult than the anger were those moods of gross sentimentality when he would appear in the playroom wanting to be with his boys and join in and do as other dads did. But he stank of the drink, and the brothers had not wanted him there – too loud, too forceful, too grimly jolly. When Alice saw it getting out of hand she would sometimes turn on him – sheer mother instinct, which was a power beyond them all, fierce and pure – and Stephen would shut himself away in the workroom or the old summerhouse, where Larry one afternoon looked in at him, his back, his boneless shoulders, as he sat among the sacking and old apples, tending a bottle, *working* it, and then, alerted by some shift in the light, turning to the window to see his son and exchange with him a long glance through the cobwebbed glass, a look that had taught Larry – those lessons that pass through the eye like a virus – that it wasn't the toxicity of alcohol which killed a drunkard, but the unsheddable burden of self-consciousness.

Alec had looked to Larry. Larry had looked to Alice. But who had *she* looked to? Whose strength or example had she called on the night a policeman stood on the doorstep, his fluorescent jacket brilliant with rain, asking if her husband had been driving a sky-blue Rover? The boys, woken by the chimes, had huddled at the top of the stairs, peering through the open hall door. They knew there must have been an accident – why else did policemen call at midnight? – but the details, the soaked road, the speed, the unlit corner, the car's flight beyond the verge, these emerged only slowly, from several sources, over months or even years. Some things Larry had never learned: the particulars of his father's wounds, whether he had been killed outright or had survived the impact, lying for a time with his face pressed against the wheel, hearing the hollow patter of the rain on the car roof. What manner of thoughts did a person have then, before the neurons started to fire at random? Would he have felt saved when at last Death crossed the wet ground to find him? Had there been time to forgive himself? To feel pleased?

He spent a moment reorientating himself, subsiding into the now by contemplating the crowd in the concourse, marvelling at how few people actually walked into each other. He was longing for a smoke, but like most of the State of California the bar was a smoke-free zone and to have lit a cigarette there would have been like Kirsty walking through downtown Tehran in her bikini. He finished his beer and went out to the taxi rank where the taxi marshal waved up a large shambolic Ford with a sticker on the bumper that read: 'If I cut you off don't shoot!' The interior of the car smelled powerfully of exotic food recently consumed. Larry asked if it would be OK to light up.

'No can do!' said the driver, a squat and impeccably mannered black man who hailed, so it turned out, from the town of Ogbomosho in Nigeria, and who, from his tone of voice, was evidently caught between sympathy for Larry's need and pride in the extravagant prohibitions of his adopted country. Larry nodded and tried to settle back on the puffed and shiny seat, gazing out at a wasteland of motels, billboards, minimalls and 'nude' diners. He had been to the city many times. Most of *Sun Valley General* had been shot at the studios on North Las Palmas, and when Doctor B figured large in the storyline Larry had been delivered to the studio in a white stretch limousine. But the place he now entered as they turned off the freeway on to Santa Monica, this megalopolis purpling under its canopy of smog, remained essentially undisclosed to him. Too bright, too big, too dirty, too foreign, Los Angeles had perhaps always been the end of his American odyssey, a last America he could never quite enter.

For ten years, ever since doing his first ads in New York when the tennis career began to fold and he had slipped into three figures on the world ratings, he had carried on his love affair with this country. His first view of New York, of Manhattan, had been through the windows of Nathan Slater's Lincoln Town Car as they drove, one October dusk, to Slater's seventeenth-floor offices overlooking Madison Square. Later that evening, with two or three other Slater 'discoveries', they had gone to the Palm on the East Side to eat lobsters. Larry was twenty-six, seduced by Slater's attentiveness, by the baseball summary on the radio (it was World Series time), by the wraiths of steam that rose from the cracks and gratings in the road, and most of all, most breathlessly, by the filigreed beauty of the towers, whose beaconed crowns he bent his neck to get a glimpse of as they passed.

For Alice – for Alec too perhaps – Culture and Beauty and Style were European phenomena, or, more specifically, French. America was Hollywood and Vegas and rednecks. It was razzmatazz and bad food. It was helplessly vulgar. But for Larry and his friends, America had felt like the last place on the planet where things actually happened, a country where a man's life could still have a mythic weight to it. After school they would hang out in Wimpy bars or Little Chefs, half a dozen teenage boys sat three by three either side of the plastic ketchup tomato, puffing on Craven As or Lucky Strike, smoking half the cigarette at a go, then carefully tapping out the embers, saving the last half for the following day. They read Louis L'Amour and Jack Kerouac and Hemingway. Some, not Larry, graduated on to Mailer and Updike and Roth. On Saturday afternoons they met up at Gaumonts and Odeons wearing American college football jackets from secondhand import stores in Bristol, and lied about their age to watch Clint Eastwood or Charles Bronson step from ever-faster cars to pull ever-bigger guns from their coats. On parents' chrome-fronted music centres they played Dylan and Hendrix, Motown, Lou Reed, Tom Petty, Zappa, Patti Smith. Their language was marbled with Americanisms: 'cool', 'peachy', 'neat', 'far out', the ubiquitous 'man'. And between them it was understood that sooner or later they would go there, go West and drive a Mustang and say 'easy over' to the girl in the diner who asked how they wanted their eggs, though as far as Larry knew he was the only one to have actually made it there, the lone survivor of all that teenage yearning.

Halfway through his first martini at the Palm – his first martini anywhere – England had appeared as a remote and underlit island he need never return to, other than on the occasional visit to Brooklands. Jet in, jet out. He had entered the future, and was half dazed with gratitude and the wildest optimism. The following night, in Slater's Greenwich Village apartment, a party had begun with tall women and cocaine, a party that lasted all through the advertising campaign for luxury cars – British, or apparently so – and then crossed the country with him to California; a pearly necklace of late and later nights as the small acting parts came in and he reached his apotheosis as Dr Barry Catchpole, becoming almost famous and almost rich, though curiously less and less content, as though, in a fatal hour he would never afterwards be able to recall or identify, he had fallen foul of some law of inverse returns, so that the more he drank the less drunk he was, and the more he partied the less pleasure he had, until the morning he had stumbled out into a San Francisco fog to discover himself, a reckless man, married to a woman who cried in her sleep and father to a little girl who had already seen more doctors than most sane and healthy people see in a lifetime.

One got weary trying to work it all out. His life resisted his attempts to comprehend it. He didn't seem to have the language, or whatever it was you needed – the books, the time, the medication. He had lost count of the number of people who had suggested therapy, who had given him the names of their own therapists, saying 'Definitely the best Jungian in town', or 'This guy *guarantees* closure'. He thought sometimes the solution would be to get back on the show, but Catchpole was gone (with ghastly irony the show had 'sent' him to England to nurse an ailing parent), and the row with Liverwitz had not been of the kind where you could go back the next week and eat humble pie. It had been savage and terminal, and in truth he was glad to be free of the programme's grinding inanity, its relentless pursuit of the trite. Why, he had bawled at Liverwitz, why were the only patients ever admitted to the hospital friends and relatives of the people who worked there? Was that usual? But there had been no serious money coming into the house for eight months. His last paid work had been a commercial for Wonder Bread in November. Since then there had been promises, a lot of talk over mint juleps and wheat-grass juice, but no firm offers. He had very slightly over ten and a half thousand dollars in the Bank of California, a few thousand sterling in London tied up in stocks and shares. He also had the cars – Kirsty drove a '93 Cherokee – and the house, which was mostly paid for. Kirsty contributed a modest income from her part-time work in a day unit for people with learning difficulties, but her salary barely covered the phone bills, which, since Alice's illness, had trebled. Cocaine wasn't getting any cheaper. Neither were the bills for Ella's asthma treatment, much of it not covered by the insurance. Then there were the school fees for KDBS, and Mr Yip's piano classes. The flights to England. Party girls. The IRS. Booze. Hoffmann. Groceries. There was no end to it.

He had long since calculated what he might inherit when Alice died, the preliminary sums done, in the teeth of self-disgust, shortly after she was first diagnosed with small-cell lung cancer in the winter of '95. It would not be much. The house would be sold off, but an old place in poor repair on a stretch of waterlogged moorland would hardly raise a fortune, and half of it, of course, would go to Alec. The good furniture, which amounted to the dining table and silver candlesticks, a couple of decent paintings, also in the dining room, and some of Stephen's collection of antique clocks, would bring in another three or four thousand. All in all he had reckoned – reckoning on despite a shame that made him sweat – he might clear forty or even fifty grand. But when? He had already started borrowing (Kirsty knew nothing of this) from men with pampered attack dogs, people who said 'We understand each other, right?' and 'You're a real nice guy', but who would certainly have a thorough and instinctual way with slow payers.

Larry and the man from Ogbomosho entered Century City and the Avenue of the Stars, a zone of high-rises and underground shopping complexes between the LA Country Club and Rancho Park. A few moments later they swung into the half-moon drive of the Park Hotel, where a doorman, dressed in the red-and-gold livery of a Yeoman of the Guard, opened the cab door and examined Larry through mirror shades. Larry paid the driver, tipping him heavily. The man only had one ear; the other looked to have been removed, clumsily, with something blunt – teeth perhaps. He was, decided Larry, peeling himself from the varnished surface of the rear seat, a man who had passed through darkness, and who might, had Larry found a way into him, have proved wise on the subject. Help, like trouble, could come from anywhere. He was sorry he had missed his chance.

Out of the cab, he lit the cigarette he had been holding in his fist since the airport, and nodded at the Beefeater's uniform. 'You're a long way from home,' he said.

'Pasadena,' said the Beefeater. 'You a dentist?'

'No,' said Larry, obscurely offended.

'Fifty thousand in town. Convention.'

Larry gave a low whistle, and tried to conjure in his mind an image of so many thousand white-coated men marching like an army, ten abreast, through the great boulevards and byways of Los Angeles. Then, recalling a line from a poem he had read in a schoolboy elocution competition for which he had won an honourable mention, he muttered, 'I had not thought death had undone so many.'

'What's that?' asked the doorman, frowning.

Larry shook his head. 'Think it's going to get hotter?' he asked.

'Bet your life,' said the Beefeater. 'Hot as hell.'

Larry took a last drag on the cigarette. He was one of those deep-lunged men who could get through a cigarette in four or five big pulls, the paper uncoiling beneath a long, sharp ember. The Beefeater relieved him of the butt and walked away with it towards some secret receptacle. Larry checked his watch. Two-fifteen Pacific Standard. Something after ten at night in England, at Brooklands. Home?

'Good night, Mum,' he said, and he went in to be among the dentists.

8

In her dream, Alice watched her elder son emerge theatrically from beneath the giant weeping willow in her parents' garden and cross the lawn towards her, telling her in French that he would save her. *'Je te sauverai, maman. Je te sauverai.'* But even while she slept, held just beneath the surface of consciousness by the ballast of her drugs, she knew that there was something clumsy and improbable in the image. Larry did not speak French, and had, at sixteen, despite her coaching, decisively failed his O-level in the subject. Alec was the linguist, but it was not Alec who smiled at her on the lawn. The dream was a fraud and she woke into the darkness, confused and agitated, feeling herself to have been tricked.

Slowly she brought herself to order, then made herself smile at the memory of a class of eight-year-olds singing the responses to her patient drilling of French verbs.

'Je . . . ?'

'SUIS!'

'Tu . . . ?

'ES!'

The slower ones, the dreamier ones, mouthing whatever came into their heads, but carried along by the others. She hadn't liked to force them. For some children that part of the brain just isn't switched on at eight. It's not laziness or stupidity. Really stupid children were a rarity, and she used to tell her young teachers, 'Never write a child off. Never assume the problem is theirs rather than yours.' There was no great mystery to it. Alec, for example, sitting at the front of the class like a baby owl, his eyes magnified by his glasses, his hair sticking up in tufts, had never had the slightest difficulty learning French. Partly, of course, because in the beginning she was his teacher and he so desperately wanted to please her, a trait charming and irksome by turns and which he had never really grown out of. She had heard the same tone in his voice telling her about the new play as he used to have when he brought her his homework, as though at any moment he might be squashed by an enormous thumb. Well done, Alec. Good boy. Go and find Larry. *Je suis, tu es, il est.* Larry's kingdom was the sports field. Captain of cricket. Captain of football. And later, as a senior, captain of the tennis team. Such a manly little boy! And she had always been there, cheering herself hoarse on the touchline, or courtside at tournaments that grew ever grander, her heart in her mouth as he swayed at the baseline and the boy at the far end reached into the air for the ball. The day he beat the Swede, whose name she seemed to have completely forgotten, had been the proudest day of her life. She had wanted to shout out from the stands so that the whole world would hear: 'I'm the mother! I'm the mother!' It was difficult for Alec, of course. The inevitable comparisons. Always being introduced as 'Larry's brother' as though he didn't have a name of his own. But she had doled out her love as evenly as possible. There had been no obvious favourite.

What on earth *was* the Swedish boy's name? She searched for a minute, but found nothing except a trace of darkness like a swipe of fresh black paint covering up the place in her head where the name should have been. Gone. Like the name of Mrs Samson's eldest, who they were only talking about yesterday morning while Mrs S hoovered around the bed and 'set things straight'. And the names of a dozen flowers, and . . . what was it, what was it she had forgotten the other day? Something else, the title of an opera she liked, or the name of the man who read the news on the radio which she knew perfectly well and had known for years. What she did remember often seemed quite random, as though her life were an old lumber room through which memory moved like a drunk with a torch, and she would find herself with a photographic recollection of the meat counter at Tesco's, or remembering word for word a conversation with Toni about her poodle. She didn't want to go with that in her mind, a last image of Toni's poodle hovering transcendentally above her like the parrot in the Flaubert story.

Ding! Ding! Ding! . . .

The little blue-and-white jasper clock in the niche at the bottom of the stairs. Only ten o'clock! How epic the nights had become! And how she longed for someone to lay a hand on her brow, someone who would say, 'All shall be well, all shall be well . . .' Even poor Stephen would be welcome now, the youthful Stephen, the way he was at teacher training college in Bristol when they first met, puffing away at that silly pipe, cracking jokes, talking politics, twang of Manchester in his voice, Stalybridge. Of course, he was drinking even then, but they all did, it was part of being young, everyone talking too much and smoking their heads off. It was never a problem until Alec was born. Then, instead of getting merry on Friday and Saturday nights, he would stop off at the pub on his way home from the school and go on with it sitting in front of the television or down in the workroom. Brooding, drinking, dreaming up new enemies for himself, building his own elaborate hell. People said it got worse after he missed promotion to head of department at King Alfred's. Others said it was because he wanted to be in higher education, not in a secondary school, that he didn't really *like* children, but it wasn't that. Something had gone wrong with Stephen before she had ever met him. God knows what. Talking personally he called 'psychobabble', and she got tired of looking in the end. Probably he didn't know himself, because it wasn't always neat. You can't always give it a name. Like the cancer. What was the root of it? Stress? Cigarettes? Bad luck? Some secret weakness. A hairline fracture that one day brings the house down. None of us, she thought, none of us survives our imperfections.

He used to shout at her, which shocked her at first because she had never been shouted at in that way before, never seen how extraordinarily ugly a person can be when they shout like that. But he only hit her once, once being enough. A push in the back after some idiotic argument about Callaghan or the unions. It was in the kitchen. She had said something to him and was walking away when he lunged at her, shoving her so that she staggered and had to catch at the wall to stop herself from falling. She had been frightened for a moment, a little dizzy from the sheer unpleasantness of it all. Then she had turned to him, slowly and calmly, because she knew by then it was the same rule for drunks and dangerous dogs. Show no fear. And when their eyes met again, when he had the guts to look at her, there was a distance between them that neither would ever cross, and almost immediately she had felt a certain nostalgia, not for him, but for some idea she had had about her own life, some understanding she had suddenly outgrown. He was on a bottle a day by the time of the accident. Vodka mostly, but anything would do. The police said they'd found bottles in the car. In pieces, one imagines.

Months later, his mother called, quite late at night, and said a better woman would have saved him. You didn't love him right, she said. You didn't love him like you should, you didn't, Alice. It's a shame, she said. Shame on you. Bitch. What? Bitch, she said. And they had wept at each other down the telephone line for a long time, then sniffed and said goodbye, and that was that, apart from cards on the boys' birthdays with a five-pound note inside.

Three men in a lifetime. It hardly made her Messalina. Rupert Langley, who had been her first beau, her tennis partner and escort, the boy she lost her virginity to. Then Samuel Pinedo. Then Stephen. A few more fumbled with at dances before she was married, or who had taken her out in the years after the accident to dinners or the theatre and kissed her goodnight in their cars.

She still sometimes played the 'if' game, wondering how her life would have been with Samuel. If he had asked her. If she had said yes. If. She was thirteen when he was introduced to her as someone 'Daddy knew in the war'. A man with black brilliantined hair, lounging against the window frame in the front room. Thin, pale, a rather prominent Adam's apple. Not a really handsome man. But something in his gaze had disturbed her. She didn't know what it was, what to call it, but when she thought about it afterwards, she decided that he was the first man to have looked at her as a woman rather than as a child, and that there was a generosity in it, a chivalry, which even after nearly fifty years she had not quite recovered from.

His people had been in the diamond business in Amsterdam. Jews from old Spain. Seraphic? When the Nazis came they sent his parents, uncles, cousins and two sisters to the camps in Poland. Samuel had hidden like the little Frank girl, though he was luckier, of course. Got out. Came to England in a fishing boat. Six months later he went back. Helped to organize escape routes for aircrew until they caught him. After the liberation Queen Wilhelmina gave him a medal that he kept loose in the pocket of his suit jacket with his lighter and cigarettes.

She was eighteen when they met again. Nineteen before they became lovers. He was at the embassy in London then, Hyde Park Gate, and came down at weekends on the train from Paddington, and she would go with her father to meet him, terrified in case he had got off at some quite different station with his coat over his arm and his little case, and smiled at some other girl. Her father called him 'the best sort of Jew'. He must have guessed what was going on but he never said anything. People didn't in those days.

Was Samuel still alive? If so he'd be almost eighty, which she found impossible to imagine. She'd seen his name in *The Times* once. Part of a UN delegation to somewhere, so he must have had some success. Become somebody.

Lord! They did it in the garden shed once, on the workbench. Torn stockings, bruised backside, the air stinking of petrol from the lawnmower. He had scars on his back. A dozen ridges of purple skin, and when she asked him about them he winked at her and said it was a girl in Amsterdam with long nails. But nails don't make marks like that. She used to touch them, stroke them very lightly, as though his back were rucked velvet she could smooth with her fingertips. What had he done with his pain? Had it come out later? Did he take to drink too? Or had someone helped him when he needed it? Making love he called dancing. She'd known next to nothing about sex before Samuel, and after him hadn't learned much that seemed worth knowing.

The year her father died he was posted back to Holland. He left her a ring – not a diamond ring, but a gold band that had belonged to his mother, and which had his mother's name engraved in curly letters on the inside. *Margot*. It had been too small to wear and it wouldn't have been right. It was a keepsake. A remnant. The little Jewess's ring. The little Jewess they had turned into ashes.

How wonderful if she could believe she'd see him again 'on the other side'; some celestial cocktail party where everyone was young and interesting and Nat King Cole was singing 'When I Fall In Love'. But she didn't believe it, didn't believe in the other side at all. The last of her faith had ebbed away during the chemo. A night on her knees by the side of the bed vomiting into a bucket, and above her just miles of emptiness. No gentle Jesus. No saints or angels. Religion was a night-light for children – Stephen had been right about that. Eyewash. Osbourne was harmless. One of the old fashioned type. 'Black cloth a little dusty, a little green with holy mildew.' She could tease him, and he had always been nice to the boys. Rather fancied her once, when she was first a widow. Popping round for glasses of sherry, offering to do the lawn, carrying out the black bin-bags of Stephen's things for the charity shop. Did he mean to try to catch her at the end? Run across the meadow with his box of tricks when he heard she was going? She would have to speak to him. No mumbo-jumbo, Dennis, dear, when I'm too weak to tell you to get lost. He could say what he liked when it was over. Whatever made it easier for the others.

But did *nothing* last? Was the 'she' who thought all this just a brain that would die when the last of the oxygen was used up? Surely there was something inside, some inward shadow, the part that loved Mozart or Samuel Pinedo. Didn't that go on, somehow? Or was the afterlife just others remembering you, so that you died, truly died, when you were truly forgotten?

The children at school would remember her for a year or two. They had made a 'Get Well' card for her, with a picture of the school on the front, and each of them had written his or her name inside with great care, and some had put an X for a kiss. 'DEAR MRS VALENTINE WE HOPE YOU GET WELL SOON.' Row upon row of scrubbed faces gazing up at her at morning assembly. Mr Price thundering away at the upright. All good gifts. Morning has broken. The extraordinary thing was that Brando's son had been one of them. She would have been a form mistress then but she thought she remembered him, a good-looking boy about Alec's age. A doctor like his father now. Another doctor! In the end they were the only people you knew, though at least Brando was human. She could vouch for that. And what a relief when he took over from Playfair, that pompous little man who talked down to her because she was a woman. Thought himself so clever, but he knew *nothing*.

On the visits she made to Brando before feeling ill again,

the check-ups, they used to talk more about the children, or about themselves, than about the cancer. His father had been an Italian POW in a camp somewhere in Somerset, married a local girl, then opened a little restaurant in Bristol that some nephew still owned. He said that in dreams sometimes he could smell his father's home-made polenta pie, and she'd told him, laughing, that sometimes she dreamed of her mother's chutneys, and of chutney-making day, when the kitchen was full of steam, a little sweet, a little savoury, that hung about the house for days.

Of course, she had seen that he was upset when she went to collect the results of her tests. The way he met her at the door and led her to the chair by his desk, then sort of perched on the corner, leaning towards her. She had said something like, it's not good news, is it, and he said no, he was afraid not. The tumours in her chest had come back, and there were mets, secondaries in the brain. *The* brain, not hers. Not *your* brain, Alice. *The* brain. He asked her whether she wanted to see the images but she said she would take his word for it. After all, there was nothing very surprising. She had known perfectly well that something was wrong, something serious. Headaches that lasted two or three days. Squiggly lights at the edge of vision. And she had read the literature, she could practically recite it. Small-cell cancer was 'aggressive'. It did not rest. She was lucky to have had the last two years.

The books all recommended that the patient have a list of questions to ask, a written list so that you didn't get in a muddle, but she didn't have one, and all she could think to ask was what everyone asks. How long? Such a silly question because doctors are not fortune-tellers and cancer doesn't run to a timetable, but Brando had nodded and paused as though doing calculations in his head, some sort of algebra, and then said she should enjoy the summer as fully as she could. Get out in the sun, he said. I know you have a lovely garden. It took her a moment to work out what he was saying, to realize that he meant there wouldn't be any autumn, yet alone a winter. She went deaf for a minute and had the curious sensation that it was the words and not the tumours that would kill her. When she could hear again he was explaining the treatment she could have. Surgery was not an option, but they could start her on another course of chemo in combination with radiation therapy, retard the spread of the disease a little, reduce the swellings. Think it over, he said. No need to make up your mind today. He said he was very sorry and she knew that he meant it. She asked about his son and he asked about her boys. He knew all about Larry and the show, and how there had been artistic differences. She told him that Alec was outside in the carpark waiting for her in the car, his old Renault, and did he know the type with the gear-shift on the dashboard, a great hook of a thing, and she couldn't imagine why they had it there when in every other car in the world the shift was on the floor, which was the obvious place, and how typically French it was, always wanting to be a little different. She was still talking, babbling on, when the tears started. She was powerless to stop them because no one can be ready for such a moment and there was a violence to it that took her unawares. What else do you have but your life? Where else can you go? And then to find yourself in someone's office with the sun squinting through the blinds and everything theatrically normal and twenty things to get done that day, and it's all over. Finished. Ground out. And so she had wept, intemperately, cried so that she felt the seams of her face would break open, and Brando had reached for her and hugged her. No awkwardness in it. Just pressing her face gently against the cloth of his suit as though he were taking into himself some portion of her grief. Playfair would rather have eaten his stethoscope. He would not have been physically capable of hugging. Plenty of people weren't and that was the pity of the world. Larry could, Alec couldn't. Samuel, but not Stephen.

There was a box of tissues on the desk. She blew her nose and dabbed at her eyes, carefully, so as not to smudge her eyeliner. She was quite in control of herself by the time she reached the carpark. That's that, she thought. She told Alec on the way home. Gave him the gist of it, very calmly, as though talking about someone they both vaguely knew, a neighbour. It was almost comical. He stalled the car three times at the traffic lights at the end of Commercial Road, and for a moment she was afraid he was going to have some sort of collapse, a 'wobble', like the one he had before, when the police found him wandering along the beach at Brighton in a perfect daze. But they got home somehow, teatime, six o'clock perhaps, and she went into the garden to find that the first of the lilac was out, and she had cried again, sitting on the bench by the summerhouse, fronds of honeysuckle round her head, crying for joy at so much beauty and wanting to float up over the potato fields like the heroine in one of those South American novels, Alec waving to her with a white handkerchief from an upstairs window. It hadn't lasted, of course. A week later she was so low they started her on the Paroxetine.

At least the will was done, though she had wondered recently whether she might leave something to Una. She hadn't been sure at first about Una O'Connell. A dreamy, rather self-contained sort of character. And it was hard not to resent the young. Their rude health. The feeling that one was being *condescended* to. But the girl had qualities. Good hands. A sweet, rather melancholy smile. And in her way she knew as much about the wretched cancer as Brando did. Alec could give the lawyers a call tomorrow (you had to be careful; she couldn't stand the thought of disputes). Then when Larry came she must speak to them both about the funeral, which they wouldn't have a clue about. Stephen's had cost the best part of two thousand pounds, and that was twenty years ago. There were cardboard coffins now, biodegradable. She had even read that you could be composted, which might be amusing. Four parts vegetable waste to one part human. The boys would decide about the house. And what would they do with her clothes? Give them away? Burn them?

Last of all there were the goodbyes (numberless, they seemed, though that couldn't be right). Goodbyes to the living and goodbyes to the dead – for the dead would go too, those she had been sheltering in her head, in memories. What made it so trying was not knowing how she would be from one day to the next, not being able to rely on herself, this slender stricken thing between the sheets, this body that Samuel Pinedo had once thought so lovely. Yet somehow she must do it, and as she slid back towards sleep she envisaged all those last thoughts and last acts like a line of delicate sun machines, those glass bulbs like the one Alec had had as a child with sails of light-sensitive paper on a pin which whirled beneath the glass when the sun shone on them.

'*Je te sauverai,*' they said. '*Je te sauverai, maman.*' And she let herself be comforted.

9

Alec dimmed the light of the lantern, then went inside to call America. The telephone in the kitchen was the farthest from Alice's room – the least likely to disturb her – and the ten-digit number he needed was written on the cracked paint of the wall beside the telephone. His own number was just below it, and at the top of the list were the hospital number and Una's home number. For a few seconds the receiver hissed like a conch shell, then began to ring. He counted fifteen rings and was about to hang up when he heard Kirsty's breathless 'Hello?'

'Hi,' said Alec.

'Larry?'

'Alec.'

'Alec! Is everything OK?'

'Fine.'

'I was in the shower,' she said. 'I just got back from the centre. Wow, what a day!'

'Zen?' asked Alec.

'Yeah. We've got this roshi over from Kyoto. Mr Endo.' She laughed. 'I think I'm in love.'

'Congratulations,' said Alec, laughing too, though quietly. He imagined her, with her wet hair pushed behind her ears, the colour of it darkened a little by the water.

'He gave us our koans,' she said.

'Koans?'

'The riddles.'

'Ah,' said Alec. 'The sound of one hand clapping.'

'That kind of thing.'

'What's yours?'

'Gosh,' she said, 'I don't think we're supposed to tell.'

'What happens when you find the answer?'

'Well, you get a Buddhist name, and it's like the first stage.'

'Enlightenment by instalments.'

'Don't be such a Brit, Alec. I know you think it's the Moonies.'

'No I don't,' he said. 'I envy you.'

'How's Alice?'

'She has to rest a lot.'

'Is Brando still coming?'

'He'll be here tomorrow,' said Alec. He didn't share the general enthusiasm for Brando. All that charm and authority. He suspected Brando did not approve of him either. The translator. The ineffectual son.

'Larry's just sick with worry,' said Kirsty. 'And it's not as if he has much to take his mind off it.'

'He's not working?'

'If he could just get back on the show . . .'

'Dr Barry.'

'I know it wasn't Shakespeare or anything.'

'I never knocked it. Is he there?'

'He's in LA. Some "business" trip.'

'He said he'd call,' said Alec.

'Well, that's Larry. But I know he wants to speak to you. He talks about you more than anyone.'

'Really?'

'I guess he thinks he should be over there. Maybe. I don't know. I mean, why would he tell me what he thinks?' The telephone bleeped like sonar. Alec heard her sniff and sigh. 'Poor Alice. I really love her.'

'Come on,' he said, afraid that she would start something in him. 'Do some Zen breathing. How does it work?'

'Ella,' she said, 'are you on the extension, honey?'

There was silence, then a tiny, hesitant, 'Yes.'

'It's your Uncle Alec. Calling from England. Say hello, honey.'

Alec waited. At last, a faintly lisped hello crossed the six thousand miles between them.

'It's night here,' he said, talking to the girl. 'A little while ago I heard an owl hooting at the end of the garden. Maybe you'll hear it when you come for Granny's birthday.'

'She'd love that,' said Kirsty. 'Now put the phone down, baby, and let me talk with Uncle Alec. Come on, Ella, put it down . . .' There was a subtle click. 'She does that all the time. I really want to get her more help but it's so darned expensive.'

'Is she still borrowing stuff?'

'Larry found one of my earrings in her booty last night. At least he knows where to look for them. She likes you, Alec.'

'I haven't seen her for a year.'

'She remembers you.'

'Has Larry picked up the tickets?'

'I guess so.'

'Why don't you all fly together?'

'I want to finish this course. I know it's selfish but Endo's too good to miss.'

'You're right,' said Alec. 'Solve your riddle. Then come.'

'Have you tried scalp massage?' she asked. 'You use your fingertips to move the scalp over the skull, like you're washing hair.'

'Is that a Zen thing?'

'Not everything's Zen, Alec.' She paused, trying to recall what she had been taught earlier in the day. 'Well, maybe it is. Anyway, you should do it for Alice. It'll make her feel good.'

'Not if I did it,' he said. He found the idea absurd to the point of comedy.

'You're not such a klutz.'

'Thanks.'

'How's your Romanian guy? Or was he Albanian or something?'

'Hungarian.'

'Right. Didn't you say he was some kind of old freedom fighter? A sort of Che Guevara?'

'Something like that.'

'I know it's a lousy time for you, Alec. Larry'll be there soon.'

'The cavalry!'

'I hope you two aren't going to fight.'

'Why should we?'

'Well, brothers do. Remember Cain and Abel? But maybe you're the one who can help him.'

'Help *Larry*?'

'People change, Alec.'

'Do they? I thought they just got more like themselves.'

She laughed but didn't sound very amused. 'I guess.'

'Has something happened?'

'Just the usual. Give hugs to Alice.'

'Sure. Kiss Ella for me.'

'Get some sleep,' she said, 'you sound tired.'

'I'm on my way,' he said.

'Take care now.'

'You too.'

'I know things are going to work out somehow.'

'Yes.'

'I'm glad you called.'

'Bye-bye.'

'Bye.'

She rang off and Alec slowly hung up the receiver. Help Larry? This was a novel suggestion. A disturbing one! What had she been hinting at? What type of trouble? He tried for a moment (staring at the wall as though at a screen) to do what he had not done in a long, long while: to have a view of his brother's life, an objective take on it, but he realized he simply didn't have the information any more – certainly not the kind of private information that might make sense of an expression like 'the usual'. But then, how did a knowledge of a person's circumstances weigh against a knowledge of his character? A character in Larry's case that Alec still believed he knew better than Kirsty, if only because he had known it first and was himself written into it. He *knew* what Larry was made of. Perhaps she had meant 'help Kirsty'. People were forever calling out in confusing ways.

He boiled the kettle for tea, brewed it in a cup, dropped the tea bag into the swing-bin and opened the fridge for the milk. On the shelves were the empty plastic tubs that had once contained the ingredients of Alice's diet, souvenirs from the time when she had sought to guard herself against the cancer's return, to make herself inviolate by consuming only the purest and most wholesome of foods. The search for these foods had been expensive and time consuming, and seemed largely useless now; all that vigilance and fibre, those trips to health-food co-ops for boxes of misshapen vegetables brought out to the car by people who looked in desperate need of a blood sausage. But nothing that might provoke the beast had been allowed into the kitchen, and the effort had perhaps rewarded her with a few extra months of comparative health, though in the end organic broccoli and alfalfa seeds would not save your life, and Alec swung shut the fridge door more firmly than he'd meant to, rattling half-empty bottles of flower remedy and vitamin C, of shark cartilage, emulsified linseed capsules, and a dozen others that had once teasingly suggested themselves as the necessary elixirs.

Sipping his tea, he crossed the living room and went the length of a short corridor of scuffed and torn lino into the 'playroom'. In the twenty years since he and Larry had used it as a den the room had become a kind of depositary, a ramshackle museum of family history, the boards piled high with junk. He had visited the room on the previous two nights at about the same hour, each time on the pretext of starting to determine what from among this tidal wash of oddments might be kept, though the truth – which standing in the doorway he now admitted to himself – was that the room still retained for him something of its air of refuge. It soothed him, and among those stations of the night that were becoming increasingly apparent to him, it was an interlude of calm, a place where he could breathe the gentle anaesthetic of nostalgia.

Some of the objects in the room had reached their last declension, existing only in a stubborn limbo of silence and inutility. Others were immediately eloquent. A beige and purple oil heater of curious design, sitting where it had been placed perhaps fifteen years before, instantly revived a scene of winter evenings after school, a scent of oil mingling with the smell of sausages or fish-fingers, and the wafting all-pervasive smoke of Alice's cigarettes. And from the box he had emptied the previous evening he had pulled out, as though lifting something precious and extraordinary from the pharaoh's tomb, a single tan boxing glove, lone memento of his slogging matches with Larry, fights which, however temperately begun, often ended with a flurry of wild punches, and Alec on the floor bawling with frustration, while Larry stood over him, anger already cooling to remorse as he glanced nervously at the door.

Tonight's box, which he dragged under the light of the ceiling bulb, was a large supermarket fruit carton with SPAR in green letters along the side. Here, with a rush of whatever chemical such recognitions released into the blood, he discovered the pieces of an elaborate toy that must have been given when he was about seven, and Larry nine or ten: a lunar landscape made of moulded plastic, and a little spidery landing craft of great simplicity and delicacy that had once had a balloon attached to it, and which was directed on to the sheet of moon by small battery-powered fans. It belonged to a period that now seemed bizarrely remote, when space travel was front-page news and children kept scrapbooks with pictures of astronauts. No self-respecting child would waste time on such a toy now. For a start, there was no screen.

Under the moon, though from the same era, was a brightly coloured tin with a picture on the lid of a man in a smoking jacket holding a magic wand. Inside were three red cups, each smaller than an eggcup, and half a dozen pea-sized balls. A booklet illustrated with sketchy and perplexing diagrams explained how, by sleight of hand, the balls could be made to disappear from beneath one cup and reappear beneath another. To do this it was necessary to obtain the knack of holding a ball pressed inconspicuously into the crease of your palm. Alec tried it a few times; it was surprisingly difficult, but it was, he thought, the kind of trick that any good uncle should be able to perform, and he determined to learn it, thoroughly, and entertain Ella with it when she came over.

Other stuff: a school gazette from King Alfred's with a grainy still of boys on sport's day – small, ghostly figures, bizarrely intent, strung out across an enormous grey field. The finishing line, which might have given the picture some context, was out of shot, and far from being redolent of a summer's afternoon, of youthful athleticism, the boys seemed to have been posed there to illustrate some idea of human futility. Farther on, another Xeroxed photograph showed a group of adolescents standing about with stick-on moustaches and frock-coats for a production of the school play, *The Importance of Being Earnest*, in which Alec had played Algy Moncrieff, 'creditably', according to the gazette, though all he could remember of it was the angry crimson mottle on his throat brought about by first-night nerves; the urge to bolt.

A box of Cluedo.

A card game called Pit.

A 'spud' gun in the style of an automatic, the spring action still functioning.

A Frank Zappa album, warped.

A hardback copy of *Struwwelpeter*.

Finally, stashed at the very bottom of the box, was an American girlie magazine from June 1977, Miss Valley Forge on the cover in a stars-and-stripes bikini and Davy Crockett hat. Inside – the month's theme was American revolutionary ardour – other models pouted beside cannon or reclined on couches wearing only tricorn hats, or leered obediently from the froth of a Jacuzzi with a provocatively handled flintlock. All sexual promise had leached away from the images, as though they were time sensitive. The models, with their huge roseate breasts, looked as if they belonged to a super-race of wet nurses. All that was missing were the babies themselves, who should have been glimpsed in the background, crawling blindly over the basques and boas. It was hard to believe that these women, now perhaps winning glamorous grandmother competitions in Amarillo or Grand Rapids, had been among the cast of his adolescent fantasies. Their nudity roused no appetite in him now, but they reminded him – as almost everything did – that he had not had sex for eleven months, and that the last occasion, with Tatania Osgood, a girl who had slept with almost everyone he knew, had been so wretched it could never be spoken of, too bleak even to be converted into one of those humorously self-deprecating narratives of sexual failure that might have seemed, in certain company, endearing and funny. Fragments of the evening, a series of tableaux, adhered in his memory with a kind of malicious clarity. Tatania at the street door of his flat in Streatham holding a supermarket carrier bag containing two bottles of a wine called Tiger Milk. Tatania on the sofa of his little book-strewn sitting room, braless in a tight black dress and exuding a wantonness that was genuinely sad. Himself at 2 a.m. kissing her and trapping his fingers in the gusseting of her tights. The pair of them on the bed, she in tears as he tried to comfort her for a succession of cheating boyfriends. Then the act itself, a pleasureless dry wrestling, Mr Bequa's TV jabbering away in the next room. And when at last the soft hammer of drink had sent her reeling into sleep, he had lain beside her listening to the thick of her breath, and thinking how the evening's meanness and failure were part of a much larger failure, and that this was the price of his timidity; that he had earned such a night and would earn others by never having the courage to ask for anything better. He had had the urge then – still associated in his mind with the dawn tinkling of milk floats – to commit some act that would close the road behind him for ever, some extravagance of love, or something violent perhaps, murderous.

He carried the cup-and-ball game into the living room, then moved softly up the stairs and peered into his mother's room to where she lay in the quarter-light as if in a body of water whose currents moved her limbs and slowly turned her face from side to side on the pillows. Her inhalations were like moments of hushed surprise, and in each breath it seemed she lost more than she gained. The sickness was weaning her off air, and however many good days she had when she could sit in the garden with a rug and drink Darjeeling tea and talk to her visitors, the process, the day-to-day business of dying, ran on relentlessly, a ferocious, semi-public labour. What sense did it have, beyond the workings of a certain crude biology? What good lesson could be learned from watching someone die? Was it just to throw you back harder against your own life, to make you see the necessity of getting on with it? a memento mori like the old gravestones with their skulls and sand timers and glib reminders that 'soon you shall be as I am'?

He had tried once, shortly after Stephen's accident, to believe in God and the overarching purposefulness of things. He had set aside time every day to say his prayers: twenty minutes in the morning and twenty at night, kneeling down in the approved manner with his hands clasped by his lips. He told no one about it, and it had felt good at first, a source of consolation and power that did not depend on anybody else, teachers or parents, people who might suddenly not be there any more. Then the two sessions had became one and the twenty minutes shrank to ten. He talked to God but God did not talk back to him. There was only the sound of his own voice, the childish litany, the discomfort in his knees, until finally, with a sense of getting out into the air again, he had given it all up. His father had reserved a special venom for religion, the 'God-botherers'. Alec didn't know if Alice believed. He hoped she did, though the last time he had seen her with Osbourne she had been ragging him, saying that she had turned into a sun worshipper, 'a bit of an Aztec', something that the reverend, sitting beside her wearing a pair of green-shaded sunglasses, seemed to think entirely compatible with modern Anglicanism. It was a curious fact, however, that she *did*, in certain lights, certain hours, her face puffed up by the steroids, her gaze refined by suffering, look more like a tribal elder of some delicate mournful people in the great plains or rainforests than a middle-class English woman, a retired headmistress, his mother, Alice Valentine.

She opened her eyes, suddenly, as though she had not been asleep at all.

'Larry?' she said.

'No, Mum, it's me.'

A pause, then, 'I was dreaming of you'.

10

Stylistically, the foyer of the Park Hotel was a marriage between an Italian bank and an English gentleman's club, but in its scale, its air of having been built the previous afternoon, the not quite convincing efficiency of it all, it was entirely home grown.

Larry made for the drink station in the well of the room and ordered a large Jim Beam from a barman in a tight white pea jacket. The convention was in full swing, and among the fountains, the marble, the plump sofas and the scurrying bellhops, several hundred mostly middle-aged men milled about industriously, peering at each other's identity tags. There were many fulsome greetings, and when they laughed they advertised their trade with mouths full of lustrous and symmetrical teeth. They were wholesome-looking men, by and large, and though they must have had their share of the world's problems – errant kids, alimonies, mal-practice suits – they wore everywhere the same expression of intense boyish delight, so that Larry was tempted to suspect them of visiting their own medicine chests. Mainstream Americans. Taxpayers, baseball fans. Serious people with a certain chis-elled gravitas. Veterans, some of them, of Korea and Vietnam. Patriots. Yet the more Larry looked at them the more he wondered how long his self-willed exile among such people, who had started to appear as exotic as Berbers or Malay fire-walkers, could possibly continue. It was as if the country were slipping away from him, or he was beginning at last to find unignorable the fine hard surface of its difference, of *his* difference. Vexing to have to see this now! To be forced to admit how much more there was to belonging somewhere than just being there. But where else could he go? Back to England? What would he do there? He would be a minor item in the evening paper – 'Local Tennis Ace Comes Home' – and then sink without trace, reduced, if he was lucky, to double-glazing ads on television, or perhaps a tennis instructorship at a local country club, where he would sit at the bar in his whites, a lush with solarium-tanned skin, making assignations with unhappily married women.

At the front desk he enquired whether a Mr Bone, a Mr T. Bone, had a room at the hotel. Anywhere but LA and he would have received the 'wiseass' look, but in a city where doormen were dressed like characters in a Gilbert and Sullivan operetta, the citizens were not given to displays of incredulity. The receptionist, Kimberly Ng, sporting an Employee of the Month badge on her lapel, checked her screen and said that they did indeed have a Mr Bone with them at the moment. Larry gave his name and she called up to the room, informing him that he was expected, and that he should take the elevator to the twenty-seventh floor of the Tower.

'Room 2714, sir. Enjoy your visit with us today.'

A broad and velvety walkway connected the hotel to the adjoining Tower, the walls serving as a gallery for photographs of the luminaries who had graced the hotel in the past. Reagan's image was prominent: a large picture of him on a spacious balcony looking relaxed under the California sun, a half-dozen smiling cronies around him. Then Reagan on the telephone to receive some historic message. Reagan with Nancy, a loving couple, tanned and innocent.

Farther along, there were images of the moonshot astronauts – Armstrong, Aldrin and Collins – and though he was now running late, Larry paused to look at these more closely. The astronauts had been honoured at a reception in the hotel entitled 'Dinner of the Century'. It certainly looked grand enough. In the foreground there were uniformed trumpeters, then about a thousand dignitaries, and finally the astronauts themselves in dark suits, looking solemn and pleased and impossibly modest.

It was just before four o'clock on a summer's morning in England when the *Eagle* touched down in the Sea of Tranquillity. The Valentines, like any other family in the country with a TV set, had sat in a breathless hush watching the crackly flag of history unfurl in front of them. Larry on the floor between his father's knees; Alec snuggling up with Alice on the couch. The thrilling ellipses of the language! Its weird laconic delivery. 'Roger, you're looking great, you're go.' 'How us, Houston?' Armstrong, cool as any gunslinger, guiding the module down, while at Mission Control the backroom boys in their white shirts sat anxiously before rows of whirring computers. How strange that today of all days he had crossed the path of these men, icons of the kind of clean-cut heroism he had never ceased to admire. It was as though their picture had been posted there as a warning, or a reminder, or in some way to mock him. He wondered how many people remembered there had been a Russian craft, *Luna 15*, in low orbit round the moon at the same time as *Apollo*, and that it had ended its flight by crashing at 300 mph into the Sea of Crises. 'How me?' he muttered, 'How me?' as he entered the elevator, ascending to the twenty-seventh floor in the company of several Japanese businessmen, who gazed studiously into the car's limited middle distance.

The meeting had been arranged by telephone the week before by a young actor called Ranch whom Larry had first met at the party of a man in the glamour industry who owned a beautiful house in Sausalito. Ranch, looking like an Armani cowpoke, had been trying to impress a very tall black model with his display of karate kata, but the girl, listless from some dieting drug, had wandered off halfway through the action, a level of interest that might have provoked a moment's resentment in most men, but Ranch had merely shrugged and grinned with chivalrous regret at the swing of her backside as she disappeared into the next room, and then immediately introduced himself to Larry, complimenting him on how 'fucking great' he was looking. Since then there had been other parties in other beautiful homes, where Larry had explained some of his predicament, and Ranch had promised to help him somehow, an idea that Larry had not, for a single moment, taken seriously.

But it was Ranch who opened the door to 2714, dressed in a dark suit and purple open-neck shirt with a large collar, his sideburns razored to knife points, his eyes back-lit by the morning's consumption of something considerably stronger than coffee. He embraced Larry as though he meant it and led him to the television screen where something wet and bloodily intrusive was going on.

'What is it?' asked Larry, wincing.

Ranch laughed. 'It's the in-house channel. The dentists have got their own TV show!' He laughed again. 'Sick fucks,' he said, then in a quieter voice added, 'TB's out on the balcony.'

For a moment Larry hoped it might be the same balcony he had seen Reagan on in the picture, but as he stepped out into the glare he saw that it was more modest, a different grade of opulence altogether.

T. Bone was on a sun chair set in an angle of shade. He didn't stand when Larry came out, but smiled, and offered a small soft hand like a mole's paw.

'Quite a view from up here,' he said, turning his head slightly to where the afternoon sun and the day's emission of CO_2 had nebulized LA to a fine haze in which the buildings seemed carved from smoke. 'Shirley Temple used to play down there. And once upon a time it was Tom Mix's ranch. We like to come here when we're meeting new friends. It creates a certain "atmosphere". Have a seat, sir. Ranch, fix Mr Larry something cool and dangerous to drink.'

'Comin' up,' said Ranch. He disappeared through the drapes into the bedroom.

'He's first rate,' said T. Bone, leaning forward confidentially. 'Found in a carpetbag in the ladies' conveniences at Union Station. In and out of institutions all his life. Convinced he'll meet his mother on "the other side", poor lamb. Tell me, Larry. Do children in England still have those little Barnardo boxes for collecting money for the orphans?'

'I'm not sure,' said Larry, who vaguely remembered that he and Alec had once had such a box. A little yellow cottage with a slot in the roof.

'One hopes so,' said T. Bone, settling back and smiling

from the shadows. 'It encourages them to think of those less fortunate. There's so little of that these days. *N'est-ce pas?*'

'Last days of the Empire,' said Larry, flippantly.

'Oh, not yet,' said T. Bone. 'No. I think we've a little more time.'

This man, thought Larry, returning the other's amused gaze, contained within himself such depths of fraudulence you would never come to the end of him. To look at he was a benign, slightly eccentric figure in his sixties with an uncanny resemblance to the older John Betjeman. He wore a Hawaiian shirt, khaki shorts and, on his very white legs, some manner of surgical support socks finished off with a pair of highly polished brogues. His accent was the sort of camp upper-class English little heard since the death of Noël Coward, but beneath it, like the faint pattern of old wallpaper under whitewash, Larry detected another voice, something grimly urban, provincial and brutish, so that it was not difficult to imagine him, somewhere in the 1950s, a little slicked hoodlum in a bombed-out and rain-damaged city like Plymouth or Slough, the type of character who carried a sharpened steel comb in his pocket.

Ranch's cool and dangerous drink arrived, blue and gin-dry and delicious. Ranch and Larry put on sunglasses, an event followed by ten minutes of small talk concerning the heat, the merits of Mexican food, the flight of the comet. Finally, after a lengthy pause during which the ice cracked and tinkled in their glasses, T. Bone said: 'We all adored you as Dr Barry.'

'Jesus, yes,' said Ranch.

'Thanks,' said Larry.

'They should have made more of you,' said T. Bone, 'but television is run by morons. Don't you think?'

'Morons,' crooned Ranch, as though he were at a revivalist meeting.

'I'm glad to be out of it,' said Larry, watching from the corner of his eye Ranch flick peanuts into the air and expertly catch them in his mouth.

'We have a little project,' said T. Bone, 'we think would be perfect for you. Nothing extreme. The kind of viewing enjoyed by thousands of healthy Americans every day.'

'Except,' said Ranch, resting a hand on Larry's shoulder, 'it won't be Americans watching it.'

'Just so,' said T. Bone. 'You would be dubbed into Portuguese and Spanish for our South American market. *Sun Valley* has been playing in Brazil and Argentina for months. You're a great favourite there. Particularly, one imagines, with the dusky housewives.'

'You got fans in places you ain't even heard of,' said Ranch. 'Bacabal, Xique-Xique . . .'

'We make our little productions very simply,' said T. Bone, looking now like Sir Ralph Richardson playing a Borgia pope. 'We remain the true auteurs. We are an industry of enthusiasts.'

'How long would the shoot take?' asked Larry.

'A week,' said Ranch, 'two weeks max.'

'For which we can offer you a fee of twenty thousand dollars,' added T. Bone. 'Naturally we'd like it to be more but these days we have to compete with the Web. However, we can arrange payment so that you need not worry about the gentlemen at the revenue.'

' And I wouldn't have to do anything I could get arrested for?'

'It's all kosher,' said Ranch.

'No Lolitas or animals?'

'I am a father,' said T. Bone, 'and a nature lover.'

'One more thing,' said Larry. 'I'm going to be in England from next week. I don't know how long for. Not long, I think.'

'I'll make a note of that,' said Ranch, flicking another peanut into the air.

Twenty-seven floors below, where Shirley Temple had once played, a lone swimmer pulled himself across the green eye of a pool. Back and forth, back and forth, like a water beetle. It was a fine day for a swim but something in the figure's progress, or lack of it, was disturbing. Presumably he was counting off his daily quota of lengths, getting himself in shape, but it looked unprofitable, forlorn, like that Greek in hell who pushed a rock up the hill all day just to watch it roll to the bottom again.

'OK,' said Larry. 'Why not? Count me in.'

'A great day for us, Larry,' said Ranch, clapping his hands.

'Delighted,' said T. Bone. 'Happy et cetera.'

'What now?' asked Larry, glancing from Ranch to T. Bone, aware that something more was expected of him.

'Ranch will take care of you,' said T. Bone, pulling a copy of the *Hollywood Reporter* from under his chair. 'Then a bite of luncheon, *chez moi*.'

Larry followed Ranch into the bathroom, wondering what the statistical incidence of people murdered in LA hotel rooms was. Inside the bathroom a card propped up on a shelf above the gleaming sink announced that 'Milagros' – the name was inked in by an uncertain hand – was the room attendant, and that she took pride in her work.

'We've only seen your face,' said Ranch, making himself

comfortable on the toilet seat under the flood of panelled roof lighting.

'Ah,' said Larry. 'This is the audition?'

'It's cool,' said Ranch. 'I like girls.'

'No problem,' said Larry. He began to undress.

11

Karol arrived at the apartment just after nine o'clock carrying a small but beautiful bouquet of coquelicots. He also brought something of the air of the streets he had been walking through, the slightly febrile atmosphere of Paris at the going out hour when the long dusk gives way to night and the lights of the great cafés begin to shine more brilliantly; a romantic hour in which it was impossible not to feel some excitement, some hope of an adventure. László hung Karol's coat on a peg by the door, smelling in the damp fabric the impeccable scent of a rain shower, then went with Karol to the dining room where he was relieved to find the atmosphere of melodrama had dispersed. For the moment, at least, everyone was behaving quite normally.

Kurt opened a bottle of champagne, while Karol, another exile from the East – though his vintage was '68 rather than '56 – told a story about a vagrant on the Métro who had approached a smartly dressed young woman and pleaded with her to become his girlfriend, and how, with a charm and sensitivity admired by the entire carriage, she had regretfully turned him down. The others began their own Métro stories while László busied himself in the kitchen. Despite the 'gun play' the food had not been spoiled; the veal in particular, served up in the little parcels of greaseproof paper, was succulent in its juice of sweet melted Parmesan and tender shallots. They had a *tarte tatin* and *crème anglaise* to finish, then cups of fierce black coffee and glasses of Calvados. With the dishes still on the table they sat at ease in the glow of a lamp and three candles. Kurt and Laurence smoked cigarettes. László and Franklin smoked small cigars. The smoke turned in lazy circles in the candle-dark above their heads. Karol, a writer who for many years was unable to publish in his own language, and thus had something of an obsession with translation, asked László about the English-language version of *Oxygène*, and László told him about the young English translator, Alexander . . .

'What's the fellow's name, Kurt?'

'Valentine.'

'Ah, yes. An auspicious name. Like the hero of a Stendhal novel.'

'And the other one?' asked Laurence. 'The one on the boat?'

'No one knows,' said Kurt. 'Disappeared into thin air.'

'Poor man,' said Laurence.

'Isn't it time, László,' asked Karol playfully, 'you wrote something with a happy ending?'

'I would like to,' answered László, 'but it would have to be a fairytale. Something for children.'

'László lacks the balls for a happy ending,' said Franklin, helping himself to more Calvados. 'It's so much safer to have everyone end in the shit.'

Laurence began to scold her husband; László held up his hand. 'No, my dear. He may be right. But at my age it's difficult to change the way you see the world. We take on a certain view when we are young then spend the rest of our lives collecting the evidence.'

'Telephone,' said Kurt.

'Let it ring,' said László.

'Tell me,' asked Karol, resting his large hand on László's bony shoulder, 'your happiest memory.'

'So you can steal it and use it in your next book?'

'Well, I'll tell you mine,' drawled Franklin, leaning heavily on the table. 'Korea, 24 December 1950. A bunch of us dogfaces sitting around a campfire on the beach at Hungnam waiting for the LCVP to take us off. The navy had loud-speakers up playing "White Christmas" and we were heating up cans of tomato soup. A week since any of us had bathed or shaved or changed our clothes. Ollie Warand from Mission Viejo. Dutch Biebal from Baltimore. Sergeant Stauffer, Walt Bateman. Three or four others from Third Infantry. We'd lost a lot of our friends in that shithole country, but we had plenty of smokes and we were going home. I remember just staring into the fire and smelling the soup – the greatest damn smell in the world when you're hungry. And hearing Crosby crooning down the beach, and all the guys talking in slow voices about what they were going to do when they were back Stateside. The girls and the hooch and the ball games. It was such a cold, still day. Christmas Eve a thousand years ago. I was nineteen. *Nineteen* years old, for Chrissakes. It wasn't until I was back in Sioux City and out of uniform, trying to make some kind of life for myself, that it hit me just how happy I'd been sitting there on the beach. So happy that for years afterwards I could open a can of Campbell's and get a rush. I swear I used to go out and buy the stuff whenever I had the black dog. I guess I was a soup fiend.'

'And did you ever paint it?' asked Kurt. 'The men on the beach?'

105

'If I'd painted it I would have changed it, so I left it alone. Anyway,' he said, grinning, 'Warhol painted it.'

'Who's next?' asked Laurence.

Karol span a knife on the table. It pointed to Kurt.

'I like to think,' said Kurt, his expression composed and serious, an expression László adored, 'that I have not had my happiest memory. I mean, that my happiest moment is still ahead of me . . .'

'The perfect definition of an optimist,' said Karol.

'But I do remember one particular day with my father on the Alte Donau outside Vienna. Papa used to work at the Semperit tyre factory. He wasn't an educated man. He worked with his hands, his back. And he worked hard. But on Sunday mornings in summer he would wake me before sunrise, and we would drive out to the river with our rods and nets. I was not a good fisherman. Not gifted. But this particular day I cast my line and caught the most beautiful trout in all of Austria. I swear to you, it was almost the length of my arm, and when I reeled it in the water of the river was the colour of the sunrise, so that it appeared I was pulling the fish from a lake of molten fire! When we went home I presented it to my mother. You know how boys are. I gave it to her as though it was the head of a dragon I had slain in single combat. She kissed me, and for reasons I did not understand at all, she was crying. Crying and smiling. I suppose she was proud of me.' He shrugged. 'I don't know why that day has stayed with me when I must have forgotten other, equally good days. Maybe it was the last completely innocent day of my life . . .'

'No!' protested Laurence, who hated the idea of any irreversible loss. 'You're still the same boy. Isn't that so, László?'

'Compared to dangerous old people like us,' said László, 'he's as innocent as a choirboy. A Viennese choirboy!'

'You're next, Laurence,' said Karol.

She smiled, wearily, and slowly twisted one of her rings. Three small sapphires.

'I'm afraid my happiest day was my first date with Franklin.'

'Oh, Lordy!' said Franklin.

'I was twenty-two and wore a cream satin dress with a pattern of roses on it. Franklin wore a suit he'd borrowed from . . .'

'Ed Sullivan, who's dead now.'

'Let her tell the story,' said László.

'We went to La Coupole. Franklin was sure it would be full of famous writers and artists, but even then it was mostly just American tourists. We drank martinis with olives on cocktail sticks, just like in the movies. I was thinking how angry my father would be if he knew. He didn't think women should drink anything stronger than wine. And then, my God, Franklin tells me he doesn't have any money, not a sou, and that we have to run away when the waiter isn't looking. That was why we had a table by the door! I didn't know what to think. Was it American humour? Was I supposed to laugh? After all, I still went to mass at St Antoine's every Sunday. But then he took hold of my hand and we ran like Bonnie and Clyde the whole way down the boulevard Montparnasse. I was so frightened I could hardly breathe. I was sure the waiters would chase us – you know how fierce they are at La Coupole – but by the time we reached Port Royal . . .' Her voice trailed away. 'I was already a little in love.'

'How romantic,' sighed Kurt.

'I remember she was wearing red knickers,' said Franklin. 'Somewhere between carmine and maroon, to be exact. It was hard to tell with the light.'

'Franklin!' exclaimed Laurence. 'You could only have seen them because you made me climb into the Luxembourg with you.'

'She was very beautiful then,' said Franklin.

'She's beautiful now,' said Karol.

Franklin nodded. 'László remembers.'

'Now you're maudlin,' said Karol.

'László?' said Laurence. 'I wonder if I could guess your happiest moment.'

'I'm sure you could,' said László, 'for I must have told you more than once. A day in November 1953 when Hungary played England at soccer in London. Wembley Stadium. No one had beaten the English on their own ground. What hope did a country like Hungary have? The government, of course, wanted victory as a vindication of the system. Real Hungarians just longed to be noticed in the world so people would see that Stalin and Rákosi had not buried us entirely. But to win at Wembley. Impossible! Yet we wanted it so badly we thought we could *will* it to happen. Perhaps we did. Anyway, that afternoon a kind of miracle occurred. Hungary won six goals to three!'

'Hurrah!' sang Karol, who of all the others understood best what the victory had meant.

'Everyone was listening to the radio, those big Oriens, and every time we scored you could hear the cheering coming from all the apartments, and from the street too. It was, in my humble opinion, the greatest moment in the history of Hungarian sport. I was fifteen. Everyone was so happy it could have been midsummer's day. Ferenc Puskás was the hero of our team. I used to know the name of the English captain. Hight . . . Bight . . .'

'Most of the team left after '56.' said Karol.

'Yes. Czibor and Kocsis played in Barcelona. Puskás joined Real Madrid but he went back in '81, back to Hungary.'

''Well, almost a happy ending,' said Franklin. 'Give or take a revolution or two.'

'*Egeszsegedre!*' cried Kurt, who had learnt a dozen words of Hungarian. They raised their glasses.

Karol was the eldest of them. He said that each phase of a life had its own kind of happiness. From childhood he could remember sleeping on his mother's lap in the kitchen – the sheer animal comfort of the warmth of the stove and of the woman who of all women will love you best. Then, in the Prague Spring, there was the excitement of resistance, the erotic fervour of revolt, the thrill of being really afraid. The opportunity to be brave! Later, the sober happiness of work, of writing books and seeing them admired and respected. Lucidity. The satisfaction of a profound ambition achieved. The relief at not having failed.

'And lastly,' he said, knitting his thick grey brows, 'there is a happiness that is truly floating, and is very hard to name, for it blows around the world like a magic dust. You know, it happened to me just a few weeks ago. I had given a reading in Dusseldorf. I met some old friends there – you know Krüger, László – and had a glass or two of wine, no more. Then the car came to take me to the station and we drove through a part of the city I didn't recognize. It was a cloudy spring afternoon, quite cool and breezy. I was thinking about the most ordinary matters. What I would read on the train.

Whether I would have time to call my daughter. I looked out from the side window of the car. We were crossing a bridge, a very ordinary stone bridge, not in any way beautiful or remarkable. And quite suddenly I experienced a sense of wellbeing that overwhelmed me in the way certain melodies heard at just the right moment can do. It lasted no more than a few minutes. It felt as though I had been seized by the present and shaken out, or had sensed – forgive me – my own immortal soul, something I find hard to believe in most days of the week. And all the while my driver made his way through the traffic quite oblivious to this little epiphany taking place behind his neck.'

László glanced up at the bookshelf, where the shot volume of Rilke was hidden in the shadows.

'"And we," he began, "Who always think / of happiness rising / would feel the emotion / that almost startles us / when a happy thing *falls*."'

Karol, embracing them all, left just after midnight. Franklin and Laurence followed a few minutes later, everyone in a mood of gentle melancholy at the recollection of joys that belonged to such a distant past. Kurt and László stacked the dishes in the kitchen, then Kurt retired to the bedroom where, before bed, he would perform certain complicated yoga exercises. László went back into the dining room, turned off the lamp and extinguished with wetted fingertips two of the candles. He did not feel tired. He sat in the light of the remaining candle. The Calvados had given him slight heartburn, and the discussion of happiness had set him off on an arc of thinking he would have to reach the end of before he could rest. It was true, the stories in themselves were somewhat banal – a fish, a tin of soup, running out of a bar, a soccer match – but happiness was a subject as elusive as love, and one that required a similar subtlety of lexis and category. To begin with, it could be divided into two broad types: the happiness when you know yourself to be happy, and that which is only apparent *afterwards*, the type Franklin had described with the young soldiers on the beach. Then there was public happiness, such as the day of the football match, joy reflected back from the faces of everyone he saw. And secret happiness, as when he was in love with Péter, almost a burden, as though he had won the lottery yet could share the news with no one. Pure happiness was rare, confined in most cases to infants, drug fiends and religious ecstatics. More common, though just as disturbing, was the condition Karol had touched upon – happiness woven into its opposite; that paradox of wars and revolutions when the heart is so inflamed it gives birth to entirely new emotions. Terror-bliss. Grief-lust. Tender, sentimental hatreds. In Hungary that year, the year the Russians came back, as many as three thousand lost their lives and thousands more their liberty. Yet those who had been there – most of them – were glad of it, proud of their effort and their sacrifice. They had played their part: history had not caught *them* unprepared. And while nothing could compensate them for the loss of their country and their friends, the remembrance of those October and November days was an article of faith.

But for László, this was not the case at all. How could he look back when there was only shame to look back on? What pride could he take in consummate failure? No. He did not want to remember. He wanted to forget. To forget for ever. Yet each year the effort of it was suddenly inadequate, and the past overwhelmed him, though rarely so thoroughly as during the previous winter when, with much reluctance, he took part in the fortieth anniversary celebrations in Paris. He had always managed to avoid these get-togethers, taking care to be out of the city, and telling whoever bothered to ask that he was allergic to nostalgia. But on this occasion he had received too many pressing invitations to have stayed away without causing offence, and so he had gone with Kurt in the Citroën to Père Lachaise cemetery to stand at the empty 'grave' of Imry Nagy, and then on to the hotel by the Gare de L'Est where, between wedding receptions, the veterans had the use of the banqueting hall.

All around László were men and women in the vigorous last third of their lives, many of them with the manner and aspect of professionals, all of them highly respectable. Greying, a little overweight, dressed in suits and dresses from French department stores, these were the freedom fighters who had flung Molotov cocktails into the engine grilles of T-34s; who had fought pitched battles at the Corvin Passage, at Szena Square, and Csepel, and seen friends, fellow workers, neighbours slain in shell-bursts or mown down in a food queue by a passing armoured car. The stories they told, the same they must have been telling each other for decades, they told again as if for the first time, and with the earnestness of people who must explain the whole truth in a single charged anecdote, or risk losing their dead a second time, burying them not in earth, but in silence.

'Jancsi was on Villanyi Ut when the tanks came. He lived

for an hour. We didn't even have a coffin for him . . .'

'We found Éva by Szabadsag bridge. She was sixteen. She still had the gun in her hand. Someone had covered her face with a coat . . .'

'Ádám was at school with me. We started work at Egyesült Izzó electrical plant on the same day. They arrested him in December at his uncle's house. We never saw him again . . .'

At various points in the afternoon, László, who had intended to stay for half an hour, shake a few hands and get out before someone started reciting poetry, found himself embracing strangers who were now not strangers at all. A lawyer who had practised for thirty years on the boulevard Beaumarchais. A woman who had come up from Lille and who wore a Hermès scarf that did not quite hide the scar on her neck. A little silvery-haired fellow with a limp who worked as a mechanic in the Eleventh (he gave László a business card), and who made them laugh with his story about the Viennese woman who had given him two oranges at the refugee camp, and how he had carefully hidden one, not believing that such riches would ever come his way again. Many like that, until, under the weight of so much reminiscence, so much Palika brandy, László had at last told his own story, the story of Péter Kosáry. As he spoke he dried his face with the sleeve of his jacket, while the little mechanic who was listening to him – confessing him – had wept too, such was the largeness of spirit there among the flummery of the banqueting room, and he had hushed László (who was in danger of giving way to some kind of attack, an hysteria), saying, 'No, no, my friend, you could not have saved him. You could not have saved him or you would have done it.'

But the logic of the answer did not comfort László, and

through the following weeks, as the streets acquired their strings of Christmas lights, and Kurt decorated the apartment with evergreen and wrote out greeting cards, László had found himself traversing the immense grey fields of depression. He slept for fourteen, fifteen hours at a stretch. He had sweating fits and panic attacks, a particularly nasty one in the Métro at Odéon, so that he had to be helped from the station by a kindly tourist. Alarmed, Kurt arranged an appointment with Dr Ourahm, a consultant at the Salpêtrière, and László allowed the good doctor to take his blood pressure and shine a light into every orifice and listen for a full minute to the stutter of his heart, and finally to present him with a bill for two hundred and fifty francs and a prescription for Prozac. László paid the bill but dropped the prescription into the first bin he came to on the boulevard de l'Hôpital. He did not believe that pills could ever be the cure for those moments when life *entered* you with a loss you can never be reconciled to. But for Kurt's sake he had forced himself to get up in the mornings and sit a few hours at his desk, and by acting like a normal man, one who was neither overly cheerful nor dangerously unhappy, he had discovered a certain peace of mind, and even a certain optimism that had teased him with the thought that it wasn't all over yet, that his life, even now – perhaps especially now – might catch him unawares and show him the gate into a garden he had never walked in before, and where, as in the conclusion of a really satisfying story, everything would suddenly be forgiven. It was absurd, of course, but still . . .

He heard the toilet flush and glanced at his watch. One-twenty. It was time to start his own preparations for bed, but the remaining candle, what was left of it, the flame teetering on the wick, seemed to mesmerize him, so that he did not hear Kurt, on light feet, cross the corridor and lean into the room and remain there a few moments, looking with tenderness and concern at his lover's back, and listening to him interrogate the air with a name he had sighed in his sleep for months.

12

TB lived in a modest building with a fake stucco frontage opposite a Domino pizza store in the heart of the San Fernando Valley. In the porch, Larry was greeted by a plump, conservatively dressed American matron. She had recently had her hair done and it shone at the tips with the weird blue of a food colourant.

'Oh my God!' she cried. 'Oh my God! It's Dr Barry!'

'Delighted,' said Larry, slipping into the doctor's clipped anglicisms, an accent as bogus as T. Bone's. He shook her hand. Was this Mrs Bone? He decided to follow Ranch's example and call her Betty.

'It's like having Dr Barry in the house!' she shrieked, leading him into the hacienda-style lounge and doing a mime of disbelief involving bracelets and fat brown arms. Ranch went to the bar and took down half a dozen bottles of liquor and a steel cocktail shaker, while Betty put out bowls of nuts and pretzels. On the whitewash walls of the room were inexpensive reproductions of eighteenth-century English paintings – Constable, Gainsborough, Reynolds – and a large framed award from the Institute of Adult Entertainment, the Blue Ribbon Award, for twenty-five thousand sales of a work called *Lap Attack!*

Larry wedged himself into a little chintz-upholstered armchair, wondering where the Jewish child he had met on the plane was, and hoping that she was happy in the arms of her father and would not grow up to resemble any of the people he was now in the room with, himself included. From somewhere out of sight came the sounds of an afternoon soap opera, a woman's voice wailing, '*You promised me! You promised!*'

'Is there a telephone I could use?' he asked. 'There's a call I should make. Mother's a bit poorly.'

'Why, that's just charming,' said Betty. 'You're a good son, Larry. We have boys too, you know. Harold and John. They're in business in Miami.' She pointed to a row of elaborately framed photographs on top of the shiny black back of a Japanese piano. Grinning boys with crew cuts. Frizzy-haired teenagers leaning against an old Chevrolet. A wedding picture with one of the boys, Harold or John, beside an overdressed, utterly anonymous young woman. The pictures stood in the shade of a tall vase of exotic white flowers. The impression was of a shrine to the dead.

'The Sunshine State,' she said, and she went to the photographs and made imperceptible adjustments to the angles of the frames. Ranch put an arm around her shoulders and kissed her cheek with a loud smacking noise.

'Betty's the best.'

Larry nodded. The last of the dangerous drinks was beginning to take effect and seemed to be numbing out certain nerve endings in his spine. If the Thunderbird had been outside he would have excused himself and driven away before this gathering, this little ship of fools, sailed any farther into the grotesque. But the car was not there and he needed twenty thousand dollars or there would be no car, and not too far in the future, perhaps, no family to drive back to.

Ranch tapped him on the shoulder. 'How about a tour of the studio before we eat? You up for that?'

'I most certainly am,' boomed Larry, in the magisterial voice of the doctor. Betty squealed with delight, while T. Bone, stretched out on a recliner chair, the demiurge on his leather cloud, smiled beatifically, and made certain weary movements with his hand, as though blessing them.

Larry trailed Ranch across the drive to the garage. The air temperature had reached into the eighties, and the light, surrounded by shadows of impenetrable blue, trembled on the corners of windows, on hub-caps, even on the white flowers of the jasmine that had twined high around the drainpipe at the corner of the house. In the bathroom of 2714, Ranch had been favourably impressed by Larry's still-athletic physique. He was softer than he had been, of course, was beginning to round out, so that in a few years, he thought, he would start to look almost womanly, but his body, despite his increasingly attritional lifestyle, had remained astonishingly loyal. He had depended on it so long, the excellent physical basis of himself, that it was hard to imagine how he would continue if it should fail him. He dreamed sometimes of a catastrophic collapse, some disaster like the amputation of a leg, or face cancer, or elephantitis. He did not believe he was someone who could 'deal' with such an event, the type who would ever be ennobled by suffering. At thirty-six (was this not one of the defining neuroses of the age?) he had begun to fear getting old, and could not share Kirsty's vision of benign elders dispensing wisdom to the young and pottering around, glamorously weathered, like Fonda and Hepburn. He thought he would make a wretched old man. But he also wondered whether he might not be a completely different person at fifty-five or sixty, and that what seemed so complicated now, the great Rubik's cube of moral dilemmas, might, from the top floor of his life, seem to have been nothing but the fruit of a temporary confusion, and that he had spent his prime like one of those circus clowns who, on all fours, can give the impression of two midgets wrestling together.

Ranch unlocked the padlock on a steel side door into the garage. The air inside was surprisingly chilly. There were no windows. He flicked the light switches. 'We like to keep it simple,' he said.

The space ahead of Larry, illuminated now by six quietly fizzing fluorescent tubes, looked as though it were used for storing the salvaged remnants of a house fire, objects retained only until someone had the will to do away with them. A dozen spare and improbable costumes hung from a mobile wardrobe rail next to two mattresses covered with the type of plastic sheeting found on the beds of incontinent children. Other props included a square of mulberry-coloured carpet, an office desk and chair, a six-foot plastic palm tree and a hat-stand from which dangled, suspended by one of its eye sockets, a latex gorilla head. It was hard to imagine a space less conducive to the performance of a sex act, and the skin of Larry's balls tightened at the thought of it.

'We got lights and multi-track sound in the back. All the dubbing and post-production's done on site. Al's our man behind the camera. You'll like him. Nadine's the sound girl. Her sister's the fluffer. That's where TB sits.' He gestured to the obligatory folding director's chair. 'Fellini's his big influence.'

'And yours?' asked Larry, fingering the inside of the gorilla head and feeling a slight tackiness as though it had recently been sweated in.

'Marky Mark. Schwarzenegger. Sir Olivier of course. TB's taught me to admire a lot of English stuff. Muffins and Shakespeare and all that shit. Can't get my head around cricketing, though.' He laughed.

'Cricketing's hard to get your head around,' said Larry. 'Have you ever been to England?'

'Been to Mexico,' said Ranch. *'Hablas español, amigo?'*

'Un poco,' said Larry. Then on a whim he asked: 'What's T. Bone's real name?'

Ranch studied him with an expression of mock amazement. 'This is LA, Larry. Who gives a fuck about his real name? C'mon. I'll show you my place. Get you fixed up.'

Ranch's place was a single-storey annexe at the back of the main house. A sprinkler near by made the grass shine. On the doorstep of the annexe two girls sat in the shade of a bougainvillaea sharing a can of cherry Coke and a joint.

'Yo!' said Ranch.

The girls got to their feet.

'Cool suit,' said the one with the ring through her eyebrow.

'This is Rosinne,' said Ranch. 'And this is Jo-babe. Say hi to Larry, girls. He used to be on TV more often than the weather.'

The girls shifted their gaze from Ranch to Larry, shamelessly assessing the magnitude of his celebrity. He knew already there would be no repeat of Betty's transports.

'I kinda recognize you,' said Rosinne. 'I think, like, my mom used to watch you. You going to make a movie here?'

'It looks that way,' he said.

'Hey! You're English,' cried Jo-babe, approvingly. 'Sick!' She offered him the joint. He grinned at her, the lovely violet blankness of her eyes. 'Thank you,' he said, 'Jo-babe.'

'You're welcome,' she answered, in the voice of a cartoon character he was not familiar with. The others laughed. Then they all went into Ranch's place.

The annexe, one-time hideout of Harold and John before they had gone to make their way in the Sunshine State, consisted of a single large bedroom and adjoining bathroom. There were three televisions of different sizes in the bedroom, a Burt Reynolds poster, a stringless Fender guitar, and a big soapstone Buddha whose lap served as an ashtray. The floor was littered with CD covers and magazines, a mix of comics and porn and fashion. Jo-babe aimed the remote at the music system in the corner. There was a pause, then the room filled with Nirvana, and she began to dance, free-form, stringy arms, stringy legs, sometimes hopping nimbly over Rosinne, who had flopped on to the floor to pool through the latest issue of *PLEASE!*.

Ranch sat cross-legged on the rumpled bed, a mirror on his lap with a picture of Bogart on it and the legend 'Here's looking at you, kid!'.

'Don't mention this to T. Bone,' he said, dividing a little heap of powder into four lines, then leaning over his reflection to snort energetically through a length of McDonald's milk-shake straw.

'Not a word,' promised Larry, hoovering up his line from Bogart's hat and passing the mirror to Rosinne, who thanked him as mildly as if he had handed her a glass of milk.

'Are these girls in the film?' asked Larry.

'These girls? They're *way* too skinny,' said Ranch. 'We only use professionals. Cindy X. Selina D'Amour. Sasha Martinez before she went to rehab. A Chinese called Patty Wang. Maybe she's Filipina. Then there's Scarletta Scarr, who's kinda my godmother. We use her if there's any S&M stuff.'

Larry thought briefly of his own godmother, a woman called Penny who had been at teacher training college with Alice in the sixties. He asked: 'Were you nervous the first time you did it in front of the cameras?'

'No way,' said Ranch. The mirror had come back and he had immediately begun to cut up another four lines, scooping the drug out of a plastic envelope with the corner of the razor. 'I was born to do this kind of work.'

'You never had an occasion when you couldn't do it? Couldn't perform?'

'You've just gotta be professional,' said Ranch. 'Stay focused.'

'Focused,' repeated Larry, nodding.

'Think of the money,' said Ranch.

'Money turns you on?'

'Dumb question,' replied Ranch, grinning. 'Hey, didn't Dr Barry fuck everyone at Sun Valley?'

'Not on camera,' said Larry.

123

'You'll be great,' said Ranch. They paused to take the coke. When Larry had given the mirror to Rosinne, Ranch put a finger to his lips, winked, and said quietly: 'C'mon, I'm gonna show you something. Put your mind at ease.'

For the second time that day Larry followed Ranch into a bathroom. This one had bulbs around the mirror. Unflushed pee glittered in the toilet bowl, and the air smelt of patchouli oil and smoke. Ranch turned to the wall-mounted medicine cabinet behind the door, opened it, and took from among the array of vitamins and painkillers, a small carved wooden box of the kind you could buy in any Chinatown.

'My little box of tricks,' he said, unhooking the catch to show two compartments containing small coloured capsules, a dozen or so on one side, perhaps half as many on the other.

'Sex and death,' he added, cheerfully. But his face, as he gazed into the box, was no longer boyish. There was a haze of fatigue, like a sediment suspended in his skin, suggesting to Larry for the first time what it cost Ranch to go on being Ranch.

'Wow,' said Larry, looking at the capsules. 'Which is which? They look the same.'

'Now that would be *too* crazy,' said Ranch. 'These ones with the red at the bottom and blue at the top will give you a hard-on you could swing a piano from. And these little critters with the blue at the bottom, they put the lights out. I mean, for ever. Kaput. *Hasta nunca*. Leaves no trace in the body. Nothing anyone could find.'

'You're kidding,' said Larry. 'That's bullshit.' He found himself laughing, a little drunkenly.

Ranch shook his head. 'More things in heaven and earth,

Larry, than you ever fuckin' dreamed of. I got them from a doctor in Vegas who wanted to do some voodoo with a girl I was seeing. You know what doctors are like.'

'Have you tried one?' asked Larry. 'I mean one of the sex ones.'

'Never needed to,' said Ranch. 'It's just nice to know they're here. Insurance.'

'They could be anything,' said Larry. He wanted to touch them.

'Could be.' Ranch closed the box and put it back in the cabinet. 'Maybe I should throw them out before some chick takes one for period pain. The thing is, I like the idea of them. You know what I mean?'

Larry nodded. He knew.

'Hey, you'll be great,' said Ranch, putting an arm around Larry's shoulders and gently leading him back into the bedroom. 'You'll be beautiful.'

13

When László was a boy, going to bed had been a matter of swilling his mouth out, stripping down to vest and shorts and jumping as quickly as he could between the sheets beside his brother János. Sleep would come to them in the music of the drains from the upstairs apartments and the rattling of the trams on Szechenyi Rakpart. Now, his elaborate *couché* was an ever expanding chore that required a good fifty minutes of light physical labour in the bathroom, and which began with what the doctors liked to call 'moving the bowels'. For quarter of an hour he would sit on the wooden O reading crinkled copies of *Voici* magazine, or frowning at Marcello Mastroianni smoking on the old film poster for *La Dolce Vita* on the opposite wall, and then inspect the resulting mess (wondering sometimes if there were not millions of men at that moment peering anxiously or even with pride at their own shit) for any ominous signs of inner bleeding. His father had died from cancer of the colon.

Satisfied that his insides were functioning as they should, he would move on to the basin and the large bevelled mirror to start work on his teeth. It was only in his forties that he had begun to put his crooked, tobacco-stained teeth in order, entering, in a fit of vanity or self-consciousness, the painful and overpriced world of crowns and laminate veneers, extractions, root work and novocaine. Between 1978 and 1981 he had spent entire afternoons in the jet-fighter seat of Monsieur Charass, whose masked and looming face had become one of the permanent props of László's dream world. When László left the surgery for the last time he had possessed a set of teeth, some his own, many not, that seemed to have been stolen from someone much younger, and which he secretly thought of as 'American teeth', still having old-fashioned ideas from his boyhood about American vigour and dollar-beauty.

His face presented a more stubborn problem. There was no Charass to take away the crimps and sunbursts of his skin, but Kurt (that marvellous boy!) had introduced him to the world of anti-ageing creams, and László had immediately become a devotee, even something of an addict. These small expensive pots peddled by elegant women in the Gallerie Lafayette, women whom it seemed were required to wear on their faces a sample of every cosmetic they sold, contained such dreamily improbable ingredients as jojoba oil, pro-phosphor, concentrated line-lift serum. His latest buy – he had been drawn to the counter by a picture of a girl with a complexion of humid alabaster, and a poster exhorting him, somewhat drunkenly he thought, to 'Forget Time!' – promised to deliver pure oxygen molecules directly to the cells of his skin via the Asymmetric Oxygen Carrier System.

In his first enthusiasm, these creams had seemed to László one of the western world's most seductive achievements. He had even claimed, in a not entirely flippant essay for *Le Monde*, that it was precisely such a product, fruit of a playful science, that had made communism untenable and helped bring about the collapse of its empire. Who could care about collective agriculture, presidiums, space labs or

Five Year Plans when the face of everyone over thirty looked so withered and unloved, while those on the other side of the curtain could rehydrate and nourish their skins with luxurious creams? Wasn't that what we feared about time, about death, its assault upon our vanity, the grinding out of whatever measure of physical loveliness we had enjoyed? How much more effective it had been, this creative narcissism of the West, than all the Minutemen missiles or the corruption and stupidity of the Party stooges. True, the lotions, teased into his skin with gently circling fingertips, had not made him look any younger, but he was convinced they had retarded the process of decay, protecting him a little from gravity and toxic air, from the effects of too much smiling or frowning, even perhaps from that scourge of all faces: guilt.

The petit four of this banquet of self-attention was a dab of Aqua di Parma, a perfume once used by both Audrey Hepburn and Cary Grant – quite reason enough for any lesser mortal to indulge. The bottle had been given to him as a parting gift by Guilleme Bernadi, producer at the Teatro Argentina in Rome where they had put on *Flicker* in the spring of 1995, and the scent, with its tones of honey and sherbet, unfailingly reminded László of the night tour in Guilleme's Spider soft-top, Beatles tapes on the cassette, warm Roman air, real southern air, blowing over their faces as they turned down streets so narrow and crowded with 2 a.m. revellers he had had the sensation of driving through the midst of an endlessly extended open-air restaurant.

He held up the bottle. It was still two-thirds full. Enough, at a dab a night, to last him into his dotage, when perhaps the middle-aged Kurt, portly and balding, would push him around the apartment in a wicker Bath chair, and all his past life would have become like the events of a single afternoon, in which much had been done, but little, nothing at all perhaps, *achieved*. His did not underestimate his work, his hard-won craftsmanship, the pleasure it gave, but increasingly it felt like something he did in order to avoid doing something else, a forty-year displacement activity, and he wondered, leaning into the mirror to watch himself think, what the true currency of human success might be. Certainly it had nothing to do with prizes, reviews, his photograph in a newspaper – it was extraordinary what little difference such things made. Neither was it a matter of figures, like the number of francs you had, or happy days, or friends at your funeral. And love?

Loving, you would not die of utter loneliness like a dog at night in a field. But love was too arbitrary. It was mere good fortune. A cloudburst. Any number of base and useless people were capable of it. Hitler had loved his Éva. Stalin, too, must have loved somebody once. No. We needed to be weighed more carefully than that. So what better than those sudden tests of worth and courage for which there was no preparation other than your entire preceding life? Those moments when you must step forward from a line of silent faces and declare yourself; say yes when the others say no; run back into the burning house without the least hesitation. Or just ask a question, like little Sandor at school on Ulloi Ut, who stood up from his desk and asked the teacher why it was necessary for certain pages in the history books to be glued together. In such moments you could fail beyond your wildest dreams. Or succeed, of course. There was that too.

He touched the precious drop of scent on to his neck, tied his robe and left the bathroom, shuffling in Moroccan slippers along the corridor to the bedroom. He grinned to himself, lugubriously, at the thought of the Bath chair. The twilight of a passionate dilettante! It was not much to look forward to.

In bed at last, in the warm lamplight, Kurt's gentle sleep-breath the most peaceful sound in the world, László lay back on the pillows, arms behind his head, and tried again to remember the name of the English football captain. Billy? Could 'Billy' be a family name in England? Mr Billy? He had visited London four times, all theatre visits. He found the city somewhat troubling. Eerie and exhausting. This time he would ask his hosts to take him on a little visit to the country. He had looked at a map recently in Galignani's and seen the most extraordinary place names. Leek! Sheepwash! He would pick out a name at random and insist on an excursion. Perhaps his young translator would drive him. They would go on what Edith Wharton used to call a 'motor-flight', and stop every hundred miles for tea and cakes.

The phone was on László's side of the bed. When it rang he was so startled he knocked over the glass of water on the bedside table as he snatched at the receiver.

'Monsieur Lázár?'

'Yes?'

'I am sorry to call you so late. I tried to call you earlier but without success.'

A voice with an accent. A voice faintly familiar.

'Who is this?'

'We have met before, monsieur. At the university. We

discussed the situation in the Balkans. Perhaps you remember?'

'Wait,' said László, 'I'll take the call in my study.' Kurt was awake. László smiled at him. 'Its nothing,' he said. 'Sleep. Dream of fish.'

In the study, he crossed the unlit room, switched on the desk lamp and picked up the extension. He knew who it was now: Emil Bexheti, leader of an Albanian students' group at the Sorbonne. A young man born for conspiracies.

'I'm here,' said László.

'I am disturbing you?'

'Yes.'

'Then I will be brief, monsieur. I wish for an opportunity to talk with you again. Somewhere in private. Not, I think, at your apartment. Or mine, of course.'

'And this must be arranged at two o'clock in the morning?'

'You received the new faxes, monsieur?'

'No. Yes, perhaps. I haven't looked at them. You want to talk about the Balkans again?'

'I would be honoured if you would agree to meet with me.'

'May I ask why me? Why in particular?'

'We think you are a friend of justice.'

' "We"?'

'You know what it is to have an oppressor in your land. To be ruled by force. By fear. You know what it is to see . . .'

'Enough of this!'

'We respect you, monsieur.'

'Not enough to stop you calling me in the middle of the

night. Are there no Balkan professors you can wake up? What about Dr Kelmandi?'

In the background, László could hear another voice, a man, older, speaking with hushed, rapid authority. Not French. Presumably Albanian.

'I apologize, monsieur. But if you look at the documents I have sent you will understand our urgency.'

'Who are you speaking for? The students? Or someone else?'

'May I believe that you will meet with me?'

'You know where my rooms are at the university. I have no objection to seeing you there.'

'Thank you, monsieur, but not at the university. You will be contacted again in a few days with the name of a safe place. Goodnight, monsieur. I am sorry. Goodnight, monsieur.'

The line went dead. László replaced the receiver and stood in the green light thinking of the room somewhere in the city where Emil Bexheti and the others were gathered to make their plans, their late night calls on behalf of the 'We'. He decided to have absolutely nothing to do with them. They were quite capable of making trouble, precisely the kind of trouble the Garbargs probably already suspected him of. He yawned, stretched and was about to turn off the lamp when something on the floor between the two desks caught his eye, and he reached down to pick it up. It was the napkin in which he had carried the gun from the dining room. He looked about for a few moments but there was no sign of the weapon and he knew it had gone. For a night at the end of May, the study seemed unseasonably cold.

14

Cutting coke on Jo-babe's belly, Ranch used a credit card rather than a razor. She lay very still on the bed, her T-shirt bunched up under her little breasts, the lines organized around her belly button like long white scars. On the other side of room Rosinne was putting a new CD into the jaw of the music machine.

'No more Bjork,' called Ranch. 'She'll make us crazy as she is.'

'I like crazy,' said Rosinne, but it wasn't Bjork, it was the King in full sail singing *America's Favorite Yuletide Melodies*.

'Inspired choice,' said Larry, who stood by the window working with his tongue to loosen a piece of meatloaf trapped between his front teeth. Lunch had been an hour in the sunlit dining room of the main house, where there were more pictures of Harold and John, the lost boys, and several piles of shiny unlabelled videocassettes. Betty, her charm bracelets jangling, had brought in the meatloaf, the peas and potatoes, and after that some odd approximation of an English steamed pudding with scoops of Ben and Jerry's ice cream, mocha flavour. As a courtesy to her the men had not talked business at the table, but when she cleared away the bowls and put the coffee on – the swing-door to the kitchen bringing gusts of another soap opera – '. . . *I'm afraid I've got some bad news for you kids . . .'* – TB had produced a folded single-sheet photocopied contract from the breast pocket of his shirt, and slid it over the table to Larry.

'The grisly formalities,' he said, winking.

Larry scanned the contract. 'Who are "Southern Enterprises"?'

'I,' said T. Bone, 'am Southern Enterprises.'

'I thought it mighta be the Mafia.'

'You wag,' said T. Bone.

'And I get the first five on signature?'

'In a lovely fat envelope that only we will ever know about.'

'What about Cindy X and Selina D'Amour and the others. Do I meet them before we shoot? It would be nice, you know, to talk to them. First.'

'My dear Larry,' said T. Bone, helping himself to another triangle of foil-wrapped cheese that seemed, like much of the meal, to have come from some museum of food, 'all shall be well, and all shall be well, and all manner of things shall be well. The important thing is to keep yourself in tip-top condition. We want you looking sleek as a young seal. Our productions should exude a sense of optimism. No bags under the eyes, please. Ranch knows all the tricks.'

So Larry had signed, and after coffee he and Ranch had been excused like children to go back and play in the annexe. The 'fat' envelope was produced, and Larry made his goodbyes, kissing Betty's hand and treating her to the doctor's penetrating pre-diagnosis stare. She blushed, deeply.

'Oh, Larry,' she sighed.

136

'Adieu, Betty.'

He knew that one of them was mad.

Close to, Jo-babe's seventeen-year-old belly was a thing of wonder, the taut surface finely atremble with the jelly and clockwork of her guts. Larry leaned down and sniffed a line through one of his new hundred-dollar bills; then, with the very tip of his tongue, he licked the stray grains of powder from her skin and nuzzled the head of a tattoo lizard that peeped from the waistband of her jeans. He wondered whether he would have sex with her, whether indeed he was supposed to, so that Ranch, presently watching a hand-held TV with a screen the size of a playing card, could examine his technique, offer advice on angle, thrust control, that special grunty kind of porn fucking.

The King was doing a South Seas steel-guitar version of 'In The Bleak Midwinter'. Larry got up to dance with Rosinne, who looked sulky and puffy-eyed, aware perhaps that this wasn't the life Santa had promised her as a little girl. She leaned her head against his chest and they shuffled round together, his hands pressed against her back, her breath moistening a patch of blue cotton above his heart.

'Snoo-ow o-on snooooww . . .' sang the King, accompanied now by a choir of children and a Detroit brass section, his voice rolling like a big sea, wave after wave of tremulous emotion, an irresistible, heartbreaking, nonsensical bawling. They danced with Rosinne's bare feet on Larry's shoes. She was so light he didn't think she could weigh much more than Ella. She had her arms around his neck. He held her very close, sliding one of his hands up her back where her skin was slick with heat as though she were running a fever. Once upon a time he had danced like this with Kirsty, the two of them leaning into each other like a pair of exhausted brawlers, those days of courtship at her father's place in Lemon Cove when he could not look at her without wanting to touch her, could not touch her without needing to lie down with her, and like some slouch-mouthed movie star had called her 'baby' and 'honey' and 'sweetheart'. On occasion – he had not dreamed this – the mere sound of his voice had made her flinch with pleasure as though he had stroked the denim between her thighs. So how on earth had he got from *there* to *here*? What was this tangle between them, this knot of ravelled emotion? It was pathetically distressing to him that he did not make love to his wife any more when he could recall so clearly the nights he used to plunder her, that look of insane concentration on her face, her arms flexed against the head-bars of their iron-framed bed, pushing against him with all her might as though she could never have him deeply enough inside of her. How had he got from *that* to *this*? From his wife to teenage coke fiends. From Kirsty to Scarletta Scar?

'. . . iiin the bleeeek mid win'eer . . . la-A-ang agOOOOO!' sang the King. Rosinne snuffled and turned in the cradle of his arms. He kissed the top of her head then gently released her, sliding out from beneath her feet.

'Got a phone in here, Ranch?'

'Under the bed,' said Ranch, pointing, but not looking away from the little screen where people very slightly larger than horseflies were doing things to each other. Jo-babe was still on the sheets, contorting herself in a doomed attempt to reach the last line of the drug on her belly. Larry searched under the bed. A Hemingway novel. A copy of L. Ron Hubbard's *Dianetics*.

A strip of passport photographs showing Ranch ten years back, grinning in a booth somewhere in America Profunda. Also a purple telephone of aerodynamic design with four yards of grey wire connecting it to the socket. He took the phone into the bathroom, slid the wire under the door, then shut the door against the King's slacks-and-rocking-chair cover of 'Stille Nacht'.

He had expected Alec, but it was Alice who answered.

'412 . . .'

'This is Ground Control,' said Larry, but Alice, her voice still wrapped in the heavy velvet of sleep, continued her recital of the number.

'It's me, Mum. Larry.'

'Hello dear,' she said. '*Ça va?*'

'Did I wake you?'

'It's still dark,' she said.

'I'm sorry. I was going to talk to Alec.'

'Oh, Alec,' she said. 'He does his best.'

'I know,' said Larry. He had the receiver wedged between his shoulder and his ear, the body of the phone in his left hand. With his right hand he opened the medicine cabinet.

'How are you feeling?'

'Not too bad, dear. I haven't gone mad or anything like that.'

'Of course not.' He unhooked the little brass catch on the box. The lid popped up. He could hear very clearly the long drag of his mother's in-breath.

'There's so much to think of,' she said. 'Hard to know where to begin.'

'I'll be with you soon,' he said, holding a red-and-blue capsule up to the light and squinting to see the tiny grains of chemistry in it. 'And Ella too.'

'Kirsty's a good girl, Larry.'
'Yes.'
'Is she there?'
'She's next door.'
'Come soon, won't you, dear.'
'I wish I was there now.'
'I know, dear.'
'Go back to sleep, Mum.'
'You too, dear.'
'Sweet dreams.'

A sigh. The phone went down. Larry shut the little box, closed the medicine cabinet and wrapped the pills in a sheet of tangerine toilet paper, before slipping them into the envelope with his money.

'Who wants a piece of the doctor?' he said, coming back through the door into the big swirl of the King's music, but the others had their eyes fixed on more private horizons, and no one answered him.

15

There was a room under the stairs they called the workshop, though like the playroom where no one played any more, it was many years since anyone had worked there. Stephen had used it for repairing his clocks, or, when his hands were not steady enough, for drinking. Some of the gear was still there – the Formica-topped bench and the Sherline lathe – and even after so long the room seemed to have preserved a faint tang of cleaning ammonia and solder, so that Alec could never go in without for an instant seeing the shadow of his father's back, the air like a sheet on which the print of the sleeper was still visible, a fragile outline that time would eventually smooth out to make the absence perfect.

Above the bench, loops of black flex with bulb sockets at eighteen-inch intervals hung from a steel hook. He unslung the flex and searched in the cupboards for the coloured bulbs, which he found, blue, red, green and yellow, neatly stowed in their corrugated boxes. These were the party lights, and though there was not the slightest need for him to test them tonight – it was another three weeks before Alice's birthday – he let himself follow the promptings of the moment without question or analysis. He knew when the bulbs had last been used: Alice's retirement party ten months ago, and the bulbs' little skullcaps of dust confirmed that they had not been touched since. How well she had seemed then! Allowing herself a measure of optimism, a bullishness the family had been quick to share in. There were plans to travel. France, of course, particularly her beloved Brittany; but she had also sent off for brochures on the Far East and India, and in a short impromptu speech in the orchard at the beginning of the party, she had announced her intention to spend more time, *much* more time, in California, with Larry and Kirsty and her granddaughter. Among her retirement presents from the school there had been a smart leather holdall, airline carry-on size, and of all the gifts she received that day, none had delighted her more. It had been used, thought Alec, three or four times. Only once to America. Not quite enough to lose its bloom of newness.

He sat tailor-fashion on the concrete floor of the workroom, moving the flex through his hands and patiently screwing in the bulbs, careful to keep the colours in sequence. The party had been a success. Nearly all the staff from the school had attended, including Alice's doting secretary, Mrs Dzerzhinsky. The neighbours, Judith and Donald Joy, lawyers who liked to wear white, had strolled over from their thatched cottage, the roof of which, topped by a pair of straw squirrels, could be glimpsed from various parts of Brooklands' garden. And Osbourne was there, paper plate clutched at chest height, moving his bulk among the guests like a flightless bird – benign, myopic, faintly comical.

In a wet month they had been fortunate to have a balmy evening; real southern air that people said excitedly was like Tuscany or the Côte d'Azur. The women in summer frocks showed off their tanned arms; the men hung their jackets from the branches of the trees. Alice, tipsy on wine, slightly hoarse from too much talking, held court at the end of one of the trestle tables. Everyone knew what she had been through the previous year, events referred to as her 'close shave', 'that nasty business', or even 'when she was away', and they were determined to show their pity and their affection. Mozart and Rodriguez and old-time jazz played on the ghetto-blaster, and there was a barbeque, a kind of brick altar, at which Larry presided, flipping steaks and searing tuna, sometimes with Ella on his shoulders, until Kirsty, fearful that the smoke would bring on an asthma attack, had reached up to rescue her.

The first guests left around midnight; a last case of white wine was brought out from the house. The late stayers made themselves comfortable on the unmown grass. Someone fell asleep under a tree and snored contentedly. Then everything was doused in a warm rain – the lights fizzled, a fuse blew, and amid much laughter people took shelter where they could. Alec found himself under the branches of an old cherry tree with Alice, just the two of them, listening to the splashing of the rain on the leaves.

'Promise me something,' she said, breaking the silence between them. 'If I get ill again you won't let me die gaga.'

'But you're not going to get ill again,' he said. 'What are you talking about?'

She turned to look at him, though to each the other's face was no more than a shadow, the obscure locus of a whispering voice. 'Of course not,' she said. 'Anyway, I've spoken to Larry.'

'Larry? What did you say to him?' He was furious with her,

but then the rain, as in Tuscany or the Côte d'Azur, ceased as suddenly as it had begun, and someone called, 'Where's Alice hiding? Come out, come out wherever you are!'

'It's all right,' she said, touching his arm, and she left him. 'I'm here!' she sang. 'I'm he-re!'

Larry fixed the fuse. Everyone cheered when the lights came on again. The party had a new lease of life. Mr Bajrami, who taught maths, performed an impromptu flamenco with Miss Lynne, who taught art. Larry dispensed nightcaps from a large bottle of Black Label he had bought at duty-free in San Francisco. Alice told a risqué joke about two nuns on holiday in Paris, a joke Alec had heard her tell once a year for as long as he could remember. The last car door clunked shut just as the light came up, the dawn mist drifting off the fields.

'Bye-bye, Alice. God bless. *Marvellous* party!'

Carrying the coiled flex over his shoulder, the extension lead in one hand and the storm lantern in the other, Alec mounted the three mossy steps from the terrace to the lawn, then crossed the lawn to the wooden gate that led into the orchard. There had been an orchard here for perhaps three hundred years, if the first trees had been planted when the house was built. The present trees were shaggy with lichen, and despite pruning some gave fruit only one year in three. But the fruit they did give, small and hard and tart, was, for Alec, the true taste of an apple, and he never bought apples in London, however sweet or polished they looked on the supermarket shelves.

He walked to the centre of the orchard, set down the lantern and lifted the lights from his shoulder. There were four trees, well spaced, which served as the posts from which the lights were always hung. He began to work, securing the bulb at the end of the flex in a nook just above his head, then walking backwards, paying out the flex until he reached the second tree, then backwards again to the third and fourth, before connecting the flex to the extension lead and running the lead to a socket by the wall. He was crouched there with the plug in his hand when he heard the ringing from the house. In the instant of hearing it he thought it was the alarm, and that he would not answer it. Then he realized it was the telephone and he sprinted across the lawn, blindly, reaching the kitchen just as the ringing stopped. He went to the bottom of the stairs. The call went on for perhaps two minutes, after which he heard the receiver returned clumsily to its cradle. He went up.

'Larry,' she said.

'I was in the garden. Sorry.'

'He's coming soon,' she said.

'I couldn't get to the phone in time. Sorry.'

'It doesn't matter.'

'No.'

'Goodnight, dear.'

'Goodnight. Mum?'

'What?'

'Goodnight.'

In the orchard he plugged in the bulbs. They worked perfectly, jewelling the dark as on so many nights in the past, nights even when Stephen was alive. The cat was back, caught in the glare as it hunted in the long grass. It froze, then leaped on to a water butt, leaped onto the wall, and away into the invisible. Alec returned under the square of lights, and after standing there a moment like a man who has entirely forgotten what he came for, he sank down with his back against one of the trees. He knew now, with a certainty that bordered upon relief, that he wasn't going to manage. No labour of the intelligence, no artifice or soft voice could help him. Losing Alice would not be difficult, it would be unendurable, and something in him would simply not survive it. With the others he would have to go on pretending for a while, but out here there were only bats and stars to see him, and he took off his glasses, folded them carefully, put his head in his hands, and wept.

16

There was a moment sometimes, on waking, the moment before she remembered to be ill, when she felt almost normal. It reminded her of a scene she must have watched in an old film: the condemned man led out of his cell to be shot, but pausing in the courtyard to register the temperature and the light and whether or not it was likely to be a fine day, as if he would be part of it, as if it mattered. Habit, like that poor Burmese Orwell wrote about, stepping over a puddle on his way to the gallows, not wanting to get his feet wet. Was that the last to go? Certain gestures, reflexes, a way of cocking the head or moving the hands in speech? Her own hands felt as if they would soon become too heavy for her, as though they were great paddles instead of fragile webs of bone and knotted blue veins. It was hard to keep her rings on now. They slipped off while she slept.

With a grunt of effort she sat up on the side of the bed, then leaned forward, a position that she found helped her to breathe. The room was fuggy. Too many flowers, too little air. She would open the window. After all, what did it matter if she caught a cold? And what if it became pneumonia? The old person's friend, they used to call it, though she doubted there was anything very friendly about it, drowning in your own bed. But which of the doors out of this world *was* easy? Stephen smashed up in the Rover. Her father, his fingers yellowed from three packets of Woodbines a day, dying from something malignant and vague like disappointment or boredom. And now herself, this. Death blooming in her skull like a flower. A black tulip.

She turned to the window. There was nothing much to see, just the stealthy undermining of the sky. 3:51 said the clock, 3:52. Not long now.

At the second attempt she stood up. The world swung, then settled. Her feet found her slippers and she shuffled to the window, struggled with the catch, rested, struggled again, and finally got it to open. Was it night or day that washed over her now? She caught a whiff of the fields, the moor, the five-miles-off sea. Somewhere out there a car was driving through the lanes. She couldn't see its lights, but the drone of its engine carried very clearly. Some man or woman with his own burden of happiness or confusion. Someone who knew nothing about her and whom she would never meet. Not now.

Her cigarettes (and a spare Ventolin inhaler) were in the blue pomander pot of Venice glass on the window ledge. Una knew that she had them there, but all she had ever said was to be careful not to have a flame near the oxygen bottle unless she wanted to blow the roof off. The idea was not without appeal. A great blue flash, a bang that would echo for miles, then no more nights to be sweated through. She took the lid off the pot and shook a cigarette from the pack, an ultra-light, a breath of fresh air she used to call them. They no longer gave her any pleasure but they gave her the memory of pleasure, and that was something. She flicked the lighter. The coughing on the first drag almost shook her off her feet. She used the inhaler, coughed again, then spat the bitterness into a tissue and pushed the window wider, letting the breeze slide like water over her skin.

Away to the right there was a glow above the orchard, almost as if there were a fire there, though the light was too steady for flames. She leaned and peered. A light in the orchard. What on earth was Alec up to? Was he outside still? At this hour? It was he, of course, who would try hardest to hold on to her. As a toddler he could not bear to have her out of his sight, following her around the house, even into the toilet, staggering after her, her little warder, her second-born, her baby. It pierced her that she could not spare him this, and a wave of tenderness went through her, followed by a sudden flush of self-hate in which she appeared to herself as a cronish, mean-spirited woman, who in the long enterprise of loving had failed those towards whom she had the most explicit duty. A mother was there to be devoured! (It was the hour for such strange thoughts: moths that only flew at dawn.) Not just her milk, but her bones and blood and brain. Had she kept something from them? Was that what Alec had come back for – to find what she had kept from him? To claim it? To eat up the last of her? She had a sudden startling image of them, Alec and Larry, in black suits like bank clerks, coming into the room and sitting by the bed, until shyly, tearfully, they reached beneath the pulled-up sheet to bite off a fingertip, an earlobe . . .

Ash dropped on to the bubbled paintwork of the windowsill and she carried her cigarette into the bathroom and doused it under the tap, careful to avoid the mirror there, for she too wished to remember herself differently. She sat on the toilet seat, panting, then crept back to the bedroom and eased herself between the sheets. Soon, the sun would break through the lower branches of the trees that grew alongside the drive. Already the first birds were beginning, single notes, tentative, as if their instinct for the light might be mistaken. She shut her eyes. For the first time in days she felt herself relaxing, almost a swoon. *Now*, she thought, now would not be a bad time; and once again she felt it, the sensation of an approach, the secret certainty that someone was moving towards her, distant still, but closer to her every hour, someone who would help her do it, who would know how to help her. It frightened her a little but she wanted him to come, and she opened her hands, thinking it would be best to be ready.

WHAT ARE DAYS FOR?

'. . . it is the breathing time of day with me.
Let the foils be brought . . .'

Hamlet (Act v, scene ii)

1

The Reverend Osbourne jogged over the grass in his mack-
intosh. The rain had caught him in the open, crossing the
meadow beside the potato field and still three hundred yards
from the shelter of the trees at Brooklands. The grass was
sopping and seeds stuck to the cuffs of his trousers, but he
couldn't run any faster. He hadn't the breath for it.

He had spent the morning at the hospital with Alice
Valentine, who had suffered some manner of seizure on the
previous Wednesday. It was Mrs Samson who had alerted
him to it, though she had not been there when it happened,
and didn't seem to know how serious it might be. He had
tried to call Alec, and when that hadn't worked, had made
enquiries of his own, finally tracing Alice to the ladies' wing
of a ward in the Royal he knew quite well. She was asleep
when he went in, so he sat on the chair beside her and waited,
feeling suddenly old and tired himself. They were almost the
same age, and he had known her for more than twenty years,
ever since Stephen's accident when he had gone to the house
to discuss the arrangements for the funeral, and had found a
handsome, businesslike woman, a clear thinker, and someone
rather brutally honest, telling him without mincing her words
that her husband had been an alcoholic and that he had never
had any time for religion, never found any consolation in it.
He had promised her that the service would be brief and to

the point, and that was how it was. A few words on Stephen's work at the school, his politics (with which the reverend had some sympathy). A little of the old poetry from the King James. At the graveside, Stephen's family had rather shunned her, but then she hardly seemed to notice them. A cold day. Frost in the shadows, and only a pair of yews to shelter them from the wind. She wore a plain dark winter's coat with no gloves or headscarf. And though there was sadness in her eyes she hadn't cried. Not there in front of them.

The boys had been with her, of course, and occasionally she stroked the younger one's hair to reassure him. The other one, Larry, had taken it upon himself to be the man of the house, and though he couldn't have been much more than thirteen at the time he did it extraordinarily well, shaking hands, putting people at ease. Everyone mentioned it. The gift of knowing what to do. You couldn't teach people that.

Then afterwards, when the cars had gone, the reverend had found that he couldn't stop thinking of her. Her stillness. Her pride. She would enter his mind at the most awkward moments. Raising the host at communion or marrying some young couple on a Saturday, his thoughts suddenly clouded with envy. For the first time in his life he had wanted something – someone – as much as he wanted God. That was what it amounted to. But he had been too cautious, too unsure of his ground, too concerned with the opinions of others. Afraid for it to be thought that he was taking advantage, a widow fresh in her loss, the earth hardly bedded down on her husband's grave. So he had missed his chance – if, indeed, there had ever been a chance. For it was hard to think she could have been interested in him. A Blimpish priest. An old bachelor even then, in his forties, with his garden, his books, his slide shows of the Holy Land. What had he had to offer a woman like Alice? It was almost comical really. What possible advantage could she have found in loving *him*?

When she woke, startling him, he was not sure that she recognized him, not at first. Heaven knows what they had given her. Yet somehow they managed a conversation, though he had found it hard to follow the flight of her thinking, and after fifteen minutes the effort of expressing herself made her irritable and tearful. She accused him of coming to see if she was dead. She demanded to know where Alec was, why he hadn't come, a question the reverend was at a loss to answer. But when it was time for him to leave (they were bringing in the lunch trolleys, those fiercely jolly women), she had not wanted to let go of his hand and so he had stayed standing by the bed until, quite unexpectedly, something revived in her, something of the old Alice, and she had smiled at him and said, 'Go on, Dennis. Off you go.'

On his way out he managed to corner the ward sister, an enormously fat young woman called Shirley or Shelly, who assured him that in all likelihood Alice would be free to go home in a day or two. It was a decision for the consultant, of course, and he wouldn't be doing his rounds until Monday, but there was no reason to suppose he would want to keep her in. This was the good news the reverend wished to pass on, in person, to Alec, though it was not the only reason for his visit to Brooklands. There was something else, difficult to pin down or explain; a nagging uneasiness that had found its way into the shadow play of his dreams, where among the scurryings, the unexpected faces, the sudden departures, he had had the sensation of an impending danger; and though the nature of the threat had remained obscure, he was convinced it had something to do with the Valentines, and with Alec in particular, and that as a friend of the family and a man of the cloth, it was his duty to try to do something. After all, Alec had had his difficulties in the past. That business a few years back when he had simply disappeared, until they found him, the authorities, somewhere on the South Coast, on a beach apparently, though the reverend had never been certain whether he was merely walking *along* the beach, or out towards the sea.

That morning, the third since his mother had gone into the hospital, Alec had woken with the idea of creating a refuge for himself in the unused summerhouse in the garden. Somewhere to go when the others came, a place to retreat to with the play. No one had used the summerhouse for as long as he could remember. It was Stephen's folly, a glorified tool-shed with a single window, some shelving, a bench outside. Honeysuckle and ivy had grown thickly over the wooden walls and roof, and probably stopped the place from falling down.

On a hook in the hallway he had found a ring of keys with a paper tag inscribed 'Garden'; one of the keys had turned the mortise lock in the summerhouse door, and he had stepped into an air, fungal and slightly sour, like old cider. His first job was to empty the place, and he began to carry out old paint tins and lengths of timber, jars of slug pellets and turpentine, and the delicate remains of field mice and butterflies. He scrubbed the walls, then broke the skin of paint in one of the tins and got to work with a wide brush, spattering paint on his jeans and wishing the summerhouse were much larger, so these tasks might last him for days, and there would be no time to brood on what had happened, to replay for the hundredth time the memory of Alice slumped in her chair on the terrace, a mouthful of tea slopping over her chin and falling in threads to her cardigan.

And if Una had not been there? This was unanswerable. How swift and calm she had been! And when the fits went on, that shuddering that seemed to require such a terrifying effort, she had sent him into the kitchen to call for an ambulance, which they had followed in her car while she explained to him that an attack like this was not unusual 'in a case like your mother's'; that she had half expected it, and he was not to be frightened. It nearly always looked worse than it was.

At the hospital they took her into A&E. He had a last glimpse of her as the porters wheeled her into an assessment ward, her arm already connected to a drip bag, her body covered to the neck in a red blanket. Una went with her, and another nurse pointed Alec towards a bench in the corridor opposite some posters about smoking, flu jabs, condoms. He sat down and waited, watching patients shuffle by in their dressing gowns, unshaven older men most of them, peering towards the exits as if still hopeful some friendly face would appear and tell them it was time to get dressed. A woman with a trolley of overused books hurried past, and several ill-looking doctors, younger than Alec, stethoscopes draped round their necks like sacred snakes. Behind the curtains to Alec's left a child was crying and would not be comforted.

Weirdly, after half an hour, he had fallen asleep, perfectly upright on the bench, and was woken by Brando gently shaking his shoulder, and then leading him to a quieter, more orderly section of the hospital where he had his office, a plain, functional room, not at all grand, with Venetian blinds at the window, and on the desk a photograph of a young man receiving some honour or accolade.

'You must have had a shock,' said Brando, perching on a corner of the desk. He was beautifully dressed.

'Yes,' said Alec. He had not thought of it like this but it was true. He felt he had witnessed something savage, like a beating.

'I'm fond of your mother,' said Brando. 'She's a very courageous woman.'

'I know,' said Alec. He wanted to get this over with. He couldn't stand the thought that he might make a fool of himself in front of this man. Might be offered a tissue from the box on the desk.

'We'll keep her in for a while. Perhaps persuade her to start a course of radiation therapy, though naturally, it's her decision. I'll give you a call once we've got her settled. Then you can come in and see her. How's that?'

In the evening Una called at Brooklands on her way home. They sat in the kitchen as the light went down and she had tried to comfort him, hinting that she could arrange for something that might help him manage. A prescription. Tablets. She had even – very briefly – held his hand, as though inviting him to unburden himself, but though it had tempted him, he had not known where to begin, what form of words, and so had kept up an exhausting and imbecilic denial. 'I'm fine now. Absolutely fine. Thank you.'

As soon as she left he masturbated in the downstairs toilet for the sheer physical shock of an orgasm, then slept, dreamlessly, curled on the end of Alice's bed. In some reach of the night the phone had rung but he didn't answer it. The next day he rose early, busying himself with small tasks, throwing out dead flowers, sweeping the terrace. He found a jar of beeswax and spent nearly two hours rubbing it into the dining-room table until his fingers ached. He made lists. Hand-washed a pair of his shirts.

When he could think of nothing else, he went out to the car and sat there with the keys in his hand, staring through the windscreen at shadows that hung like phantom laundry from the trees lining the drive. It was the same on Friday, though then he had gone out to the car three or four times, even starting the engine and letting it idle for a while before he switched it off again. In his head, time moved with the starts and silences of a faulty machine. He did not wind his father's clocks and they began to chime more erratically. Some had stopped altogether. The house grew stiller.

Osbourne startled him, tapping on the glass of the summer-house window. For a moment they peered at each other like utter strangers. Then Alec came out and they shook hands.

'Have I come at an awkward time?' asked the reverend. The rain had stopped, and on the shining lawn the bric-à-brac from the summerhouse was like a small exhibition illustrating the past. There was, for example, the type of old-fashioned

Dutch hoe his father had used in the garden at Meer. The reverend silently greeted it.

'I saw your mother this morning,' he said. 'Much more her old self.'

'Did they say when she can come back?'

'Not exactly. But not long. A few days, perhaps.' He looked for somewhere to sit but the bench had puddles of rainwater on it, and there was nowhere else. He thought: how miserable he looks, poor devil. Shifty too.

'Larry will be here soon,' said Alec.

'Splendid.'

'The day after tomorrow.'

'You'll meet him at the airport?'

'Yes.'

'Heathrow, I imagine.'

'Yes. The early flight.'

With his handkerchief, Osbourne cleaned the sweat from his face. He didn't care for running. 'And how are *you*?' he asked.

'I'm OK,' said Alec.

'Keeping yourself busy?'

'There's a lot to do.'

'Is there? I suppose there is. The house. The garden. Your work, of course. Making some progress?'

'A little.'

'Lázár, isn't it?'

'Yes.'

'I've certainly heard of him.'

'They didn't say when she would be back, then?'

'The doctor's making his rounds on Monday. With a bit of luck he'll give the green light then.' The reverend nodded, squinting at things quite randomly. It was foolish of him to have come without a plan, and now he was unsure how to go on. 'The thing about faith,' he began, quietly addressing a spider's web that glittered and trembled with raindrops, a thing of fabulous intricacy under the eaves of the summerhouse, 'is that it doesn't have to come all at once. Road to Damascus, et cetera. You can believe for a morning. Or an hour, if that's all you can manage. It doesn't matter.'

'Sorry?' said Alec.

'All I mean is that saying a prayer can help. It's very natural when things are difficult. Some people think it's hypocritical because they don't pray when things are going well. But it's perfectly all right.'

'Don't you have to believe that it will make some difference?'

The reverend paused. 'Perhaps not even that.' He pressed his hair into place with the flats of his hands. 'We're not alone,' he said.

'No,' said Alec, feeling as he spoke the weight of his conviction that quite the opposite was true; that aloneness was what lay at the beginning and end of every argument. 'Do you want some tea?' he asked.

'That's very kind,' said the reverend, 'but I've decided to plant out my arum lilies today. If I see your mother first, any message for her?'

Alec shook his head.

'Righto. I'll tell her you're keeping busy, then.'

They looked at each other; a silence that made evident both the purpose and the failure of their conversation. Then they shook hands again and the reverend made his way towards the stile that led from the garden back to the meadow. He had meant to say a few words about how even the worst situations had something salvageable in them, that the picture was never entirely black. The important thing, however, was that the elder boy was on his way. Things would improve then, somehow.

He looked up. The clouds now were slashed with a blue as clean as starlight, and he smiled, feeling the grateful inhalation of his soul. It was hard to believe there could be any atheists in Somerset, and by the time he was halfway across the meadow, his coat flapping over his arm, he had quite forgotten his dreams.

2

The moment László set out for his meeting with Emil Bexheti he felt a constriction of the chest, as if on the previous evening he had smoked an entire tin of Havanitos rather than his customary two. The Paris air seemed thin and innutritious. It was like breathing through a straw and it began to worry him. He wondered whether it was the beginning of something.

In the science room of his old school, dissected organs, human and animal, had been preserved in sealed bottles for the instruction of the pupils. He was sure there had been a lung there, floating in its syrup, an object that looked to have grown on the side of a tree or on a submerged rock, and which even as a young boy he had found improbable as the organ that funded human speech and laughter. And from that same schoolroom, he could recall certain mysterious and exotic terms – alveoli, pleura, gaseous exchange – that meant almost nothing to him now. It was shameful that he had so little idea of what took place in the world beneath his skin, though it seemed inevitable that in the next ten or fifteen years he would undergo some manner of enforced education. He knew, for example, that the heart was chambered like a weapon, but were there two or three chambers? Four? Was the body entirely dark inside? Was there colour?

He paused outside the Air France offices on rue de Rennes, leaning forward a little in a posture that seemed to ease the intake of air. Don't let me be old today, he thought. Today he needed clarity and vigour, a will unsapped by any thoughts of mortality, and he turned his mind once more to the meeting, and to the note he carried, which yesterday morning, or the night before, had been slipped in among his papers at the university. A single sheet of A4 in a brown envelope. Unaddressed, unsigned.

'The café terrace at the Monde Arabe. Wednesday 1600.'

His first reaction had been to drop it into the wire tray on his desk – both his 'in' and his 'out' tray – where he collected all those matters he did not intend to look at for a very long time. There was work to do. His Hrabal lecture, a dozen postgraduate essays to wade through. But several times during the next hour he had reached for the note and examined it as if the message, which could hardly have been more blunt, more laconic, were somehow encrypted. Finally, with a grunt of impatience, he had screwed it into a ball and lobbed it into the waste basket on the other side of the room, only to fish it out a few minutes later, carefully fold it, and put it in his wallet next to the photograph of himself holding his mother's hand outside the old house on Szechnyi Rakpart.

Back at the apartment – it was Kurt's yoga night – he had held the note under the lamp in the study. He had, of course, been expecting something of the kind since the call the night of the dinner, but now that it had come he felt suddenly and unreasonably implicated, as if he had agreed to it all, even solicited it. He decided to destroy the note by tearing it into pieces so small it could not possibly be reconstructed (by whom? Kurt? The Garbargs, fingering the communal rubbish?). Alternatively, it might be wiser, more complete, to burn it in an ashtray, or even to flush it away in the toilet, though in the first case there would be the lingering odour of paper smoke, and in the second, he risked the reappearance of scraps of paper from the mysteries of the U-bend. The plumbing of the Fifth Republic – or in the case of his own toilet, possibly the Fourth – was good but far from perfect.

He had paced about the study, laughed at himself, read a paragraph from the previous days *Libération* (Kurt kept all the papers for recycling), then flicked through a dozen pages from the last draft of his latest work-in-progress, *L'un ou l'autre*. To be absolutely safe he resolved to throw the note away in a street bin a good distance from the apartment. People threw things away all the time. There could be nothing remotely suspicious about it.

He spent that evening with Laurence Wylie in a bar on the boulevard Ménilmontant, the same bar in which Franklin had acquired the gun from the policeman. She had quite obviously been drinking at home before coming out, and it did not take more than a glass of Ricard before she began to repeat herself. Franklin had not been keeping his appointments with the doctor. Franklin was mysteriously sick in the night. Franklin made 'jokes' about killing himself. Most recently there had been a row with the gardienne, Madame Barbossa, whom Franklin had accused of snooping. She probably was, said László. Snooping was part of her job. But Franklin had made the poor woman weep by calling her a *'collabo!'* This to a woman whose father had died heroically in the street fighting of August '44, saving his comrades, saving France. Naturally the neighbours had become involved. It was a miracle the police had not been called. László agreed it was a mess, a tangle, and had promised that he would have another talk with Franklin, though he drew the line at Laurence's suggestion that he also talk to Franklin's doctor, a German of indeterminate sexuality whose waiting room was always full of painters and novelists and dancers with their STDs, their imaginary brain tumours.

At midnight he walked her home to the rue du Deguerry, hugged her in lieu of any more substantial consolation, then caught the Métro from Parmentier. There were bins in the Métro station, bins on the street, but the note had remained in his wallet. He could not quite understand it, this sudden blossoming of the neurotic. Was it some old reflex of secrecy? After all, he had grown up with Rákosi and the ÁVH, where it was taken for granted that there were informers everywhere. But he had lived in France for forty years! Was it possible that the old instincts were so easily provoked? He was not convinced, and as he took the cage elevator up to his apartment, it struck him that he was acting like a man who had decided upon a course of action he could not yet justify to himself, as though reason – or what passed for it, those little narratives of self-justification – were loping behind his true intentions like an idiot.

Kurt was at home, standing in the kitchen in his underwear eating a slice of bread and honey. He demonstrated a new contortion from the yoga class. László passed on the story of Franklin and the gardienne which, in the retelling, lost its character of melodrama and seemed merely comic. They sat up a while, then retired to the bedroom and went through the preliminaries of love-making, but after twenty minutes, such was the laming effect of his secret, László, lying over Kurt's back like the last survivor of a disastrous cavalry charge, was forced to admit defeat.

'Too much wine,' he said. 'Sorry.'

'Sleep,' said Kurt, good-humouredly. They were old lovers now and failure was part of the repertoire. This was Tuesday night.

On the Wednesday afternoon, having decided he would walk to the Monde Arabe, László chose to come up the rue de Rennes on to the boulevard St Germain, rather than cut through by the Panthéon and run the risk of encountering colleagues from the university. At three-thirty the day was hot, the cafés crowded with gleeful Americans. Backpackers stared at maps, and outside the St Germain Métro the hurdy-gurdy man ground out sentimental tunes while his little dog slumbered in its basket. Walking, László rehearsed his speech to Emil Bexheti, which he would be at pains to ensure was neither too indulgent, nor overly stern. I am a playwright, my friend, and my function is to observe, and then to write as honestly as I can. That is all. Naturally I sympathize with your cause. But seriously, what do you expect of me? If it's a matter of signing a petition, or even perhaps of writing to a newspaper, these things I am prepared to consider, though you should not overestimate my influence. Above all, do not ask me to meddle in other people's business. Such actions, however well intended, end badly . . .

He imagined them concluding the meeting with glasses of mint tea at the terrace café, after which he, László, would go home and tell Kurt everything and they would laugh and open a bottle of Sancerre and put Puccini on, and life would go its way with barely a ripple. How simple it was! And this fiction comforted him for several minutes, almost as far as the tower of the Monde Arabe itself, which, standing by the river in its cladding of steel tiles – each with an aperture like a camera's, narrowing or expanding according to the strength of the light – was, he conceded, an admirably theatrical choice for a rendezvous.

Inside, glass-walled elevators ferried the visitors to the library or to the roof, and László ascended in the company of an Arab scholar – a tall, bearded, effortlessly superior type – and two teenage Parisiennes who wore the kind of tight cotton camisoles that might have earned them a flogging in some parts of the world. (He himself, or course, in such stern theocracies, would not escape so lightly.)

Just after four o'clock he stepped on to the terrace. A dozen people lounged against the rail, while another twenty or thirty sat at the wooden tables. The interior of the café was almost empty. He stood for a minute in the middle of the terrace, then, feeling awkward, foolishly conspicuous, he found a space at the rail and took the view. Notre Dame, the 'Genie de la Bastille', and in the distance, shimmering in a smoke of exhaust fumes, Sacré Coeur, looking oddly like the space shuttle, its creamy dome targeted at the sky. On one side of him, an oriental girl recorded the scene on a digital camera; on the other, a pair of lovers gazed out as if from the deck of a liner towards the coast of a country they had once been happy in.

He waited fifteen minutes. The lovers drowsily departed. On the far bank of the river, some curious effect of sunlight and water made it appear that a torrent of molten fire coursed behind the first-floor windows of the houses on the quai de Béthune. He told himself he was relieved that it had turned out to be nothing, that this was for the best, and after a last look around, he took the lift again, crossed the courtyard, and waited at the corner of rue de Fosses for the lights to change. Next to him, a young man in a sports jacket also waited, pulling on a cigarette and staring ahead. They crossed together, and as they reached the other side the young man touched László's arm with a gesture so slight it might almost have been accidental. It reminded László – awkward reminiscence at such a moment – of his few casual encounters in Paris in the years after he first arrived, days when blinded by an inassuageable loneliness he had gone with strangers, using lust like a hammer to smash at the tenderness in himself.

'Yes?'

The young man flicked the end of his cigarette into the gutter, where it span in the water among the fruit peel and the Métro tickets. 'There is a car, monsieur. Please hurry.'

He walked ahead, and after a hesitation that lasted no more than three or four seconds, László followed him on to the quai de la Tournelle, where a grey Volkswagen was parked at the rear of the taxi rank. A second man, older than the other, more heavily built, leaned over to open the passenger door. László was ushered into the back seat and the young man sat by his companion. Two policemen in shirtsleeves strolled past, glanced at the driver, glanced at László, at the vehicle itself (which had a dent on the offside door), but kept moving, as if on such a warm afternoon it was much more pleasant to continue their conversation than stop yet another car with someone vaguely foreign at the wheel.

'Where are we going?' asked László.

'Not far,' said the younger man.

They pulled out into the traffic, driving fast where it was possible, but never too fast. László leaned back, staring out at the city, its public beauty. As they went west along the river, past Pont Neuf and the Musée d'Orsay, he tried to prepare himself, marshalling arguments and defences, rebuttals to imaginary accusations. Am I afraid? he wondered. He thought that he wasn't.

At the Pont de l'Alma they headed south and circled round until they were on the avenue Bosquet, driving back towards the river again. Then, with a lingering look in the rear-view mirror, the driver accelerated and turned hard into the kind of street László always imagined to be inhabited solely by homesick *filles au pair* and widows with lapdogs. A place with no bars or restaurants and which by 7 p.m. would be deserted, shut down.

They stopped fifty metres from the end of the road, and László followed his young guide through a passageway at the side of one of the buildings to where a flight of narrow stairs wound like an iron vine up a corner of the interior courtyard. Several times the younger man stopped for László to catch him up. 'Please,' he said, anxious now, as if he might fail in this, the last part of his task. 'Please . . .'

At the top of the building they entered a corridor with walls barely wider than László's shoulders. They were, he realized, in one of the city's secret places, where doors with worn handles led into rooms where any kind of life might be lived, almost invisibly.

At the second door on the right hand-side, the young man knocked with the conspirator's three quick taps. The door was opened by Emil Bexheti.

'Thank you,' he said, ignoring the young man and shepherding László into the room. 'I was sure you would come.'

'In which case,' said László, still husky from the climb, 'you knew more than I.'

The room was extraordinarily small, a *chambre de bonne* in the shape of a blunt wedge, almost directly under the slates of the roof. Stifling in summer, bitterly cold in winter. László had done his time in such rooms; he had not thought to see one again.

In the middle of the room were three chairs – two facing one – and along one wall a single bed with a sagging mattress, stripped bare. On the table beside the bed were an alarm clock and a cellphone. From one of the chairs a young woman in a black dress, her face so pale it seemed somehow scraped down, examined László with a coolness, a hauteur, he found almost intolerable.

'This,' said László, 'had better be very good indeed.'

'But that depends on you, monsieur,' said the woman, sharply. Emil waved her to silence.

'On me?' László repeated. He took the chair opposite her, and as he did so he entered again, quite suddenly, that other room in that other house where men and women had come to have their parts explained to them, street maps spread over the table top, gunfire echoing across the wintry city. And now he knew he would be asked again, told what would depend on him, not by Feri or Joska, but by a young woman whose name he did not know, and who, however well informed, could not possibly understand the character of his need. He locked eyes with her and smiled – a little fiercely, a little sadly – and because she was unable to see the origin of the smile, its long roots, she was momentarily disconcerted.

'Go on,' said László.

And so they began.

3

There was a rumour, perhaps true, perhaps no more than a high-altitude urban myth, that passengers in economy received less of the piped oxygen than those in superior classes. Larry could not remember who had suggested this to him – it might even have been Ranch – but coming round from the slough of another mid-flight doze he was inclined to think the rumour had substance, for in happier days he had travelled on the other side of the mysterious curtain and thought he had indeed inhaled a richer mix and been the better for it. Pinker and more optimistic.

He knuckled his eyes and looked round for Ella, but her place beside him was empty; nor – turning and twisting in his seat – could he see her in the aisles. They had been allotted the middle two seats of four in the central section just to the rear of the wings. At one end of the row was an American college student on his way to summer school in Oxford, a young man with troubled skin who addressed Larry as 'sir'. On the other side was a nun, an ethnic oriental, who had crossed herself and prayed audibly during the take-off from San Francisco, for which Larry had been grateful. Like most people he had only the haziest idea of how this communal defiance of gravity actually worked and believed that at least one person on the plane needed to offer up a prayer if they were to arrive in safety. He waited five minutes, then leaned over to ask her if she had seen his daughter.

'Daughter?' She spoke the word as though it were new to her, but she had evidently understood because she looked at the empty seat with real alarm, as if the child might somehow have tumbled out of the plane and fallen through miles of air into the unlit Atlantic.

'I guess she wandered off while I was napping.'

'We look for her,' said the nun, decisively.

'No, no,' said Larry, 'I'll go.' But the nun was already out of her seat. 'My name Sister Kim,' she said.

'Larry Valentine,' said Larry. He noticed that along with the more usual accoutrements – habit, beads, cross – she was wearing a brand-new pair of green-and-white sneakers blazoned with the Greek for victory.

They set off together, looking left and right along the gently vibrating body of the plane. Sister Kim stopped a passing stewardess, explaining to her, in an idiom all her own, that the gentleman had lost his little girl.

'She's an asthmatic,' added Larry, hoping this would justify the presence of a nun.

'Don't worry,' said the stewardess, in a voice sharply English, 'she can't get very far on a plane, can she?'

They went on as a party of three, just as the screens came down for the next film and the lights in the cabin dimmed. After a discreet check of the toilets, the stewardess consulted with the chief steward.

'Does she have her inhaler?' asked the steward.

'Yes,' said Larry, recalling that he had put it in the bib pocket of her dungarees as they waited in the departure lounge after a tense farewell to Kirsty, who had driven them to the airport and come as far as the check-in, crouching to hug Ella for several teary minutes. Larry had been somewhat offended, as if flying with him implied some imminence of danger for the girl. This, however, was not a good beginning.

On the screens, young women in Regency dresses were receiving a gentleman caller. Long-haul somnolence had seized most of the passengers. They gazed up, shoeless and weary. Some already wore the complimentary black eye mask and slept, or attempted to. There was little sense of any progress.

The search continued for another fifteen minutes; a man, a nun and two aircrew, processing in the aisles until at last they discovered the child on the top deck, wide awake in one of the unoccupied multi-adjustable seats in club class, apparently thinking. The steward and stewardess expressed amazement. How could she have got there without being noticed? But Larry knew that his daughter had several mysterious talents, and that not being seen by the coarse-grained gaze of adults was merely one of them.

'You always stay with Papa,' said Sister Kim, wagging a finger at the girl, though at the same time winking at her and then telling her how pretty she was.

Larry took Ella's hand and walked her back.

'You want to watch the movie, El?' A horseman was riding through the rain, a shining black figure atop a shining black horse. But Ella preferred the colouring book she had been given in the child's pack at the beginning of the flight, and she began filling in the patterns, her brow furrowed with concentration, as though colouring were a chore some authority required her to complete in a responsible manner for a purpose Larry was not privy to. The flora of her inward life was increasingly foreign to him. He could no longer be sure even of the fundamentals, such as whether or not she was happy, or at least content. Hoffmann's view was that the trip would be good for her. A therapeutic encounter with a fundamental human experience. He liked, he said, his 'little people' to meet Mr Death and shake his paw. Kirsty had been in favour too, so Larry was overruled. But was it good for a child to be exposed to the events waiting for them in England? What's wrong with Granny? Where's Granny gone? No. He could not share Hoffmann's faith in a child's capacity for truth in the raw. Why should a child's capacity be so much greater than a man's?

Sister Kim was studying a book with photographs of other nuns in it. Her hands were small and careworn, working hands, and Larry wondered whether her heart were in the same condition, chapped and chaffed from the difficulty of having to love indiscriminately. He asked her if she would keep an eye on Ella while he went to freshen up. She said she would, and he took his blue leather wash bag from under the seat and made his way to the toilets, shutting the folding door of the cubicle and confronting himself in the mirror. The light in there was peculiarly unforgiving. He seemed to have acquired a grey tan, and even his hair, the brown-blond thatch to which the California sun gave threads of gold, looked ordinary and glamourless. From the shallows of his skin, an older, feebler man peered back at him.

He took a pee. Someone rattled the door. He badly wanted to smoke, but if the man who had lost his daughter were discovered endangering the flight and setting off the smoke alarm he would be met at Heathrow – another of his fantasies of imminent arrest – by social workers and transport police.

He grinned at the thought of how Alec might deal with such a situation and, thinking of his brother, realized how badly he wanted to see him, and that in some way he was counting on him. What kind of shape was Alec in these days? Five, six years now since he had had his 'wobble' (Alice's term), and had left full-time teaching at the comp in London. How serious had that been? Were doctors involved? He had never asked, because five, six years ago he was in San Diego doing promotion for Reebok and talking to Ray Lumumba about a part in *Sun Valley*. Ella had just been born, and Alec's trouble had been like a reminder of everything he – Larry – thought he had escaped in escaping England, those Fates who naturally crowded into old used-up countries, and who had already sent his father into the dark. He had no clear idea how he and Alec were going to get through these coming weeks, what dread pressures would come upon them, but the fact was that soon now they would be orphans, a thought terrible and curious that pricked all manner of childhood anxieties.

Kirsty, whose own mother had died at forty-seven years of age when her Cessna spiralled into the Gulf of Mexico on a flight into Tampa, had made the mistake of trying to comfort him with a yard of undigested Zen the night he returned from LA. She had told him about Alec's call, and then said, 'You know, suffering comes from our inability to accept transience.' And while he had accepted the truth of this, he had also known that her understanding of it was as feeble as his own, that she was pretending to a wisdom she had not earned, and it immediately sparked one of their sadder and more frenzied exchanges. In the lamplit kitchen, amid all the gleaming domestic hardware

Sun Valley General had provided, they threw out remarks reckless of any consideration for justice or accuracy, a blind verbal lashing-out.

'You want Ella to hear this?' she had asked, when Larry, still fogged with the drink and drugs he had consumed at T. Bone's, began to raise his voice. Hands on hips, a cartoon of the shrewish wife, she demanded to know what he had been doing in LA, and when she seemed, quite rightly, not to believe his heavily edited version of how he had spent the previous twelve hours, he had almost choked on his indignation. Her own life offered him little in the way of material for reproaches (he had come to think of this as a form of meanness) and, for lack of anything intelligent to say, anything pertinent, he accused her of carrying on with her guru, her Jap, Mr Transience, and for this, quite rightly, she had flung the remains of her OJ at him and walked out, pausing at the door to hiss: 'I used to *admire* you.'

What was depressing was how quickly they could reach this stage, as if each had become specifically what the other could not tolerate, though on the following day he had apologized – a mute, somewhat cowardly apology – buying her a jar of her favourite black olives from Molinari's on Columbus Avenue. He had left them on the breakfast bar and then spied on her from the hall as she fished them out of the oil with her fingers. It was the moment he might have gone to her – there were only three good steps between them – the moment he might have settled his hands on her shoulders and said the necessary things. But distances in a marriage – in his at least – were deceptive, and he had remained by the door, perverse and voyeuristic, watching his wife eat olives and slick her cheeks with grease when she pushed away a tear.

Someone tried the door again. 'Later!' called Larry. He was busy with the contents of his wash bag, turning them out on to the narrow steel shelf by the basin. Safety razor, multivitamins, deodorant, painkillers. Two spare canisters for Ella's inhaler. A smoke-brown plastic bottle of Deroxat; five foil sheets of Xanax; a bottle of Luvox, a box of Paxil, a condom, nail-clippers, toothbrush, eye-drops, tweezers. He swallowed a Xanax and a Deroxat, and cleaned his teeth, then blew his nose, noting that his snot was streaked with blood from a last big line of adulterated powder woofed up from a CD cover in the spare room while Kirsty and Ella had waited outside in the Cherokee.

The blue-and-red capsules he had taken from Ranch's cabinet were in a vinyl side pocket of the wash bag, still wrapped in the same sheet of tangerine toilet paper. He had not looked at them since that afternoon in the Valley, though he had often brooded on them, their nearness inspiring dark and melodramatic thoughts. There were three of them – one slightly larger than the other two. Sex and death. Or nothing at all, nothing but a crooked doctor's invention, or some story dreamed up by Ranch to amuse the girls, so that even now he was down there in the annexe with Rosinne and Jo-babe, laughing at how the soap-opera guy had fallen for his spiel. Shoulda seen his eyes pop! Man, he just wanted to eat them right there!

Yet something in the sheer improbability, the fantasticalness of it all, suggested to Larry that the pills were precisely what Ranch had said they were, and that somewhere in Las

Vegas there was a man with the necessary lethal knowledge to prepare them. But whatever the truth of it, this was the perfect occasion to be rid of them, right now, as they flew over one of those dwindling zones of the planet nobody pretended to own. Yet even as he imagined them spilling almost weightlessly from some duct in the plane's gleaming underbelly, he was watching his hands carefully wrap them again and return them to their pocket in the wash bag. They were an asset he was not yet prepared to relinquish. Soon, of course, very soon. But not yet.

Going back to his seat, he watched the film continue its run on a score of angled screens. There were bonnets and carriages, and English hills of surpassing loveliness. The gentlemen frowned at each other and bowed, while the ladies waited for secret notes to be passed.

Ella, her colouring book on her lap, her crayon held in the tenseless curl of her fingers, looked as though sleep had caught her very suddenly. Sister Kim smiled and nodded. Larry thanked her. Her smile widened.

'I know what you are,' she whispered. 'At convent we have television too, sometimes.'

'Will you say a prayer when we land?' asked Larry.

She said that she would. 'Jesus is pilot,' she said.

He laid a blanket over his daughter's legs and reclined his seat. He was tired again, physically sluggish, but agitated by what seemed like a great backlog of *thinking*. He could not decide whether there were a great many decisions to be made, or none at all; whether his situation warranted some explosion of energy, some drama of action, or if he should simply wait and see; if indeed there was nothing he could do that would make the slightest difference. He could not save Alice – what manner of angel could? It seemed unlikely he could save his own marriage. And if that should fail, he did not, in all honesty, know if he would have the mettle, the knowhow, to save himself.

He took the earplugs from their bag and sealed off his skull from the sighs and little disgruntlements of his fellow passengers. He closed his eyes and made an effort to focus on transience, but it was too harsh a lesson. He was a child still, and like everyone else, with the possible exception of Mr Endo, he was swimming against the current and would be swept away. At the back of this was the spectre of an overwhelming loneliness, of a place where nobody would stay with you because nobody could. And *this* was what he was supposed to accept? Where was the comfort in it? What kind of courage did this letting go require? Clearly more than he had to offer. He would have to rely on quite different weapons – weakness for example – and, as he fell, not into sleep but into some parallel condition unique to the long-haul passenger, he began to imagine, and even to believe, despite the fact that in such a dearth of good air one could not entirely trust such ideas, that the last good road left open to him was failure itself. And this he decided to call hope.

4

The discussion in the little room lasted for over an hour.
The window was closed – indeed, it looked to be *sealed* –
and it was not long before they started to sweat and grow
irritable. Emil, his beard shaved to the contour of his jaw,
delivered a concise though thoroughly partisan analysis of
Balkan politics, while the young woman, with her narrow
skull, her high cheekbones, her face sloping back to the eyes,
where the skin was slightly puffy and discoloured as if she
were not quite well, a chronic insomniac perhaps, confined
herself to asides about the international conspiracy of indif-
ference that ignored those disasters it found unprofitable to
address: the 'no oil' argument. László played devil's advocate.
When Emil asserted that the Albanian people, in the guise
of the ancient Illyrians, had been the true first inhabitants
of Kosovo, he pointed out that there was no real evidence
for this, no monuments or reliable texts, nothing but a few
fragile linguistic coincidences. Was it not the case that the
independence movement in Kosovo was another scheme for
the old ambition of a Greater Albania? And what of the
legality of it? Why *should* the Serbs give it away?

'You defend Milošević?' asked the young woman. She
could barely keep her seat.

'Milošević,' said László, 'is a cynical and dangerous man.
In fact I believe he is mentally ill. But is this about Milošević?

It feels like a tribal matter. A blood feud.'

He thought she might slap him for this, but Emil laid a hand on her arm and switched the talk to Bosnia. He spoke of the massacre at Srebrenica, the camps at Omarska and Manjaca, of killers like Arkan and Mirko Jović, and the systematic rape of women and girls by men who masked their faces because they were neighbours.

'This will happen in Kosovo too,' he said. 'Trust me. It will all happen again. At least the Bosnians had an army of sorts. They could fight back.'

'And you have exhausted all peaceful means?' asked László. He glanced at the young woman, from whose slender limbs there seemed to emanate a convincing shimmer of violence. 'Ibrahim Rugova seems a genuinely good man.'

'Rugova is a good man,' said Emil, 'but he is not a man of action. He could not stop a hundred and fifty thousand Albanians being thrown out of work. Doctors, teachers, all those in state employment. He has not stopped the apartheid in the schools or the suppression of our language. He has not stopped detention and beatings. Did you know, monsieur, that any remark critical of Serbia is considered a "verbal crime" punishable by two months' imprisonment? Did you know that thousands have been summoned to police stations for what the authorities call "informative talks", interrogations that last for three days and for which no justification is ever offered? They are making their lists, monsieur, and one day they will use those lists and they will not be interested in talking. You know what the Serbs call the Albanians in Kosovo? "Tourists." They mean to get rid of us, monsieur, and only when it is too late will the world take notice. Is it not accepted everywhere that a man has the right to fight in defence of his life? His family?'

There was a great deal more of this, though from the moment Milošević had stripped Kosovo of its autonomy, László had entertained no serious doubts about the justice of the Albanian cause. The unhappy Serbs with their deranged leader were in thrall to a mythology cooked up in the nineteenth century and reheated by nationalist communist demagogues a hundred years later. What was it he had heard it called? 'The politics of fantasy and hatred.' But it was one matter to denounce a regime while sitting at the dinner table among friends, quite another to assist the operation of a group committed to its violent overthrow. There could be no doubt any more whose company he was in. Did Emil Bexheti already have blood on his hands? Where had he been when the rector of Pristina University was attacked in January?

Twice during the meeting the cellphone rang. Most of the talking was done by the voice at the other end, to which Emil paid respectful attention. Towards the end of the hour he poured László a glass of lukewarm water from a bottle of Volvic.

'In '56,' he said, coming to the point László had been expecting for some time, 'did you question the legitimacy of armed resistance?'

'No,' said László.

'Though you knew it was not a game? That people, many people, would be killed?'

'We were a country under occupation.'

'You fought for your freedom.'

'Yes.'

'You still believe that was right?'

'Yes. But it might be worth your remembering that we lost. A good cause is no guarantee of victory.'

'So the sacrifice was futile?'

'No,' said László. 'Something was achieved, though it's hard to say exactly what. They showed us our weakness, but we also showed them theirs. Certainly nobody who saw what happened then was surprised at the speed of the collapse in '89.'

'It was more than that, monsieur. You set an example for the entire world.'

'The best of them did. Though in an affair like that there is always much brutality. Lynch mobs. Summary executions. It wasn't always very edifying.'

'I know that some consider you a political fatalist. I am, of course, familiar with your work. But I ask you once more, in all earnestness – were you and your comrades wrong to take up arms?'

László shook his head.

'Would you deny to others the right to do likewise?'

'Obviously I could not.'

'Then may I assume you would not oppose a movement that pursued objectives comparable to those you once fought for?'

'Why would I oppose it?'

'Would you support it?'

'Perhaps.'

'Actively or passively?'

'You would make a good Jesuit,' said László.

'Religion,' snarled the young woman, 'is essentially fascistic.'

'And you,' said László, 'would have made an excellent Party member. You have a head full of slogans.'

Emil said: 'You can help us, monsieur. The risk would not be great. You are now a successful and respected man. I do not ask you to throw this away.'

László frowned at the other's conceit. 'Perhaps I want to throw it away. Perhaps I am not at all what you think I am, Monsieur Bexheti. Do not have too much confidence in your research. But suppose you now tell me, in the most specific terms, what it is you want of me.'

There was a pause. Emil nodded. 'I have your solemn word that you will speak of this to nobody?'

'Very well.'

'Not even to Monsieur Engelbrecht?'

'Not even to Monsieur Engelbrecht. Not immediately. Here, however, you must trust me to manage things as I see best.'

Before the woman could object, Emil signalled his agreement. 'We are in your hands, monsieur.'

'Let us say we are in each other's hands,' said László. He wondered what would happen if he betrayed them. Would a police launch fish him out of the Seine? He prepared himself – ready now to imagine almost anything – but what they wanted of him was so simple his first reaction was a sharp disappointment. They wanted a courier. A postman. Someone who would carry a case abroad, and then come home.

'Nothing more?'

'Nothing more.'

'And what does the case contain? Documents?'

Another pause.

'Money?'

'As I am sure you already know,' said Emil, 'for several years there has been a tax on all émigré Albanians to pay for the parallel republic. For the schools and the hospitals we were forced to establish for ourselves. Now there are many who want us to be more active in the defence of our rights. They are prepared to give generously in order to make that possible.'

'Money to buy guns.'

'Also food, medicine, clothes . . .'

'Uniforms.'

'You want us to buy books?' asked the woman.

'I would prefer it immensely,' said László. 'But tell me, where would this case have to go?'

'Can you not guess?' asked Emil.

'No,' said László, 'not at all.'

'Where are you most qualified to go? Where would you not be a stranger? Where do you know the language . . .'

'The *language*?' So that was it! He had been chosen not because he was "a friend of justice", but because he spoke an impossible language!

'You want me to go to Hungary?'

'To Budapest,' said the woman.

László threw back his head and laughed: he couldn't help it. What fun the gods were having with him now! It was strange, however, that he had not seen it coming.

'Who,' said Emil, leaning forward and lighting a cigarette, 'could suspect your motives in going there? You know the city . . .'

'I have not been there since '91.'

'How much does a city change in six years? And you have relatives there.'

'Two rather dim cousins. A very elderly aunt. My brother . . .'

'. . . is in America. We know all this. The point is that I

188

would be a foreigner there. My presence would immediately be suspect. I am also well known to the Serbian informers in Paris, of whom there are many. The moment I left my apartment it would be reported.'

'But why Budapest?'

'That is more than you need to know,' said the woman.

László shook his head. 'You will have to do better than that.'

'We go,' said Emil, 'wherever there are people who will provide the items that we need.'

'I know Budapest has its share of Ukrainian mafia,' said László. 'Are these the people you are dealing with?'

Emil held up his hands, palms out. 'As my colleague has said, that is more than you need to know. Or rather, more than I am at liberty to tell you. Suffice to say that when one goes shopping one does not always admire the character of the shopkeeper.'

László tugged a handkerchief from his pocket and carefully wiped the sweat from his eyes. 'Supposing,' he said, 'that I considered doing as you ask – and for the moment I commit myself to nothing – when would I have to leave?'

'Six, perhaps seven days' time.'

'And I would receive this case in Paris?'

'We will give you the details when we have your answer. You must please inform us by fifteen hundred hours tomorrow. If we have not heard from you by then it will be assumed that you do not wish to help us. You will not be contacted again. And this meeting will not have happened.'

He passed over a slip of paper with a number on it. 'Call from a public telephone. Do not say who you are. Simply ask "Is Françoise there?" Nothing more.'

'Is Françoise there.'

'We will take care of the rest.'

'One more thing,' said László. 'You mentioned Kurt Engelbrecht. If I find that you have involved him in any of this I will go directly to the authorities and denounce you. Is that understood?'

'Yes,' said Emil. 'Perfectly.' He went with László as far as the head of the stairs, where the young man in the sports jacket was waiting for them.

'You know,' said László, 'whatever anyone may have told you about me, the truth is I was never much of a "freedom fighter".'

Emil smiled. 'I did not think you were Che Guevara, monsieur.'

'You see,' said László, looking down into the well of the courtyard where the late afternoon sunlight was heaped up in a corner, 'I couldn't pull the trigger. Did you know that?'

'We do what we can,' said Emil. 'Each in his way.'

'Yes,' said László. 'But I did nothing.' He turned to his guide. 'Let's go.'

Emil watched them from the top step. As they came to the turn in the stairs he said: 'Sometimes we have a second chance, monsieur.' He was not sure, however, if the playwright had heard him.

5

At 6 a.m. British Summer Time, flight BA902 from SFO floated through cloudbanks suffused with morning light, Sister Kim praying serenely, until England appeared in a rush of housing estates and tiny fields. An A-road, a motorway, an athletics ground, an industrial estate. It was a landscape without much grandeur to it, but from the air, at least, it had some quality of the homely, the delicately human, pleasing after so much time amid the towers and deserts of the American immense.

Alec was waiting for them as they came through the automatic doors at arrivals; a pale, weary-looking figure among the huddle of early greeters. He waved and smiled. Larry, carrying the big suitcases, smiled back, thinking how there was always at such moments a disconcerting adjustment to be made, as if the person who had come to meet you could never quite be the person you had expected. Even a face, a posture as familiar as his own brother's, seemed subtly misremembered.

When he cleared the barrier he put down the cases. Alec held out his hand but Larry pulled him into a hug, immediately learning more of the true history of the last weeks than any amount of talking could have produced. Not just the fizz of tension in his brother's body, but that smell of unhappiness, like a room in a house where children have been punished.

Ella turned up her face. Alec kissed her forehead.

'Good flight?'

'Crappy flight. Thanks for coming to get us.'

'No problem.'

You're looking good,' said Larry.

'Really?'

'Sure.'

'I'm glad,' said Alec, raising an eyebrow as though every-thing were irony.

As they crossed the road to the carpark, he said: 'She's coming back today. Una's bringing her from the hospital around four.'

He gave this news so conversationally that Larry, the mesh of himself strung weblike between time zones, was unsure for an instant who Alec was talking about.

'Mum?'

'Of course.'

'That's *fantastic*! You hear that, El? Granny's coming out of hospital!' He was profoundly relieved. A hospital-bed reunion had been a miserable prospect, not least because hospitals had such odd associations for him. Places of entertainment. Places where he pretended to be someone else.

'Is she better now?' asked Ella.

'Maybe a little better,' said Larry, glancing at Alec. 'But just a little.'

'She has to take her medicine,' said Ella, sternly.

On a steadily filling motorway they drove with the sun livid in the rear-view mirror, the Renault creaking and rattling, never quite making seventy. The brothers talked of Alice, though always with an awareness of Ella wide awake in the back seat. It did not take Larry many questions to discover that Alec had not visited her in the hospital. For this, Alec offered no explanation or defence. He didn't say 'I couldn't. I tried but I couldn't', and Larry did not pursue it, though it angered him a little. After ten hours in the air it was difficult to have much patience with other people's fear, their shortfalls. And Alec's failure to do something as simple as drive to a hospital indicated that things were rather worse than he had imagined. He told himself that this was OK, that they would manage, but it gave him a sinking feeling, as if having run almost to the end of his breath he had looked up to see ahead of him vast distances still to be travelled.

They came off the motorway at Coverton – 'Can you smell the sea, El?' – then drove over the moor. The villages they passed were tidy and prosperous, almost suburban, the barns and old village schools converted into private houses with expensive foreign cars outside, but the hedgerows were still tall and in their way unmannerly and uproarious with June.

When they turned into the drive at Brooklands, Larry leaned forward, wondering what changes he would find. He had not been here since the retirement party the previous August when he had become shit-faced on duty-free and kissed the art teacher, Miss Whatshername, behind the summerhouse. In the light of what had followed, it was tempting to recall the whole of that night as though it were one of those movies set on the eve of a disaster no one is expecting, but which everyone is secretly preparing for. Tempting but false, for surely they had all been perfectly innocent of the future, and Alice had not said, or at least not *meant*, what she had whispered to him in the minutes before the fuse blew. Absurd request! What did she have in mind? That he would smother her with a pillow the moment she stopped making sense?

Then the house swung into view, its walls more bowed, more overrun with creepers than he remembered. A dozen of the terracotta tiles were missing from the roof at the gable end, the guttering above one of the upstairs windows had ruptured, and the wooden side gate into the garden was jammed ajar, turning it into a kind of trellis for weeds. He shook his head. 'This place needs a lot of work,' he said, 'a lot of work.' He felt quite nauseous with fatigue.

Napping in the twin room downstairs, Larry dreamed pleasantly of Sister Kim, and when he woke, half expected to see her beside him, his guardian angel, but there was only Ella, in shorts and T-shirt, sitting on the other bed, swinging her legs and watching him. She had opened one of the suitcases and Larry automatically looked to see what she might have helped herself to, but the case contained only clothes and toiletries, a couple of books, nothing that was likely to be of interest to her. He sent her off to find Alec while he shaved and showered and drank a cafetière of coffee and smoked three cigarettes and swallowed another Xanax. Then, feeling different rather than better, he patrolled the house with a last cup of coffee, looking into rooms and out of windows, recovering the place, trying to *arrive*.

He left Alice's bedroom until last, uncertain how he would react to it, but the room had been thoroughly tidied and aired and smelled only of furniture polish, and very faintly of pine disinfectant. The curtains were pulled back and tied. There were no clothes draped over the chair, no shoes on the floor, no sickroom litter of pillboxes and tonics and half-read magazines. The double bed was made up under a patchwork cover, though at the foot of the bed the material was rucked, as if someone had been sitting there. He smoothed it out, then went to the chest of drawers where the photographs had been angled so that they could be seen from the bed. The largest (it chilled him) was of himself, sixteen, waiting in his whites to go on court at a youth tournament in Eastbourne. Then a formal portrait of Alec in his academic gown at the graduation ceremony at UEA, smiling bravely yet somehow contriving to look as if he'd lost something. Beside this, in a pretty frame of lacquered wood, a softly monochrome photo of the teenage Alice standing in front of a weeping willow with her father, and another man, younger, who has turned away from the camera, frowning at something out of shot that the others have not yet noticed.

He picked up a picture of Ella, nude on a blanket, one year old. Then an enlarged, overcolourful snap of the wedding reception at Lemon Cove, Kirsty with her hair cut page-boy style, laughing at some remark thrown from the group of delighted onlookers, while her father proffers an elaborately wrapped package. The fondue set? The engraved cocktail shaker? The steak knives?

He stood, listening for any sound of movement in the house, then slid open the underwear drawer and disentangled one of Alice's bras, an elaborate and robust garment of elastic and wire and pastel lace with a little silk butterfly bow at the front. He thought of the stuff he used to buy for Kirsty.

Nathan Slater's party girls had taught him about lingerie – the difference between the crass and the sexy, how to match colour to skin tone, what styles enhanced a curve, what cuts most flattered. He tried to remember the last time Kirsty had worn any of it, then realized he could not remember the last time he had *seen* her in her underwear. It had not been recently. It had not been for months. And this, surely, was as good an index as any of how things stood between them. Their steady retreat into strangerhood.

He turned the bra in his hands then pressed one of the cups to his face like a mask. A whiff of washing powder, of dried lavender. Little or nothing of Alice. He tucked it quickly back into the drawer and pushed the drawer shut.

'Fuck it,' he said. 'Fuck it, fuck it, fuck it.'

In the playroom, Ella was letting Alec show her various old toys. Some of them had been laid out on the table like exhibits at a trial – a boxing glove, a spaceship, a little black gun. But the toy that had caught the girl's interest was a glass bulb with a wire spindle at its centre and six small square sails of black-and-white card. Larry remembered it. He was surprised that something so fragile could have survived so long.

'You have to put it in the window, El. The sunshine makes the little sails spin round.'

She wanted to know what it was called. He shrugged. 'Make up a name,' he said. 'I expect you can have it if you want. Ask Uncle Alec.'

'Of course,' said Alec. He was pulling out the old collapsible baize-topped card table from behind a pile of boxes.

'I don't think she knows how to play bridge,' said Larry. 'Shouldn't we be getting ready for Mum?'

'What's there to get ready?' said Alec. 'There's nothing to get ready.' He carried the table out into the passage, Ella, the sun machine held gravely in front of her, walking behind him like an altar girl following the priest with some curious relic of the faith.

At three-thirty, Dennis Osbourne arrived to be part of Alice's welcoming party. He brought a bunch of pink and carmine peonies from his garden. He shook Larry's hand. 'America treating you well?'

'Like royalty,' said Larry.

They were waiting in the living room. It was twenty years since the place had last been decorated. The paint was crazed around the light fitting in the ceiling, and on the walls the turquoise paper curled outwards at the joins.

'I expect you'll be doing a new show soon,' said Osbourne.

Larry nodded, wondering how Osbourne would get along with a man like T. Bone, what, trapped in a lift, they might find to say to each other. 'Only a matter of time,' he said. 'I'm looking for a new agent.'

It started to rain. From the window Larry watched the garden grow lively with countless little movements of water. He had forgotten how much weather the place had, this incessant shifting of the light.

Ella and Alec were sitting either side of the card table. The reverend touched the child's hair. 'Hello, young lady,' he said. Ella smiled up at him with an expression Larry thought she must have learned from one of her doctors. On the table in front of her were three red plastic cups. She was trying to decide which of them was hiding the ball.

'And your good wife?' asked Osbourne.

'She's well,' said Larry.

'When I think of California,' said the reverend, 'I think of long roads lined with palm trees. And a violet sky. And Rex Harrison leaning on a balcony smoking a cigarette with a kind of ebony filter.'

'That's it,' said Larry.

Ella tapped the middle cup but she was wrong. Alec was still a move or two ahead of her. Larry wondered how long his brother had been practising. He had never seen him in the role of magician before.

As each car passed on the road at the top of the drive the adults' attention – Ella's too perhaps – was held there for an instant, so that the atmosphere in the room was constantly tightened and released in a way that was becoming difficult to bear.

Larry said: 'It's eight o'clock in the morning for me. Is there a drink in the house?'

'Maybe some sherry,' said Alec. 'Look in the cupboard under the TV.'

In the cupboard there was a lone bottle of Harvey's Bristol Cream, two-thirds full, a fine patina of dust on the bottle's shoulders. 'What happened to Dad's clocks?' he asked. His watch had just bleeped the hour.

'They need winding,' said Alec. 'I've been busy.'

'I can testify to that,' said Osbourne.

'Well, she'll be here soon,' said Larry. He poured the sherry

198

into a tumbler. Osbourne thought he wouldn't just yet. Larry knew there was no point in asking Alec.

'I used to know a card trick,' said the reverend. 'All the queens came out on top.'

'Hey, we could have a magic show on Granny's birthday,' said Larry. 'What do you think, El?'

'Balloons,' she said, watching Alec's hands like a cat.

'Quite right,' said Osbourne. 'Can't have a party without balloons.'

Alec was shuffling the order of the cups. There was a certain amount of patter involved. Larry stepped up to the table. 'She'll get it this time,' he said.

The cups were lined up in their final positions. Ella immediately tapped the left-hand cup. Alec lifted it.

'Clever girl,' said Osbourne. 'Clever girl.'

Before the trick could begin again, they heard a car on the gravel of the drive. They froze for a moment, then filed from the room and came out of the front door just as Una was switching off the engine. Though the rain was very light, Alec had taken the big golf umbrella from the hall and was holding it over Larry and Ella's heads. The reverend stood at the back, still holding the peonies. Una got out of the car. Larry let go of Ella's hand and went around to the passenger door. He opened it and reached down for Alice, and though the moment before she had seemed almost inert, an elderly lady lost in the midst of some sad reverie, she was suddenly animated, gripping his arms and hauling herself from the seat. 'Oh, Larry,' she moaned, 'oh, my Larry . . .'

She clung to him, the material of his shirt bunched in her fists, and he held her, eyes closed, whispering to her, crooning to her like a sweetheart, while the others, awed by so much undisguised need, looked on, not daring to disturb them. After a minute, Ella edged towards her father and threaded a finger through a belt loop on his trousers. Larry freed one of his hands and pressed the child against his thigh. Osbourne whispered something canonical. Una smiled at Alec, her mouth unsteady. To Alec the scene was the most profoundly embarrassing he thought he had ever witnessed, and he stared fixedly at the gravel, afraid he would make some shocking noise, a bark of grief.

'Can we go in now?' he asked. But nobody moved, and it seemed they would be there for ever, stupefied by emotion.

On the following day, like a failing queen surrounded by her courtiers, Alice Valentine lay in her old bed at Brooklands and explained to them all what she required of them, and how, in these, her last days, they were to conduct themselves. Despite the labour of it, the poverty of air in her lungs, she spoke at length, though among her medicines now there were new drugs that threw longer, deeper shadows, so that she strayed from the light into the dark with a suddenness that meant she could not always be sure she was making any sense. Even so, it was surprising to her that the only one who appeared to understand her was Alec.

She couldn't move her right hand, then saw that Larry, sitting beside her on the edge of the bed, was holding it. And there, between his knees, was her granddaughter, solemn as a little Chinaman. Girl should be out in the garden, not stuck inside seeing things that would give her dreams. She asked who had bought the flowers. Alec nodded to Dennis

Osbourne and she laughed, wheezed, coughed, and told the reverend that he was putting on weight and there was not the least hope of her going with him now, even if he dug up his entire garden. Samuel, she said (*did* she say it?), Samuel knew how to make a woman happy.

Finally, she turned to Brando and instructed him to make sure that everyone did as she asked, though rather rudely he talked across her to Una. She thought she might get very cross if he did that again. He was a foreigner, of course, really. A pastry chef. She said the funniest thing she had ever heard was Kenneth Horne in *Round the Horne*. Am I repeating myself? she asked. No, said Alec. Thank you, dear. She told him she didn't mind him not coming to the hospital. You could die of sheer heartbreak in those places. And when you were too weak to make trouble, people did what they liked with you. She said she loved them all and would they please get out and come back later. Goodnight, she said, though it was still a little before midday, and when the curtains blew the light danced over the walls.

Larry walked Dr Brando to his car, a silver-blue Audi estate parked in the shade of the trees. He thanked him for coming. He asked: 'What do you think?'

'Well,' said Brando, glancing at his watch, 'she's obviously a bit disorientated but that should settle down. I'm sure this business of speaking in French will pass too, though at least you have an expert on hand. How's your French?'

'I don't,' said Larry.

'I'm sure Alec will pass on anything relevant.'

'What comes next?' asked Larry.

Brando had the key in the door of the car. When he turned

it, the locks snapped up in unison. 'It's difficult to make predictions, Larry. Particularly at this stage. The tumours have been more aggressive than I'd hoped. A lot of it's up to the individual, of course, though clearly she's going to need an increasing amount of nursing care. Isn't your wife coming over soon?'

'Next week.'

'So there'll be another woman in the house. That's good. Call me if there's anything at all you want to discuss. And talk to Una. She knows her stuff. She'll be able to give you plenty of good advice.'

'OK,' said Larry. He had other questions. About pain. About what exactly happened at the end. But the doctor was in a hurry and the questions would have to wait. He watched the car move up the drive with that big-car hum and crunch of gravel, then shut his eyes and turned his face to the sun. He was still struggling with the jet-lag. The previous evening, after speaking with Kirsty ('Sure, sure. Everything's just fine'), he had fallen into a profound sleep, only to wake two hours later and spend the remainder of the night listening to the labour of his heart and to his daughter mouth-breathing in the other bed. He knew he would be no use to anyone until he could relax, but he was working in a range of emotions the Xanax was not equipped for. He decided to run a bath. A long soak might unlace him a little, then perhaps he could nap for an hour and get some of this weight of sleep off his shoulders. He went back into the house, fetched his wash bag, and set off for the bathroom at the far end of the first-floor corridor. On the stairs – where he managed to avoid more than a fleeting glimpse of the *PLEASE!* spread – he met Ella and the reverend coming down. Evidently, Osbourne had shaved that morning without the use of a mirror. His throat was nicked and there was a little crust of dried shaving cream by his left ear. When Larry asked Ella what she wanted to do, she bunched her lips and shrugged. The reverend said he'd go into the garden with her and see whether there were any early cherries.

'Got your inhaler, El?' asked Larry.

She showed it to him.

'OK.' He tousled the girl's hair. 'Play nicely.'

On the landing, Alec was coming out of Alice's room, pulling the door shut.

'Una still with her?' whispered Larry.

Alec nodded.

They moved away from the door towards the window that overlooked the garden.

'What was she saying?' asked Larry.

'Una?'

'Mum. All that French.'

'A lot of things.'

'Such as?'

'Such as who brought the flowers. What it was like at the hospital. She said she wanted to go back to the old house. To Granny Wilcox's.'

'Wow. I don't even remember how to get there. Do you?'

'Not exactly.'

'You think she's well enough to go anywhere?'

'I don't know.'

'We practically had to carry her up the stairs.'

'It's what she wants.'

'Does she *know* what she wants?'

'You think you know better?'

'Of course not. Jesus. No need to bite my head off.' He almost said: She's my mother too. Being back at home he suddenly felt about fourteen. 'Maybe we should talk to Una about it. Brando says she knows her stuff.'

'She does.'

Pause.

'I'll be in the summerhouse,' said Alec.

'Fine.'

'She's got a bell.'

'I know.'

'She said she was glad you're back.'

'Yeah. Me too.'

Passing the orchard, Alec heard the reverend counting.

'Sixty-one, sixty-two, sixty-three . . .'

Ever since coming down from London he had longed for others to share the burden with him. Shield him. But now that they were here he found he missed the solitude of the week before when the garden's great resource of quiet had begun to tease out something equivalent in himself, which now all these voices drove away. It made it hard to be civil. It certainly made it harder to think.

The air in the summerhouse was flat with heat and heavily scented with the honeysuckle. He left the door open and set the manuscript on the table by the window. On the shelf, where clay flowerpots had once been stored, he had put his dictionaries and other useful books, including copies of *Sisyphus Rex* and *Flicker* in the Eliard translations. His own effort had ground to a halt a third of the way through the second act. After Alice's fit, which had taken on in his mind the dimensions of mythology, he had found it almost physically impossible to concentrate. It was like lying with his head below a finely suspended anvil, trying not to think of what would happen when it fell. He couldn't do it. Not even a letter from Marcie Stoltz, forwarded by Mr Bequa, in which she confessed herself 'intrigued' to know how the work was progressing, had made any difference. Anything beyond the white front gate of Brooklands had a remoteness that beggared the imagination, though he thought Stoltz might start to phone (she had his number at the house), and he would have to start lying to her, saying how well it was going and how excited he was.

He polished his glasses with the tuck of his shirt, then took a pencil, sharpened it, and opened the manuscript:

Mineur un: J'ai revé de ce moment cent fois. Même quand j'étais éveillé.

Mineur deux: Et comment termine le rêve?

He didn't think Larry understood a thing. Larry was thinking about Larry. Or about Kirsty or America or something. But not about Alice. Of course he cared, they all *cared*, but the others were just looking on, and that wasn't enough. He didn't believe any of them could see what he saw: the complete impossibility of letting it go on and on for weeks and months. But what could he do? Did he still believe in fairytales? In stumbling across a magic cure? He thought perhaps he did, and this seemed funny in an utterly bleak sort of way, and he was laughing to himself when Una tapped on the timber by the open door.

'I didn't know it was a comedy,' she said.

'Only in parts,' said Alec.

She stepped into the shed. 'Is that him?' She pointed to the portrait of Lázár in the Luxembourg which Alec had pinned to the edge of the shelf. 'What's that he's carrying?'

'A cake perhaps. Or a bomb.'

'I'd say he's got a kind face, so it's probably a cake.'

'Probably.'

He studied her while she studied Lázár. A slight pout to her lower lip. Pale lashes. Grey eyes touched with violet. A little round scar on the side of her nose as if once she wore a stud there. She had on a blue cotton dress, sleeveless, and her shoulders were tanned, honey-brown against the just visible plain white strap of her bra. She must have been lying in the sun at the weekends, and he imagined her with a boyfriend, a doctor perhaps, who had a boat or a convertible. Someone like a young Brando.

'What was your mother saying?' she asked.

He told her about the house.

She nodded. 'Let's see how we get on. You're going to need to keep a closer eye on her now.'

'I know.'

'I've put the Dexamethasone on top of the chest with a note explaining the routine. Will you make sure she takes it? We don't want her back in the hospital if we can help it.'

'I'll put it on the list,' he said.

'I like your brother,' she said.

'We're very different.'

'Oh, I'm not so sure of that,' she said. 'Are you nearly finished with the play?'

'It's coming on.'

'That's grand.'

Dennis Osbourne, red-faced from his exertions, was trying to conceal himself behind a slender tree in the orchard. Una waited, smiling at him, until Ella came through the long grass and captured him.

'Your daddy wants you,' she said, holding out her hand to the girl. 'Sorry to spoil your game, Reverend.'

'I need a sit-down,' he said. 'How's Alice?'

'Back on the English now. She's getting quite mischievous, isn't she?'

'Poor woman,' said the reverend, squatting awkwardly on the grass. 'Is there anything I can do?'

'She's sleeping. Best let her get on with it.'

'Yes,' said Osbourne. 'Sleep's the great healer, I suppose. I shall see you later, Ella.'

'Thank you for playing with me,' said Ella, who had been carefully drilled in the importance of such remarks. She took Una's hand and together they went into the cool of the house. Una said goodbye to her in the living room. She was running late for an appointment in Nailsea. A young haemophiliac with Kaposi's sarcoma. Mother going out of her mind. Afraid to sleep. Asking why all the time. Why him, why us. Why why why.

'Be a good girl now,' she said. 'Keep an eye on them all till I come back.'

Ella waited. When she heard the front door shut she switched on the television and started flicking through the channels, though without a remote control she wasn't sure at first how to do it, and even when she had worked out how to use the buttons she couldn't find MTV. She settled for a cartoon, and had curled herself on to the sofa to watch it – the manic pursuits, the crash-bangs – when her father appeared, wrapped in a white towelling bathrobe, the wash bag in his hand. He switched off the television and knelt on the floor in front of her.

'We have some talking to do,' he said. 'Some very serious talking.'

6

The evening that followed his meeting with Emil Bexheti, László dined with Kurt at Marco Polo's on the rue de Condé. *Asparagi di campo, risotto alla sbirraglia, tortellini bolognese* – all the good things. Then they walked home together, hand in hand, past the church of St Sulpice and along by the side of the Luxembourg. It was a little after twelve. A scattering of stars showed faintly above the lamplight, and the air was redolent with that mix of gutters and public gardens, tobacco smoke, restaurant steam, and the sour but somehow likable breath of the Métro exhaled through broad grills in the pavement, which give to Paris nights their inimitable savour.

Kurt squeezed László's hand; László squeezed back. He was never entirely comfortable with this way of walking, and he reserved it for those moments of especial tenderness when something more than mere proximity was required. It was not that he was ashamed of Kurt. On the contrary, he was often joyfully incredulous that such a sweet-tempered young man should agree to stay with him. But László was a homosexual who retained a certain abstract disapproval of his tribe. In San Francisco, during his tenure at the Théâtre Artaud, he had been appalled at some of the things he had seen, men using each other much as dogs use table legs, a corrupt and worthless version of the Dionysian. In truth he had never really thought of himself as queer or Gay. A mariposa. A fruit. His case, he believed, was much simpler. There had in his life been certain people, beginning with Péter, whom he had needed, and who happened to be men. He did not want to make a vocation of it, to go on marches, wear badges. And anyway, he was from a time and a place where the notion of 'coming out' had been utterly unimaginable. Homosexuality was illegal in Hungary until years after he had left. His parents might have stood it – they were doctors, liberals, readers – but the Party would have destroyed him. Two men in a bed in the act of adoring each other was as subversive as a secret printing press, and it had not been much easier when he came to France – except in the theatre, of course, where nobody cared what you got up to, or who.

But tonight he wanted to think of the past he shared with Kurt Engelbrecht, rather than the one he possessed alone, and where, increasingly, he felt himself a ghost among ghosts, a wanderer in the Fields of Asphodel. At the apartment on rue Delambre he threw open the windows, lit the candles and fetched a bottle of Sambuca from the drinks cabinet beside the bookshelf in the dining room. He filled two small glasses, added a coffee bean to each, and with his lighter heated the surface of the liquor until it ignited with ghostly blue flames. He passed one of these entertaining glasses to Kurt. 'Venice,' he said.

'Venice,' replied Kurt, grinning.

'La Fenice e des Artistes.'

'Murano.'

'San Michele.'

'The Cittadi Vittorio . . .'

'Ah!'

They had not done this for a while, this resuming of those ten or dozen stories that constituted the official history of their intimacy. As always, it began with Venice, and the morning they woke in their hotel to find the city furled in freakish snow, and had sat, wrapped in blankets, watching it for hours, wonder-struck as ten-year-olds.

Then Seville – the Triana district at 4 a.m. Footsore, irritable, hopelessly lost, wandering into a riverside bar to hear *cante hondo*, the crowd smoking as though in a trance, the singer, a middle-aged man in a dark suit at the far end of the bar, delivering his song in spasms of grief, ecstasies.

'Next?'

Vienna. A melancholy hour at the grave of László's mother, followed by a difficult, somewhat comical weekend with Kurt's parents, kindly people only a few years older than László, who had addressed him during his entire stay as 'Herr Professor', preferring to think – could they really have believed it? – that his interest in their son was exclusively pedagogical.

And the holiday in New York with László's brother, János, a divorced optometrist with an apartment full of prize-winning schnauzers. It had been Kurt's first visit to America and they had driven from the airport in a yellow cab at dusk, rocking on bad roads through canyons of electrified tower blocks, Kurt almost in tears at the romance of so much light . . .

Evenings at the theatre. Nights on the town. Weekends in the country. Do you remember? A history with very few of the pages glued together, though each time they played the game, each occasion inspired by some unvoiced disquiet, the recollections were reworked a little as the line between memory and imagination became subtler, or just unimportant. It nearly always worked, and if not, well, there was the sambuca to make up the difference. This, thought László, was entirely the point of such drinks.

It was ten-thirty by the time he let his eyes open to the daylight. Kurt was long since up, the duvet on his side thrown back as if he had *leaped* from the bed. László slouched to the bathroom. He felt excited and slightly ill, his cock half erect, a persistent buzzing in his left ear, a taste of alcohol and fire on his tongue. He stood under the shower and coughed for a while, trying to clear his lungs, then shaved, catching the scrawn of his throat and emerging into the kitchen thirty minutes later with three scraps of toilet paper stuck to his skin by the adhesion of his own blood.

Leaning by the stove he ate a *croissant beurre*, a painkiller, a vitamin pill, then dressed himself in grey slacks and a linen shirt and went down into the street feeling like a Hemingway character, some old boxer ennobled by weakness, hauling himself into the ring for a last big fight. The day was for settling things, and it was in this spirit he intended to have his talk with Franklin Wylie, though quite what he could say to him that would be of any use he was not at all sure. Something to shame, something to encourage. It was impossible, or at least unacceptable, that all their years of friendship should end in silence, a dull glare of mutual incomprehension.

He caught the Métro from Montparnasse Bienvenue, changed at Sebastapol and arrived at Parmentier shortly before noon. At the greengrocer's on the corner of Rue Jacquard he bought a large bag of cherries, then walked to the rue du Deguerry and tapped in the code to the outer door, but as he crossed the vestibule to the stairs, Madame Barbossa spied him from her office and flagged him down. She had met him on many occasions, knew he was 'like family' with the Wylies, and revered him as a man of culture whose name might be found in the newspapers from time to time, though she had no practical idea of what he did. She told him that Monsieur Wylie had gone out early, eight o'clock, just as she herself was coming in. Madame Wylie had left two hours later to have lunch with her mother at the old folks' place in Epinay.

'I should have called,' said László, though he was surprised; it was almost always safe to assume Franklin would be at home at this time of the day, working or mooching, sleeping even. He offered the gardienne a cherry. She was looking at him as if he might, handled in the right way, reveal some item of scandal, something she could add to her collection of Wylie stories. Something to amaze a neighbour.

'The spare key?' asked László. He was not averse to a little gossip, but this was not the occasion for it. 'I'll put the cherries in the fridge so they can be enjoyed cold.'

'As you like, monsieur.'

She fetched the key from her office. László wheezed his way to the fourth floor and let himself in. It was an old apartment, and little had been altered since the Wylies had bought it in '78 or '79, choosing it for its high ceilings, the pretty church across the street, the flood of the evening sun. The walls in the hallway formed a little gallery, densely hung. There were things by Franklin there, but most of the pictures were the work of dead friends, including a Phillip Guston, and even a Beuys sketch of what looked like a severed head, Orpheus perhaps, 'his gory visage' floating down the Hebrus.

He moved into the kitchen, where pans and skillets hung in rows from butcher's hooks. It was the scene of many fine suppers together in the past. Laurence was a first-class cook; she was also a tidy woman, even a meticulous one, for whom the kitchen was a serious space, a place to be respected, so it was surprising and unnerving to see in the middle of the room a bottle of red wine left where it had fallen or been dropped or, God knows, thrown. A starburst of glass, the wine pooled in the hollows of the tiles and spattered on to skirting boards and cupboards. The record of an impact, very exact.

He tiptoed around the debris and placed the cherries on a shelf in the fridge, then looked beneath the sink for some newspapers to clean up with, and was crouched there reading the front page of an April edition of *Libération* when he heard what sounded like the soft opening or shutting of a door somewhere in the body of the apartment. He stepped into the passage.

'Franklin?'

Not even Madame Barbossa's vigilance was perfect. Franklin might have returned long ago, slipping past her while she admired someone's dog or baby. When he wished to he could move very quietly, a tall ghost, padding up behind people, startling them with a sudden tap on the shoulder.

László moved along the corridor to the studio, the largest room in the apartment, with big windows overlooking the church, and a door at the far end leading into a small washroom.

'Franklin?'

Along the length of the wall opposite the windows was a

long table – an old dining table – its surface covered with a guano of slopped and dried paint. Brushes and palette knives stood to attention in a score of tins. Above the table, the shelves were loaded with coiled aluminium paint tubes, aerosol cans and plastic bottles of pigment, fabulous colours that would have exhausted László's vocabulary had he attempted to name them all. And there were tools for gouging and scraping, boxes of charcoal, print rollers, a staple gun, all the paraphernalia of the artist, which writers, condemned to pen, keyboard and ashtray, feel such envy of. But there was nothing on the easels or pinned to the walls, not even a sketch, though on the floor there were half a dozen large canvases stood up with their backs to the room, as though in disgrace. No scattering of rags, no endearing mess, nothing to suggest the sanity of work. The place looked to have been finished with, abandoned. László could remember a time when there had always been flowers there – fistfuls of them in jars of discoloured water.

He lifted the outermost canvas on to the pegs of an easel, and stepped back. Though the greater part of Franklin's output had always been abstract, large-scale, incensed with colour, the painting on the easel was figurative in the style of the German expressionists – Kokoschka, perhaps, or Barlach – and depicted a newly married couple on the steps of the *mairie*. The bride, in her costume of rose blooms, was immediately recognizable as Laurence Wylie. Not the young Laurence (a woman centred in her smile, in the warmth of her regard), but Laurence as she was now, Laurence the martyr, the victim, the dupe. It was grievous to see, but such was the quality of Franklin's attention to her, the scrupulous depiction of an unhappiness he himself had authored, that László felt his throat constrict and his eyes become moist. Confronted with such a face, with the perverse love that had laboured over its depiction, blame or anger was beside the point. Useless.

He turned from the woman to the figure at her side. A man in a black suit, his head tightly wrapped in what appeared to be cellophane, or that plastic film used to preserve food, so that his features were flattened and distorted like a bank robber's in a stocking mask. His back was arched in the agony of a suffocation, his fists bunched in rage, but his bride, oblivious to his torment, or just helpless to relieve it, ignored him, and looks directly forward, engaging the gaze of the viewer as if searching for some deliverance beyond the frame, though there was something else in her expression, some mute communication painted into the eyes like a code, that László could not immediately make sense of. He had to stand farther back – two, three steps – before he saw that it was a look of warning.

In the telephone box on the corner of the road by the church, an Arab girl was hunched down on the steel floor, smoking and talking intensely. László checked his watch, then leaned against the railings to contemplate the sparrows bathing in the gutter, scrupulous little birds, shivering the water from their feathers and hopping about in the sunshine. Ten minutes later the girl came out and László went in. The receiver was warm from her hand still, faintly scented. He dialled very carefully. After three rings he was answered.

'Is Françoise there?' he asked.

7

It was twilight at Brooklands. Larry came out on to the terrace and sat in the canvas chair opposite his brother.

'Ella in bed?' asked Alec.

'Yeah. Mum?'

'Asleep. I think.'

Larry had a bottle of Teacher's from the off-licence in Coverton. He had driven out in Alec's car before lunch and since then had worked his way through half the bottle. He poured himself another two fingers, drank one of them, then leaned forward and said, 'Ella's taken something.'

'Hardly the first time,' said Alec. He was drinking tea.

'No. This is different. This isn't a bracelet or a ring.'

'Money?'

'She's taken a pill,' said Larry. 'I don't know how but we've got to get it back.'

'One of Mum's?'

'One of mine. From my wash bag.'

'What kind of pill?'

Larry shook his head.

'A painkiller? Sleeping tablet?'

'I wish.' He took a deep breath and started to explain, though he knew the story required more context than he could ever hope to provide. He said he had gone to LA to discuss a film deal. He omitted to mention the nature of the film, though he gave Alec something of the characters of T. Bone and Ranch, despite the fact that talking of them in the calm of an English garden made them seem like figures in some outlandish cabaret. He mentioned the hotel, the lunch party, the bathroom, the box. The pills. He'd hoped to make it sound casual and mostly normal, but actually it didn't sound normal at all.

'*Suicide* pills?'

Both of them – a reflex with its roots in the hinterlands of childhood – glanced up at the window above as though the light might suddenly flick on, and Alice lean out, wise to their secrets and demanding explanations.

'Fucksake . . .' said Larry, wincing. He had not introduced the 'sex' pills. Nor did he know which of the two Ella had taken because he could no longer remember Ranch's explanation of the difference. Either way, it didn't bear thinking about.

Alec blinked behind his glasses for a while. 'You're sure it was Ella?'

'Of course it was Ella.'

'You talked to her?'

'For an hour, yesterday, as soon as I found the thing was gone. Again today. She blanked me completely, both times. When I told her how dangerous it was she seemed to understand, but with Ella you never know. I even phoned Hoffmann . . .'

'Hoffmann?'

'Her shrink in Frisco. He's away at some child homicide convention in Detroit, so I left a message on his machine, then had a panic attack thinking what if he tells Kirsty? Can you imagine? So I called back and left another message saying he was only to talk to me about it. Not that I trust him much.'

'Did you tell him what she took?'

'I said she was having a regressive episode. After a while you start to speak like them.'

Alec sipped from his mug. Larry the athlete, Larry the party king, Larry the handsome, Larry the successful, Larry the happy husband. And now Larry the man who kept suicide pills in his wash bag. He hardly knew who he was sitting next to.

'What on earth were you going to *do* with it?' he asked.

Larry shrugged. 'I meant to chuck them away in the plane.'

'Why didn't you?'

'That's not the point any more. The point is getting it back. I'm pretty certain it's not in the bedroom. I stripped the mattresses. Emptied out the drawers. But she's good at this now. It could even be in the garden. Can you talk to her? She likes you.'

'What am I supposed to say? Give Daddy back his pill?'

'Just try and get it into her head how serious this is.'

'I'll try.'

'Thanks.'

'I can't believe you had it.'

Larry rubbed at his eyes with the heel of his palm. 'I feel like I haven't slept in a year.'

'What did you do with the others?'

'Others? Flushed them away. A little late, I know.' He shook a cigarette from the pack and lit it.

'I didn't know things had been so difficult,' said Alec.

'Since *Sun Valley*. Before then, I guess.'

'You didn't say anything.'

'You've had troubles of your own.'

'I'm all right.'

'Yeah?'

'Yeah.'

Larry laughed – sheer fatigue as much as the whisky. He put a hand on his brother's knee. 'You're a complete fucking mess,' he said.

'I manage,' said Alec.

'Sure. Do you remember when I went to America for the first time and you were about to spend your year in Paris? You remember that?'

'Yes,' said Alec.

'It feels like the last time I spoke to you.'

'That was ten years ago.'

'I know. I'm sorry.'

Alec shrugged.

'Did you like it?'

'What?'

'Paris.'

'Yes.'

Larry nodded. 'That's good.' He was looking over the potato field to where night was finally tidying away the tower of the church. It was a view so long etched on to the retina of memory it made him soulful. He saw himself as a boy, and Alec too. He saw Alice as a vigorous woman, and even his father as a man not yet on the edge, his shadow striding across the garden. All of them, their lives flitting like the little bats that dived and swooped around the eaves of the house.

'I suppose we should have a plan,' he said. He was starting to drawl. 'What do you think? Should we have a plan?'

8

On Thursday evening Kurt Engelbrecht returned to rue Delambre with two plastic bags of groceries in either hand. He carried them into the kitchen, put them on the table and called for László. He had bought more cassis, and there was still half a bottle of white wine in the fridge from the previous evening. At eight o'clock it was early and late enough for an aperitif.

At the bottom of the sink he saw László's plate, knife and coffee cup from lunch, the plate still with its debris of apple skin and olive stones and cheese rind. It was one of László's habits – if something so casual, so unconsidered, could be called a habit – together with getting flecks of toothpaste on the bathroom mirror, and now and then forgetting to flush the toilet, that Kurt found mildly provoking, but which he never mentioned in the belief that László was operating a similar restraint in regard to the little blindnesses of his own.

He began to unpack the first bag, putting the vegetables on the wooden rack and arranging the fruit in the big glass bowl. Then he went into the passage and called a second and a third time. There were several reasons for László not to be there: he had stepped out with the mail, or had gone to the *tabac* for more cigarillos (though with his chest troubling him he had promised to leave them alone for a while); or he had simply gone down on to the boulevard to enjoy the warmth of the evening, buy a paper, chat to Madame Favier at the patisserie. He might even be taking the rubbish out, all credible explanations for his absence, so it seemed strange to Kurt, looking back on it later, strange and significant, that he should immediately have gone to the study with his heart thudding, and opened the door there with such a feeling of dread.

What had he expected to find? A smashed glass? An overturned chair? A body? But the room, quarter lit by the setting sun, was quite innocent. No sign of any haste or trouble. No air of menace. Yet far from reassuring him, this calmness, the sheer order of the place, convinced him that something had indeed occurred, and that his unease of the last week, the fear of some unspecified event, some violent alteration to the steady progress of their days together, had at last been realized. On László's desk the papers of his manuscript were gathered into a neat pile, the pens lined up at the side, the little ashtray emptied and wiped. Even the chair had been slid under the desk, as though no one would ever need to sit there again, as though it were all done with and finished.

Propped against the bottom edge of the computer monitor on his own desk was a blue oblong envelope with his name on it. He stood a moment, looking at it, then went back into the kitchen and touched the china of László's cup as if he hoped to feel some trace of warmth in it still. Then he washed it, washed the plate and the knife, and put them away in their proper places. There were spits of grease around the gas rings on the cooker. He cleaned the cooker. There were crumbs on the floor beneath the breadboard. He swept the floor, then vacuumed it, and was on the point of filling a bucket with hot water to scrub it when he recognized the folly of such tactics. He left the half-filled bucket in the sink, rolled down the sleeves of his shirt, and went back into the study. It was darker now. He turned on the green-shaded lamp and slit open the envelope with the little Opinel penknife he kept in his desk drawer. Inside the envelope were two sheets of paper written over on both sides in black ink. He could tell from the handwriting that they had been written slowly and were probably not a first draft. He carried them to the window and read them standing up, one hand, the tips of his fingers, pressing on the surface of László's desk.

My dearest Kurt,

I am writing to you in some confusion, though also with a clear sense that what I am doing now is necessary, and that could I possibly lay it all before you in the right way you would approve. You will be angry that I have not shared my plans with you, but there were reasons for this that have nothing to do with you. It has no significance. I would trust you with my life and without a moment's hesitation. There is no one in the world I can be surer of.

I will be away for some days – I do not know precisely how long – performing a small task that is, I hope, a valuable one. The task is political and covert, though not dangerous, and will require from me no very particular talents. Of course, in an affair like this there is always the old problem of intentions and consequences – meaning to do good we do harm and must take responsibility for that harm – but the group in whose interests I am undertaking this journey (into the labyrinth?) have a just and urgent cause, and for far too long I have left it to others to act

*in the world. I have made futility into a fetish, as though
nothing effective could ever be done, all endeavour doomed
to end in confusion, treachery or failure, an evasion with its
origin in that episode from my past of which you already
know something, the broad strokes if not the detail. That
day long ago when, as a result of my weakness, a young
man lost his life. Since then I have never been entirely free
of the guilt and sorrow that hour brought to me, and while
it may be precisely such difficulties that made a writer of
me (the most confessional of the arts) as a man I have
been weakened in ways I can no longer accept. I cannot
– to borrow an image from Jules Supervielle – go into the
garden and just see the garden. There is always an extra
shadow. Always, in any silence, the shout that I did not
answer.*

*Do you think, my friend, that it is possible to put things
right? To make amends? To atone? The Ancients believed
in it. Not just the possibility but the necessity. Or is this
some dementia I am suffering from? After all, I cannot run
the film backwards. I cannot be eighteen again. So who can
be saved? What can be rescued?*

*No doubt there is something grossly selfish in all of this,
but will you believe me if I say it is also us I want to save?*

*You and I were never the people to spend hours gazing
moodily into each other's eyes. We are sparing with our
endearments – it is how we manage our lives together. But
let me say this, so that whatever happens, whatever our
futures might be, you will have at least some poor idea
of how I value you. You have given me ten or fifteen of
the happiest moments of my existence. Knowing you, I
can never lose faith in life, nor in the sheer generosity*

of another's heart. I carry the memory of your face with
me now like an icon to be adored secretly among strangers.
Trust in this. Destroy this letter. Forgive me.

L.

When he got to the end he read it through again, then
tore it methodically into small pieces, placed the pieces in the
ashtray, and using the same lighter László had used a week
earlier to ignite the sambuca, he burned them and crushed
the embers into a black dust. Then he moved the lamp closer
to the window and leaned towards the glass, looking south
to the boulevard Edgar Quinet, and the walls of the cemetery
where Sartre and de Beauvoir and the glorious Beckett lay.

9

At six o'clock, Larry stood at the kitchen stove, labouring over the evening meal. A pillar of steam broke across the red of his face as he prodded the rice with a wooden fork, frowning at it like a soothsayer investigating the liver of a slaughtered ram for those striations and whorls that would betray the future to him. Beside the hob, propped against a mostly empty bottle of white wine, was one of Alice's cookbooks, an Elizabeth David, open at a recipe for risotto, though it had, of course, been necessary for him to find alternatives to the chicken stock and the beef marrow and the diced ham, and everything that would, in his opinion, have given the meal flavour and nutritional profit, but which his wife – 'I don't eat dead animals, Larry' – would have refused to eat, to touch even.

He had collected her the previous morning – Alec's old car again – from Terminal 4 at Heathrow, where she had come out a little dazed and fragile in the wake of a sports team of blazered young men with crew cuts, who were joshing each other loudly despite the early hour. When he had called her name it had taken her a moment to locate him, and as she searched the faces at the barrier her expression was unmistakably a look of distress, as though this were not an orderly airport in an orderly country, but somewhere more fluid and dangerous, and still half asleep, time in a tangle in her head, a voice from the crowd had marked her out. But then she had seen Ella and let out a joyful 'Hi!', and for a while they had been like any other family there, grinning hard and trading hugs. Only a very practised eye could have seen it for what it was: a tenderness shot through with shared and private fears. She was upstairs now, in the room above his head, tending to his mother.

He checked the recipe and ladled more stock on to the rice. He was wearing one of Alice's blue canvas aprons and handling the food with a certain alcoholic swagger that made him wonder whether he might not be very suitable for some kind of low-budget cookery programme. Catchpole in the kitchen: classic English cuisine from steak and kidney to spotted dick with television's best-loved medic. There appeared to be an inexhaustible demand for colourful types who could chatter to camera while dicing peppers or flipping Thai prawns in a wok. Set against his present difficulties, this didn't seem such an outlandish idea, and while being a TV chef was not, he thought, a wholly proper way to earn a living, it was preferable to what awaited him in the chill of the garage at San Fernando. It would certainly be the better option when KDBS organized the next Take Your Daughter to Work Day.

Ella was on the terrace; he could hear her through the open glass doors chatting in her considered way with Alec. Her stubbornness in the matter of the capsule had, in the last week, provoked Larry to extreme tactics. He had offered her money (twenty dollars). He had threatened to spank her (though they both knew he wouldn't). He had spied on her through the keyhole of the bathroom, and even followed her into the garden, trailing her from tree to tree, stalking her as she gathered daisies and buttercups, crouched to turn a beetle with a twig, sang to herself. Did she know he was there? Or was this conspicuous innocence unfeigned, so that he was persecuting an entirely blameless child? What if one of the capsules had rolled off the shelf while he was in the toilet on the plane? Would he have noticed? Could he trust himself any more not to make such a mistake? What confidence could he have in his own judgment?

Alec had had his little chat with her. Apparently she had heard him out without giving the least hint she knew what he was talking about. And then Hoffmann had phoned, back from Detroit, telling Larry he would have to bill him for the call, and speaking to Ella while she stood in the kitchen holding the receiver with both hands, wide-eyed, nodding, saying yes, no, yes, I will, OK, uh-huh, OK. It had done no good. She was like a child in an Edward Gorey cartoon, a little thing in a taffeta party dress wandering about the house with a pistol in her hand.

'Alec!'

Alec leaned into the kitchen.

'This'll be ready in twenty minutes, max. We should start getting Mum down.'

'Right.' He didn't move.

'You want to do it? Or you want to stir this and I'll go up?'

'I don't mind,' said Alec. But he came over to the stove and took the wooden fork from Larry's hand.

'Don't let it dry up,' said Larry. 'And lets put some candles out. Make an evening of it.'

'Good idea,' said Alec, without the least enthusiasm.

'And as for you,' said Larry, as Ella appeared in the

doorway, regarding him shrewdly with her head cocked to one side, 'as for you . . .' But he had no idea what to say next.

In Alice's room, Kirsty Valentine, only daughter, only child of Errol and Nancy Freeman (formerly 'Friebergs') of La Finca, Lemon Cove, California, sat on a stool at the end of the bed holding her mother-in-law's feet in her hands, palping the soles with her thumbs in the way she had been shown in a class on reflexology at the day centre in San Francisco. Alice leaned against a bank of pillows, already dressed for her evening downstairs. Earlier in the afternoon, Toni Cuskic had come by with her wallet of scissors, her clips and dryer, her poodle, and had brushed out the snags from Alice's hair, plaiting it, at Alice's request, into a neat silver rope.

Her hair, and the blusher she had rubbed into the absolute white of her cheeks, put Kirsty in mind of a Bette Davis film she had watched recently, part of a gay icon series on AMC. Yet somehow the fashion suited Alice, suited the newly blatant nature of her stare, the startling bluntness of her questions – 'Why don't you have another child?' 'Do you still love him?' 'Are you faithful to each other?'

This, perhaps, was 'disinhibition', a term Kirsty had picked up scanning the cancer literature in Barnes and Noble: the tumours, weevil-like, eating away at the furniture of adult judgment; an irresistible, irreversible decline that ended in full-blown dementia, when the mind was of no more use than a fancy mirror in an unlit room. Nicer then, infinitely more consoling, to imagine there was something rather Zenlike in

Alice's new directness, that her manner derived not from the perishing of the intellect, but from her impatience with the conventional. If people had to die – and Kirsty was enough of an American not to accept the absolute inevitability of it – she wanted them to go full of a profound and liberating knowledge of things. When else should you be wise, if not at the end? But several times in the last twenty-four hours she had witnessed the shadow of vacancy or panic fall over the blue of Alice's eyes, and in her heart she knew that here was a woman being shut up inside herself. That she bore it at all seemed nothing less than heroic.

But how should her questions be answered? It wasn't just the problem of balancing tact with honesty, the etiquette of talking with someone so terribly sick, it was her own painful uncertainty as to what the answers really were. *Did* she still love Larry? She supposed that she did, but her 'Yes, of course' had about it the ghost of a qualification, as though she had said 'probably', or 'most of the time', or 'not like I used to'. The difficulty was being able to see him clearly, to have, as she had had in the past, a single clear idea of him. These days he seemed to shimmer, being at the same time the man she had strolled with on Muir beach in the weeks before the wedding, the pair of them lit up, laughing because they were getting away with it, this remarkable trick of happiness, and some stranger who shambled in and out of the rooms of the house in shorts and sweatshirt (his favourite had 'Barney's Beanery' printed over the heart), tumbler in one fist, cigarette in the other. He reminded her sometimes – still a big man, still solidly built – of a boxer who, the night before the fight, has unaccountably lost his nerve and begun to unravel. What *was* his problem? What had so bent him out of shape?

His father? The drink? Losing his job? Was it something organic? Something in the air? Lead insult? How was she supposed to tell?

As for having another child, to Alice she said, 'I'm not sure this is really a great time.' But the reality was simpler and sadder: how could they have a child when for months they had slept with a wall between them? (Two walls: the bedrooms were separated by the passageway.) And what of the child they already had? Hoffmann had rung the evening before she was due to fly with some talk of another episode, though, oddly, he had seemed more concerned about Larry, who, according to the professor, was 'struggling to articulate the appropriate responses'. What exactly he had meant by this she was unsure, she preferred not to ask, but the phrase looped through her head during the flight over until it acquired some ominous quasi-mystical significance that had threatened to bring on a migraine. Worst of all, it seemed to support her own most private misgivings, the unpalatable fact that she was less and less comfortable leaving Ella alone with Larry. She had seen the way he crossed roads, jaywalking through the traffic, not yet trying to stare it down, not raging at it, but playing with the danger. And he laughed at the television – news items, sad movies – in a way that spooked her. When Natasha Khan, her friend over in Sunset, asked if Larry had a gun in the house (Natasha's ex kept an assault rifle in the games room) she had immediately gone home and turned out all the drawers in the guest bedroom, uncovering a small stash of pornography and sports magazines, a quart of bourbon, a flight schedule (SF to Vancouver) and, most miserably, a pair of her own panties, not even clean, which he must have fished out of the laundry basket in the shower room. But no gun. And then at Heathrow, Ella on Larry's shoulders holding up a sheet of paper saying 'HELLO MOMMY', they had looked fine together, just fine, and she had felt ashamed of herself. Whatever Larry was, whatever he was *becoming*, there was a reserve of sweet water in him it was mean of her to doubt. It was Hoffmann perhaps, Hoffmann she should give up trusting.

From the landing Larry called: 'Decent in there?'

'We're decent!' sang Kirsty.

He came in, flushed in a way she immediately and wearily recognized.

'What are you doing?' he asked.

'It's nice for her feet,' she said.

He nodded. 'Supper in fifteen minutes. Let's get your shoes on, Mum.'

She had a pair of trainers, large white cushioned shoes with Velcro straps in place of laces. These had been Una's suggestion, and though they looked cartoonish on the end of Alice's skinny legs, they were gentle to her skin, and after the first time she wore them she no longer complained of their ugliness. The thought that they were in some way fashionable had even made her smile.

'You want some gas?' asked Kirsty. The bottle, industrial black, was at hand's reach on the covers.

'Just the inhaler, dear.' Larry passed it to her, watched her spray it twice into her mouth; the inadequate in-breath followed by the inevitable, miserable coughing. He slid his arms beneath her shoulders and righted her. She stood, leaning her head against his chest, then they shuffled on to the landing.

'I'll go get Ella to wash her hands,' said Kirsty.

Larry asked: 'How do you want to do this?'

'Slowly,' said Alice. 'Very slowly.'

The stairs were too narrow for them to descend side by side, so Larry went in front of her, and by keeping two steps below her she could hold on to his shoulders. Her arms were trembling, a feeble electricity that Larry felt through the whole length of his body. When they reached the dining room the others were standing by their chairs, waiting.

'Here I am,' she whispered.

Larry guided her to her chair at the head of the table. Alec had found the candles and set them in their silver stems, but the flames, paler than the light that came through the windows, barely showed.

It took another five minutes to get her settled, a cushion wedged behind her back, a linen napkin tucked into the collar of her dress. Sometimes, as she moved, she let out a low, involuntary moan.

'Hey,' said Kirsty, 'don't you think Alice's hair looks great? I wish I had someone like Toni at home. Doesn't her hair look great, Alec?'

'Yes,' said Alec. 'Toni's very good.'

'Oh, he doesn't know,' said Alice. 'Everything's a mystery to him, poor soul . . .'

She looked at Alec, who had the place on her left. Larry, serving out the risotto, noted it: another of those exchanges he had seen three or four times during the last week, part of some on-going wordless discussion between them. Something he was outside of. He didn't like it.

'I hope you're going to eat this, El.' He put a spoonful of the sticky rice on to her plate, passed it to her and sat opposite.

'*Bon appétit*, everyone! You see, Mum, I learned that much.'

'Ella's been learning some cute French songs at school,' said Kirsty. 'What's the name of your teacher, honey? They start the kids real early.'

'Is this a mushroom?' asked Ella, holding up a grey comma on the tines of her fork.

'Yes,' said Larry. 'A special kind of delicious mushroom. Try it.'

Ella scraped the mushroom on to the rim of her plate and started picking out the others.

'Ella!' He turned to Kirsty. 'Make her eat something, will you.'

'You mean force her?'

'I mean she's old enough not to play with her food like that.'

'So she doesn't like mushrooms. It's not a major failure, Larry.'

'Look at him,' said Alice. She nodded to the photograph on the sideboard of Grandpa Wilcox in uniform. 'Look at him watching us all.'

'We're going to the house, right?' asked Kirsty.

The visit had been arranged the previous week. Larry had managed to contact the couple who lived there now, Rupert and Stephanie Gadd. When Larry had explained things they were understanding, Rupert Gadd promising to be 'on stand-by' the following Sunday. Apparently they were just back from Italy.

'I remember Granny Wilcox showing me Grandpa's medal,' said Larry. 'You remember it, Alec?'

'The DSO.'

'Is that like a Purple Heart or something?'

'The Distinguished Service Order,' said Alec.

'Wow.'

'Where is it now?' asked Larry.

'Arnhem,' said Alice. She had put some rice on to her fork but hadn't actually eaten anything. 'Saved his sergeant. Saved him completely.'

'I guess he was the real thing,' said Kirsty.

Larry drew the cork on a bottle of Montepulciano. He was the only one drinking.

'Go easy today,' said Kirsty in a low voice.

Larry smiled at her. 'Do you know what side your Grand-father was on? Old man Friebergs?'

'Je-sus,' said Kirsty, rolling her eyes.

'Latvians fought with the Nazis,' explained Larry.

'They had more reason to hate Russians than Germans,' said Alec.

'How's your guy?' asked Kirsty.

'Lázár? He might have shot a few Russians, I suppose.'

'I think it was called the Condor legion,' said Larry. 'Is that right? Or the White Eagles. A kind of Latvian SS.'

Kirsty glared across the table. 'You don't know what you're talking about. And my father fought in Korea, so don't you dare say my family are some kind of Nazis.'

Ella, who had shown no interest in her risotto, asked if she could have a banana. Larry said no, but Kirsty took one from the fruit bowl and peeled it for her.

'I hate this kind of talk,' she said. 'I don't want Ella to even have to think about it.'

'A great American tradition,' said Larry. He pushed away his plate and reached for his glass, but the wine was too light. He needed a real drink. He needed to get out.

'Granny's crying,' said Ella.

It was true. Head bowed over her uneaten supper, one sticky tear had made it to the end of Alice's nose.

'Hey, hey . . . what is it?' Kirsty went to her and put her arm around her shoulders. She sounded close to tears herself. 'Are you tired? Huh?'

Larry crouched on the other side of the chair. Alice was saying something but he couldn't understand her.

'You want to rest a little?' asked Kirsty. 'You want to go back upstairs?'

'She's just come down,' said Larry.

'For Chrissakes! If she wants to go back up. You want to go back up, Alice?'

Alice sniffed. 'So sorry,' she said. 'What a mess.'

'OK,' said Larry, 'we can do this another night.' He took his mother's arms, drawing her from the chair. Over her shoulder he hissed: 'Where's Alec?'

Kirsty looked round, shrugged. Ella, her mouth crammed with banana, pointed to the open door.

After this, the evening failed at its own pace. Ella was sat in front of the television set, as if, in any emergency, this was the natural thing to do with a child. Kirsty stayed upstairs with Alice, coming down half an hour later to make fruit tea for her. Alec, lurking in the kitchen, knew that he should go up and check the pillbox. It was his job – the only one of any consequence that he had – but to go into that room now and take the risk of catching Alice's eye, of not being able to defend himself from what he saw there, of her seeing

237

how utterly split he was between pity and disgust, this was too much. And really, what did it matter if she took her medication? Her *fucking* medication. It was rare for Alec to speak an obscenity, unusual for him even to think one, but he found himself alone with the supper dishes, muttering to the soapsuds like a derelict. *Fucking* Larry with his *fucking* wife. Their idiotic *fucking* behaviour. His own behaviour. His own *fucking* stupidity. His *fucking* cowardice.

'Not the hugest success,' said Larry, breezing in with a tray from the dining room.

'Are you surprised?' asked Alec. 'When you go on like that?' He didn't look at Larry but he heard the sharp offended intake of air.

'Like what?'

'Bickering.'

'Who was bickering?'

'Who do you think?'

'So it's all my fault?'

'Can't you see how *ill* she is?'

'Of course I can see! What do you expect me to do about it?'

'Show some basic consideration.'

'Well, that's pretty rich coming from you,' said Larry, prodding his brother's shoulder as if to remind him who, between the two of them, had the physical power. 'Where were you hiding? Eh? Where did you run away to?'

'You know who you remind me of these days?' said Alec, scrubbing the non-stick surface off the rice pan. 'Dad.'

'I was wondering how long before someone came out with that crap. I just didn't expect it to be you. Christ! A couple of drinks would improve you no end.'

'Yeah. I can see how much good it's done you.'

'And try getting laid once in a while. I'll even lend you the money.'

'Is that what you do? Is that why you two can't talk to each other any more?'

'Keep your nose out of it, Alec.'

'Or were we supposed not to notice?'

'Go to hell!'

'*You* go to hell.'

'What's going on?' asked Kirsty.

'Nothing at all,' said Larry. He picked up a cloth, and with elaborate care started to dry one of the glasses.

Kirsty frowned, then slid Alice's mug into the hot water, resting her other hand on Alec's back. 'I think she took all her drugs.'

'Thanks,' said Alec.

'She said some weird stuff when we were in the bathroom. Still, I guess she was tired.'

'What kind of stuff?' asked Larry.

'Stuff you say when you're tired.' She yawned. 'I'm gonna put Ella to bed.'

An hour later she went to bed herself. She had moved into the downstairs room with Ella; Larry had shifted his gear upstairs to Alec's room, where there was an old-fashioned camp bed of tubular steel and wire mesh. There were only single beds in the spare room so this new arrangement had been passed off as a purely practical matter, though who this was intended to fool or reassure, Larry didn't know.

The brothers finished the clearing up then sat on the sofa in the living room to watch the evening news. After the May election the government was getting busy, declaring a Year Zero, salvaging the nation's future by making it modern and fashionable. Among the politicians they interviewed there was a strange, compulsive use of the word 'new'.

Think it'll work?' asked Larry.

'*Plus ça change*,' said Alec. But he admired them for trying. For doing something.

Larry said he thought they were some kind of Khmer Rouge, and that he intended to visit a good old English pub while there was still one left to visit. He remembered a place called the Blue Flame, fifteen minutes' walk across the fields. Flagstone floors, wooden barrels, not quite clean. A place with pickled eggs and cheap cigarettes.

'Do you mind?' It was understood that one of them would have to stay for Alice.

Alec shook his head. 'I might do some work.'

'No hard feelings about tonight?'

'No hard feelings.'

'Just letting off steam. It's bound to happen.'

'I know.'

'Catch you later, then.'

'Sure.'

When he was gone, Alec switched off the television. Out of the quiet came the sound of his mother's coughing, a muffled hacking and retching that reached its crescendo, then slowly died away. He hurried into the garden, crossing the lawn and gulping down lungfuls of milky air. In the summerhouse he struck a match, lit the storm lantern and set it on the shelf by the portrait of Lázár. Then he sharpened his pencils, opened the manuscript of *Oxygène*, and for twenty minutes performed a kind of mime of work until the deception was no longer tolerable, and he leaned back on the rear legs of his chair to watch the insects that came to the light through the open window, among them a pair of large butter-coloured moths that knocked the dust from their wings on the glass waist of the lantern and flew like manic angels around the playwright's head.

A little before midnight, Larry returned, crooning some country-and-western number as he clambered over the stile and weaved his way back to the house. Alec extinguished the flame in the lantern and sat on in the dark, long enough, he hoped, for Larry to have got to bed. He didn't want to speak to him again tonight. Though they had made their peace, he was still shaken by the row in the kitchen, could still feel where Larry had jabbed his shoulder. *And where were you hiding? Go to hell!* They had fought often enough as kids, as teenagers, passionately against each other for half an hour. But tonight he had seen something new, an anguish that mirrored his own, a depth of trouble he knew nothing about and could not have explained. Kirsty had been right the evening he called San Francisco (and he had been wrong): people change. And how credulous of him, how unthinkably naïve, to imagine that his brother would just go on the same, untouched by the disorder that found its way unerringly to others lives – to *every* life in time. But how was he to understand himself now? What more telling definition of himself could he hope to find other than being what Larry was not? He had never questioned it. Had anyone? It was the easiest way to think about him. So what now? If Larry wasn't 'Larry' any more, who was Alec?

At a quarter to one he recrossed the garden. Flower-heads showed silvery against the dark of the foliage, and the night felt heavy, liquid, the stars not quite in focus. Perhaps it meant a change in the weather, a heavy dew tomorrow. He locked the terrace doors, drank a glass of tap water in the kitchen, and was on the point of switching off the lights in the living room when his attention was caught by the card table in the alcove beneath the stairs. He had put the table there the day after Alice came out of hospital, and at the same time had put the pieces of the little conjuring game back in the box. But now they were out again, the three red cups in a line across the centre of the table. He went closer. Who had taken them out? Larry? Why should he? Certainly not Kirsty. Ella, then. Ella, of course. If nothing else, her obsessive nature betrayed her: the intervals between the cups must have been uniform to within a centimetre or two. But when? And who had she wanted to play with? He crouched, studying the cups in turn, then lifted the middle one.

'You win,' he whispered. He picked up the right-hand cup. Still there was nothing. He turned over the last.

Nestled on the baize, like the egg of some giant hornet or dragonfly, was the capsule – shiny blue and shiny red. He picked it up. It was almost weightless, its little load of pharmaceuticals just visible through the slightly dented glycerin skin. The hair prickled on the back of his neck, and he swung round as though expecting to catch Larry or Ella or, God knows, Alice, standing by the door, watching him, seeing the expression on his face, and knowing what he must be thinking. But he was quite alone. Nobody was going to disturb him.

He placed the capsule between his lips, tore a strip from the evening paper, wrapped the capsule, and slid it into the breast pocket of his shirt. Then he put away the cups, closed the box, turned out the lights and went upstairs, pausing for a moment, in a kind of passion, outside his mother's room.

10

At 8.45 on a morning of dazzling sunlight, László Lázár stepped down on to the platform at Westbahnhof. In one hand he carried his old blue 'pilot's' bag; in the other a black holdall of tough imitation leather handed to him at the Gare de l'Est the previous evening by a middle-aged man he had never seen before.

It was not, of course, the money – that would come later – and when he had looked inside it, locked into one of the toilets on the train, he had found it to contain nothing but a dozen newspapers – *Le Monde Diplomatique* – and two large white bath towels, presumably for the sake of bulk. In Vienna he kept it with him, depositing the blue bag at left luggage and taking a taxi to the Opera House, killing time in Kärntner Strasse, Singer Strasse, the Hoher market. Several times he paused to watch the street in a store window, trying to catch from out of the animated sheen of passers-by a glimpse of any figure that stopped when he stopped, but the only persistent face, the only face his trick surprised into a guilty stillness (a face like milk splashed on dark wood), was his own.

At 12.30 he returned to Westbahnhof and took a seat in the station restaurant, a table between a pillar and a large pot plant, from where he had a clear view of the glass and steel doors. There were still twenty-five minutes before the

rendezvous, but this time he did not intend to be startled by an unseen approach, as he had been at the station in Paris, turning to find a face too close to his own, a stare like a policeman's, a voice reciting, 'Françoise said to give you this,' in an accent he was starting to be familiar with.

The waitress came, a plump girl, profoundly bored, and stood beside him with her pad of paper. He had no appetite – the fag of tramping with the holdall through a hot city he had little affection for had triggered a nagging headache – but he selected something at random from the menu and ordered a bottle of Kaiser beer. She brought the beer immediately. It was cold and it seemed to do him some good. He relaxed a little, closing his eyes, trying to come to terms with the fact that he was here at all – in Vienna! – when in a saner, more orderly world he would be at his desk in Paris, picking at lines of dialogue and starting to wonder what there might be in the fridge for lunch.

The rhythms of the train were in his blood still, a sensation distantly familiar to him, for he had once known the night train well. Four or five times a year he had taken it to visit his mother and Uncle Ernö. 'The Orient Express' – an exotic name for a conveyance that was neither luxurious nor even particularly fast. Six berths to a compartment, eleven compartments to a car, and along the length of the carriage a narrow corridor where people smoked and leaned at the windows, gazing moodily at dark blue fields and the lights of strange towns.

And there was always some incident, some curious encounter. On this trip he had spent an hour somewhere in Eastern France calming the fears of a red-haired American girl who had heard, or perhaps read in one of those tedious guidebooks

no one seemed capable of leaving home without, that there were criminal gangs who sprayed knockout gas into the sleeping cars in order to rob, or even to murder, the unconscious passengers. His English – unused since San Francisco – was shaky, and she spoke nothing else, but with the help of some schnapps he had at last succeeded in making her see the absurdity of her fears, though privately he suspected that farther to the east (Romania?) such gangs did indeed exist, for these were desperate times.

Once the girl was asleep, and the Frenchman on the berth below her ceased to grind his teeth, László had stretched out on his own bunk, and thought back to to his last journey on the Orient Express, the winter of 1989, when he had come to Vienna to watch his mother die. János had flown in from New York (where his marriage to Patty was ending in the divorce courts), and the pair of them had carried on a three-day vigil at their mother's bedside in the Allgemeines Krankenhaus, János muttering in László's ear about justice and love and private detectives, while László watched the February snow, silver and dark, building drifts on the sill of the narrow window above his mother's head.

It was the type of end that people call 'peaceful': the old woman, skeletal after months of wasting, suddenly absent, the breath gone out of her mouth, her eyes shut like a pharaoh's. A brief, apparently untroubled translation. But at the instant of her going he had been shaken by the sense that in that cramped and curtained space at the end of the ward something revelatory had taken place, sacred even, and he had clutched at it in the hope that his grief could be meaningful, a noble effort to reconcile himself to the will of the transcendent. But the moment didn't stay. He was

too much of the materialist, brought up on dialectics, the True Path, the Victory of Socialism. He had no grounding in religion, no child-learned texts with which to dress the moment up in language, no consoling images of souls in flight. So her death, like that other, earlier death, in Budapest, had remained untransfigured, and merely what it was: an enigma that outstared reason, and left him for a while in a perfection of loneliness that had frightened him badly.

Afterwards, when the formalities were done, the papers signed and the porters had taken her to the morgue (a little flower of bruises on her wrist where the drip needle had been), the brothers had clung to each other in the corridor outside the ward, two middle-aged men, unshaven, raw-eyed, foreigners in a rage with death, while either side of them the nurses went about their business, walking on soft-soled shoes that seemed to make no noise at all.

'*Bitte?*'

His food had arrived: a slab of pork surrounded by a mess of green which, consulting the menu, he discovered to be creamed spinach. He picked up his fork, afraid that it would look suspicious if he made no attempt to eat what he had ordered, but after the first mouthful he decided that it would look more suspicious to eat such food, and he pushed aside his plate, glancing up from the table at the very instant his contact emerged through the swing-doors.

She had cut and dyed her hair (auburn) and was dressed in faded jeans and a man's blue shirt with the sleeves rolled up to her elbows, but there was no mistaking her: Emil's

friend, though shorn of that aura of severity which, in Paris, had shivered from her skin like smoke. She looked now like someone's favourite niece – his, perhaps! – smiling and crossing to his table with a confident swing of the hips. Over her shoulder she carried a bag identical to his own, though from the tautness of the strap, the way she lowered it carefully to the floor beside his chair, it was evidently much heavier.

She kissed his cheeks. 'You had a good trip?'

'Thank you,' he said.

She sat opposite him and lit a cigarette. When the waitress came she ordered a Coke.

'You should eat,' she said, looking at his plate.

László shrugged. 'The heat . . .'

'There may be a storm later,' she said.

'You think so?'

He would have liked to have known what the rules were here, whether he was to assume they could be overheard, despite the fact there was no one at the tables either side of them, and there was music, the inevitable dreary waltz, seeping from speakers hidden in the walls. He thought they should have given him some training in Paris. He didn't want to make a fool of himself.

He leaned towards her. 'Will you be coming with me?'

'No,' she said. Then with a trace of her old impatience, 'Of course not.'

She drank her Coke and crushed an ice cube between her teeth. 'Listen,' she said. 'The Budapest train leaves at fourteen-twenty. When you reach the city you will stay at the Hotel Opera on Révay utca. Do you know it?'

'I know the street. Near the Basilica.'

'Correct.'

'And what do I do there?'

'You go sightseeing.'

'For how long?'

'Two, three days. Leave the bag in the hotel safe.'

'Wouldn't it be safer to keep it with me?'

'It is important that you do exactly as we ask. Nothing more and nothing less. When everything is ready you will be contacted.'

'How?'

'That is for others to decide.'

She tapped out her cigarette, then reached down, very casually, to take hold of the strap of his bag.

'You have everything you need?'

'But that depends on you,' said László.

She allowed herself the briefest of smiles. 'Enjoy your vacation,' she said. He wanted to ask her whether they would meet again, but already he felt quite sure that they would not. He was sorry for it. Having so thoroughly disliked her at their first meeting, he now decided she was admirable, pure as a blade, though he suspected it was a purity that might one day feel justified in leaving a device in a crowded bar. Charlotte Corday, Ulrike Meinhof. Joan of Arc! How odd he should find himself her confederate in this affair. He watched her walk away. Was she 'Françoise'? It was a long time since a woman had interested him like this. He was pleased to find it was still possible.

He signalled for the bill, paid in cash and left a tip, but when he came to lift the bag the weight of it astonished him. He had to adjust his grip, bend at the knees a little, hoist the thing on to his shoulder. How much money felt like *this*? Quarter of a million? Half a million? Impossible, of course, to guess the value without knowing the currency. Deutschmarks or dollars, presumably. Krugerrands? Perhaps. Whatever it was, the donations of the diaspora had obviously been generous, though many of them were *gastarbeiter* and must have felt the loss of what they gave. For the rest, a tycoon like Bexhet Pacolli could have made the bag heavier without much sacrifice. So, too, those who had become wealthy in more sinister ways (the heroin racket in Zurich was said to be run by Albanians, and the capos there might have welcomed the chance to buy influence). Unlikely that Emil and his friends would be greatly worried by the provenance of the money. In times of need, hard currency could always justify itself.

He bought his ticket in the station hall, collected his pilot's bag, and went on to the platform, where the train (the 'Bela Bartók') was on time, the engine and a score of dusty carriages creeping in under the afternoon shadows of the station. László boarded and edged down the aisle until he came to a compartment emptier than the rest, with two unoccupied seats facing forward. Here, he stowed the blue bag on the overhead rack and sat on the seat by the window, the black bag at his feet, one loop of the strap wound around his wrist. Behind him, two Hungarian voices, city accents like his own but with an argot he didn't always understand, discussed the latest Ferencváros game. The carriage was stifling – old rolling stock with no air-conditioning – and he longed to sleep, but waking up in Budapest with the bag missing would be a very expensive mistake indeed. It might, quite literally, be more than his life was worth.

A whistle blew, a child was held up to wave goodbye, a little air began to eddy in at the tops of the windows. He sat back, took, or tried to take, a deep breath, but his lungs were sticky, and when he tried a second time, forcing it, there was a pain, like a ravel of irritated nerve ends threaded through his ribs in a line beneath his left armpit. Now here was another thought to play with. After all, there would be nothing extraordinary about a man of his age having a coronary on a hot day, travelling. In casualty they would open the bag looking for his medication, or just made curious by the weight of it. A pity he would not be there to see their faces.

He put on his sunglasses and retrieved a crumpled copy of *Die Presse* that had been pushed under the seat in front. He was becoming exasperated with himself, his relentless self-concern, his fantasies of collapse, of finding himself looking up from the floor at the faces of strangers, someone – there was always someone – shouting 'Don't move him!'. Did he *wish* for it? The failure that would excuse all others. Poor László! What could he do? A sick man! Helpless!

At Hegyeshalom, an hour out of Vienna, customs officers boarded the train. The Austrians, with their snappy berets and blue-grey tunics, were almost dapper; by contrast, the Hungarian trio, in caps and rumpled khaki, had the hapless look of young military conscripts, though for László, uniforms of any description could still provoke in him the old fear that those who wore them were spiders who moved along the web of the law, and whose interest could snare him in a tangle he would never escape from. He unwound the strap from his wrist and took off his sunglasses.

'French?' asked one of the Hungarians, in English, as László passed over the passport, which in 1971, after the success of *Sisyphus Rex*, the French government had at last seen fit to grant him.

'From Budapest,' said László, replying in Hungarian.

'Budapest?'

'Forty years ago.' He wondered if the other understood. How much would he know about '56? People would not remember it forever. Another generation and it would be a paragraph in a textbook memorized by schoolchildren for the sake of an examination question.

'You've been about,' said the young man, scrutinizing the stamps in László's passport.

'For my work,' said László, and he prepared himself to deliver an acceptable explanation of what his work was. He knew from experience that customs officials were often nervous about writers, a tendency at its worst in those places with a long tradition of locking them up, and where the habit, the reflex of persecution, was hard for them to break. But he then realised that the young man was only envious of those enticing little stamps, and was, in fact, not particularly interested who came into Hungary, or who left. Hungary would be in the Community soon, another branch of the great European department store. The world had moved on; the grey-faced men, those who had worn coats lined with frost, were lost in the very history they had thought themselves the masters of. The country was open now, though László did not think he would ever quite get used to that. It had come too late for his generation.

They stopped again at Győr, then continued across the plain, where the heat rose in a silvery haze from grasslands and cornfields. Broad, low, farmhouses floated past; cars queued patiently at a level crossing; shadows indolent as moat water surrounded the blackened walls of an old Soviet-era industrial plant. László leaned his head against the window and fell asleep. Immediately, he began to dream, discovering himself in a street he did not quite recognize, one of those urban settings collaged by the unconscious from a dozen different cities; places lived in, or seen from the window of a taxi, or on a cinema screen. He was dressed in a baggy black suit like a type of circus clown, and dragged behind him an enormous overpacked suitcase tied shut with lengths of string. At the corner of the street, garbed in the outfit of a Mexican *bandido*, Emil Bexheti leaned against the wall with his arm around the shoulders of a beautiful woman, who laughed shrilly to see László stumbling up the dust of the street. And yet the mood of the dream was not oppressive. In spite of the sense that he could not possibly carry his burden much farther, he was content, almost cheerful, in the dogged fashion of a man who acts out his fate knowing that there can be no other. And after a while he ceased to hear the woman's laughter. The city abruptly ended and he was out in the country, hauling the case – which now he dimly recognized as the one he had left Hungary with, his father's case, a thing of solid burnished leather with the initials 'A.L' stencilled on the top – along a white road that undulated into the remote distance; a white ribbon threaded through a deserted arcadia, which would lead him, unerringly somehow, to his final destination . . .

He woke as they were pulling into Kelati station, the spell, the unexpected peacefulness of his dream, replaced by a great agitation of noise and movement. In a panic he reached forward, cursing himself and scrabbling under the pages of the newspaper that had fallen from his lap while he slept, and then, in his relief, laughing out loud as his fingers grazed the waxy sides of the bag.

He clambered with it down on to the platform, weaving through the gangs of accommodation touts, tough-looking women mostly, holding up cards with 'Room to rent' spelled out in English and German and Italian. Above their heads, pigeons flew in swift formations, their wings rippling the light that fell in a wash from the great fan window at the city end of the station. Émigré, playwright, international courier, László Lázár was back, and in his old language he silently greeted his old home.

11

On Sunday morning, Alice Valentine waited on the sofa in the living room at Brooklands. She was wearing a fawn winter coat, and round her neck a stole of mink fur, with a mink's desiccated head on either end of it. The stole had belonged to her mother, and fifty years ago might have bestowed some glamour on a young woman with an evening dress and a powdered throat, but time and hordes of golden moths had done much damage to it. The creatures, with their glass eyes and ragged ears, seemed to be suffering from acute alopecia, and Alec thought of the old dog skin at the end of Lampedusa's *The Leopard*, dropped from a window on to a dust heap. But Alice had wanted it, and after long searching he had found it coiled in a hatbox at the back of a wardrobe on the landing. None of them knew *why* she wanted it; perhaps in tribute to her mother on the visit to the old house. No one asked her for reasons any more.

It was a quarter to twelve by the time they left: Larry, Ella and Kirsty in the back of the car, Larry with his knees almost up to his chin; Alice in the front with her stick, her oxygen, her tissues, her supermarket carrier bag of pill bottles. They travelled on minor roads under the looped shadows of the trees, Alec leaning forward at the wheel like a card player, though there was almost no traffic. Ella, in a green frock and sandals, sat between her parents, poised and silent. Larry scratched the top of her head and she gazed up at him.

'How you?' he whispered. 'How we?'

They had had their little talk about the return of the capsule ('our secret'), though he had spoken to her more in gratitude than reproach. He was grateful to Alec too. Evidently his conversation with her had been more effective than they had realized. The thing was gone now; Alec had sent it the same way as the others (extraordinary what gets flushed down people's toilets!), so *that* particular crisis was over. He had been unexpectedly reprieved, and the escape had invigorated him, so that for the first time in months he felt that better things might be possible. If he could rein back on the booze, the powder, the tablets, the mood swings, the lying, this time perhaps he would defy the lengthening odds and make the world right again. But the change would have to be convincing. It would have to show on his skin like a light, for there were only so many times a person could promise reform before the words 'I'll change' began to sound like 'I want to change but I can't'. It might, of course, be too late; he was so cut off from Kirsty's private thinking now, the tendency of her thinking. For all he knew she had already instructed someone in the States, some lawyer, and he'd go home to find the paperwork waiting for him. She'd had a week on her own over there, and that Khan bitch might have talked her into something. But it was his instinct that he still had one last chance, and he intended to reach for it.

With his left arm laid along the top of the seat – his hand behind the nape of his wife's neck so that she would only have to lean back a little for them to be touching – he gazed through the side window of the car and saw a half-dozen rabbits scattering across a field. Sheep grazed; lion-coloured cows stood by troughs in the shade of trees, swishing their tails. There was corn growing and oilseed rape, and red tractors raising a dust in the hayfields. In spite of everything – motorways, pesticide, a million new homes – here at least the country had retained its riches, its mannerly beauty. In his hurry to put England behind him he had underprized this. Now he felt the tug of it, as though this landscape – the first he had opened his eyes to – had some authoritative claim on him, something at the level of blood, which he was finally ready to acknowledge.

He looked at his mother, hunched in her seat as though the air were hardening on her shoulders. Could she take any pleasure in this? Was that still possible? It was a long time since she had been out of the house – a long time since going somewhere meant anything other than going to the hospital – and when he and Kirsty had gone in with her morning tea (into the shaded room no breeze seemed to freshen) she had been so flustered and confused they had wondered if the outing would be possible at all. She had complained wretchedly that she could no longer find any position to be comfortable in; how at night she wanted to turn on to her side but was afraid she would suffocate. Then, when Kirsty left them alone – Ella calling 'Mom!' from the bottom of the stairs – she had said she knew what a 'kind doctor' would do, a remark that Larry had refused to understand, though she had followed him around the room with her eyes until Kirsty came back and he could escape into the garden for a smoke.

For days now (months?) he had been trying to gather in

himself the courage to speak to her. He needed – and the need was urgent – to appear before her as he truly was, to make himself visible to her: no more the shining target of her old pride, but a man who had proved unequal to those imperfections in himself he had barely suspected the existence of five years ago. And though he supposed she had already resigned herself to the loss of the old dream in which they had been such loyal partners, he was afraid that she would slip away (say 'die', Larry!) while some pretence still clouded the space between them. He needed to be recognized. It would take no more than a moment's attention, a hand raised in blessing, but he would have to choose his moment with the utmost care. And choose it very soon.

To the right of them was Salisbury Plain: low, pale green hills jointed to the sky by fragments of dense, dark woodland. Then as they came within twenty miles of the house, Alice began to point things out. A church where she had once been a bridesmaid. A haunted pub. The gates of an estate behind which some local character had lived out a lordly decline.

To Ella, Kirsty explained: 'This is where Gran'ma lived when she was a little girl.'

'OK,' said Ella, and she put on a short mime of looking out with interest, though there wasn't much to excite a child from North Beach who had seen canyons and mountains and giant sequoia trees.

When Alec missed the turn-off, Alice waved a crumpled tissue at him and called him a fool, as if they drove this way every week. He apologized, reversed, and turned into a lane that ran between unmown verges, the ruts and potholes blue with last week's rain.

'Wow,' said Kirsty, 'real countryside.'

'We may see some bears,' said Larry. 'Better wind up your window, Mum.'

But she wasn't listening to them any more. She wasn't interested in their chatter. This was private.

Larry leaned forward and touched his brother's shoulder. 'You remember this?'

Alec nodded. There were fields here they had once played in together, greening their knees. And certain small farms they had worked on during the holidays or at weekends, baling or scrumping, earning a few pounds, then drinking milk in the farmhouse kitchen when it was too dark to work. It stirred them, seeing it again, the lane twisting into the hills like time itself, and for the last fifteen minutes the journey was processional and solemn and they rode in silence.

The house stood alone on a stretch of road at the outskirts of the village: two storeys of red brick with the year '1907' pricked out in black paint on a stone above the front door. From the outside at least, the place did not look very different, though there were new high gates, and a yellow alarm box prominent beside an upstairs window, and in the centre of the driveway a little fountain – cherub and urn – as in a country hotel. Alec parked the car between a Range Rover and a green MG, and as the brothers gently levered Alice from her seat, an old Labrador limped over the gravel to meet them, snuffling at the hem of Alice's coat, as if the mink, dead half a century ago, still leaked some subtle feral stink.

'Shoo,' sighed Alice, but the dog was full of doggish interest in her, and followed them to the front door. Larry tugged at the craftwork iron bell-pull (a plain electric buzzer in Grandma Wilcox's day), and after a minute the jangling was answered by a young man, twenty, twenty-two, who stood in the door frame, pale and pretty, his shirt unbuttoned to his navel, looking at them as if good style meant a level of unresponsiveness that bordered on the moronic. Evidently, no one had told him who this gaunt and weirdly dressed woman might be. He leaned against the door and drawled, 'I'm Tom.'

'Yes,' said Alice, and letting go of her sons she staggered past him into the dark of the hall.

'We've come to visit,' said Alec, hurrying after her, afraid that she would crash disastrously on to the tiles.

'Name of Valentine,' added Larry, grinning at the boy's discomfort and following the others inside.

'We're Valentines too!' said Kirsty. 'Do you have a bath-room for my little girl?'

By the time they were all in the house, Stephanie Gadd had emerged from one of the downstairs rooms, a woman in the vicinity of fifty, youthful, vigorous, dressed casually but punctiliously in navy blue slacks and a chiffon blouse. She had a string of pearls at her neck, which she turned and tangled in her fingers as she spoke.

'Well done!' she cried. 'Did you have an *awful* journey? Tom had a B of a time coming down from London.' She smiled at her son, lingeringly, then, without turning, gestured to the man behind her. 'And this is Rupert, my other half.'

'Really pleased you could make it,' said Rupert. He grimaced and shook hands, squeezing hard as if he hoped to communicate dumb sincerity through the force of his grip, though when Larry squeezed back, much of the colour left the older man's face.

Tom was asked to show Ella and Kirsty to the downstairs loo. The others were led into the dining room where an elaborate buffet lunch was laid out on snowy tablecloths.

'Just finger food, I'm afraid,' said Stephanie. 'I don't think people want anything *substantial* when the weather's this warm.'

Alice was seated between Alec and Rupert. She would not be parted from her coat or stole, and sat in her place like the last days of a Hollywood starlet, or one of those women undone by absinthe in a Toulouse-Lautrec painting.

When Kirsty and Ella came back, Stephanie handed out the plates and invited everyone to help themselves. On Sundays they were very informal and she hoped that was all right. Rupert drew the cork from a bottle of wine and held up the bottle to the light. He said he belonged to a wine club – 'nothing too serious, just some chaps' – but they had been impressed by this red from Peru.

'Just pour it, darling,' said Stephanie. She made an elaborate female solidarity face at Kirsty, who did her best to return it.

At the window end of the table, Tom Gadd, still unbuttoned, occupied his chair with a kind of doomed elegance, toying with a slice of Parma ham, a stuffed olive, then, with a blatant yawn, excusing himself to make some phonecalls.

Alice sipped at a glass of mineral water but ate nothing. For several minutes towards the end of the meal she appeared to be asleep, but when Stephanie returned from the kitchen carrying a tray of sliced peaches and freshly made meringues, saying how sorry she was she didn't have more, that it wasn't more special, that it was just something to 'fill a hole', Alice silenced her, calling out in a voice retrieved with visible effort, and saying, '*Please!* Please can we see the house now?'

There was an instant's confusion. The skin on Stephanie's face tautened, as though her self-control might be far more fragile than her manner had so far suggested. But she recovered herself, set down the tray, and touched her pearls. 'How very thoughtless of me,' she said. 'Of course you can see the house now. Rupert!'

'Absolutely,' said Rupert, springing from his seat. 'Are we all going together?'

They started in the lounge, filing in behind Stephanie, who, sketching freely in the air, explained how they had knocked through and enlarged and finally forced upon these simple rooms a type of luxuriousness. In each of the rooms there came a moment when they gathered around Alice as though to witness a public act of recollection, but her gaze was distracted. She frowned as if they had brought her to the wrong house, or she was searching for something in particular, something that wasn't there, the fine end of a thread that would lead her back.

They went upstairs, Alice at the front clutching on to Larry's arm, the others inching up behind them.

'You have a beautiful home,' said Kirsty.

'How kind,' said Stephanie. 'We keep our little place in London, but it's not the *old* London now.'

'Can't buy a morning paper,' said Rupert, 'unless you speak Portuguese or Urdu.'

'*Un moment!*' called Stephanie, striding to the head of the column. She opened the door at the far end of the corridor and announced the master bedroom. 'We brought the mirror in Italy,' she said. And then to Alec: 'Do you know Siena well?'

Larry, who thought he might be able to have a lot of fun at these people's expense, picked up a photograph from the mantelpiece beside the mirror. Two boys in cricket whites in the school grounds of some middle-ranking English public school. The boy with the bat was recognizably the languid Tom. The other boy, slightly older, blond-brown hair in a flop over one of his eyes, held up a ball as though he had just taken five wickets and was trying not to look too pleased with himself. At the far left of the picture there was the green flutter of a woman's dress, and the dark green brim of her hat. Larry put the photograph back on the mantelpiece, catching sight in the mirror of Stephanie Gadd staring at him with an expression he had last seen on Betty Bone's face in the San Fernando Valley.

At the window, Alice was gazing down into the garden. It was smaller than the one at Brooklands, and neater, running down a slight incline between beech hedges to the bank of a stream. The others joined her.

'There,' said Alice, a voice barely audible. 'There . . .'

'Do you mean the old willow?' asked Stephanie.

Alice nodded, pressing on the glass with her fingertips.

'You want to go into the garden, Mum?' asked Alec.

She turned to him and smiled, beamed at him as if she were surprised to find him there, and his suggesting that they go out somehow made it possible. 'What an angel,' she said. And then turning to Stephanie Gadd, she repeated it: 'My son is an angel.'

'Oh, yes,' said Stephanie, her hand straying towards the pearls again. 'Yes, I can see that.'

For a few minutes the garden gave Alice new strength. With her stick she moved on her own across the trimmed lawn with more energy than she had been able to muster in weeks. It was mid-afternoon, the velvet hour. At the point of farthest visibility, the air was silver and slate, darkening nearer the horizon, almost purple. Something was building out there, new weather, but it was still a long way off, and might, in the end, come to nothing.

'The place doesn't look too bad on a day like this,' said Rupert. He was standing with Kirsty in the shade of the house.

'Oh, I think it's heavenly,' she said.

'Old fellow from the village mostly. Can't understand a word he says but he's reliable. Steph's the brains behind it all.'

'It was kind of you to let us come.'

'Not at all.'

'I think she's OK now,' said Kirsty, watching Alice pause to lean her face into the heart of a large yellow rose.

'Still,' said Rupert, 'it must be wretched for her.' Then in a voice that was quite different, he added, 'We lost Tom's brother to leukaemia two years ago. They used Tom's bone marrow but it didn't help much.' He grinned, as though his face suffered from a poverty of expressions. 'Poor Tommy seems to think it was his fault. You know. Thinks he should have done more.'

When Alice started to slow down, a toy unwinding, they brought out a chair for her and tried to coax her into the shade. They were solicitous and complained that she was overexerting herself, but she insisted they set the chair on the grass in front of the willow. Alec helped her to sit. She clutched at his hand and told him it was the garden she had come back for. Nothing in the house had helped her – who were those people? – but the tree was miraculously unchanged. The perfectly kept secret of itself! The same tree she had seen each morning from her bedroom window as she got ready for school. The tree behind whose branches she had hidden with Samuel, her head on his shoulder, Sunday afternoons before he took the train back to London. The tree she had stood beside the night she went out to rescue her father. The night he told her about the flame-throwers. Did he know about that?

Alec nodded. He had no idea what she was talking about. And could this really be the same tree? He had his doubts. But her face had acquired that particular waxy glaze that meant her pain was on the flood. 'We ought to go,' he said.

She gestured with her hand. She wanted to stay a little longer. Sit there on her own. She was expecting someone.

She didn't know who. Not yet. But *someone*. 'I'm very tired,' she said. 'Don't know if I can stand up again.'

'I'll help when you're ready,' he said.

'Will you?'

'When you're ready.'

He crossed the garden and joined the others on the patio, where they had gathered under a sun umbrella.

'Everything all right?'

'Fine,' he said.

Stephanie brought out a jug of home-made lemonade, and for twenty minutes they made small talk, a shrill to-and-fro of pleasantries that only Ella felt free to ignore, twisting in her seat to stare at Alice's back, at those fascinating creatures slung over her shoulders, those little savage heads, their glass eyes prinked with sunlight. It was a sight she would remember even into middle age, long after she had forgotten the house and the people who lived there, or even why they had gone. She asked about it when her mother came to visit her and the grandchildren in New York (the Thanksgiving of 2037), but Kirsty had no memory of mink heads, though she could recall, she said, clear as day, the storm on the drive home, and, of course, the birthday party the following week. And all that that entailed.

12

When the phone rang he snatched up the receiver, certain
it would be his contact giving him a time and a place to
hand over the bag, but it was the automated wake-up service
informing him that it was 8.30 a.m. He lay back on the
pillows. He was in a large clean bed in a large clean room.
Muted colours, everything new. A large window with a net
curtain looked over the narrow street. There was very little
noise. Filtered sunlight fell on the glass-topped table.

For another half-hour he drowsed, then dragged off the
sheets and went through to the bathroom, opening the complimentary bottles of shower gel, shampoo, conditioner, and
standing under the shower with his face turned up to the jet.
He had, he reckoned, stayed in over two hundred different
hotels in the last twenty years, sometimes for pleasure, but
mostly on work trips, 'business' (as if he had a business!).
Places where he waited for an interview, for a discussion with
a producer, a call from home. Rented space where the life of
the last tenant was often still apparent in a trace of tobacco
smoke or a hair laced around the plug chain. Sometimes much
grosser evidence. In a hotel in London he had once found a
splash of blood on a bathroom tile, and in a good hotel in
Dublin – recommended – an unflushable human turd.

At the Hotel Opera on Révay utca, breakfast was included
in the price of the room and served in a restaurant on the

ground floor. On his way past the front desk, László raised a hand in greeting to the waist-coated receptionist with whom he had left the black bag the previous evening, though not before he had looked inside it in his room, disappointed to discover that whatever was in there had been thoroughly wrapped: an outer skin of waxed brown paper and beneath it what felt like a thick layer of plastic sheeting. He had been tempted to make a small incision, just big enough to see the stuff itself, but kneeling beside the bag with his nail scissors he had lost his nerve, afraid that his trespass would be discovered and somehow punished. He had the receipt for the bag in his wallet: a slip of green paper like a ticket for clothes at the dry-cleaner's.

The restaurant was doing a brisk trade. A lot of German was being spoken, some English, some Japanese. When he asked for a table the waitress seemed slightly surprised to be dealing with a Hungarian. She found him a quiet place next to a pair of fine-boned, grey-haired ladies, whom László immediately decided were artistic spinsters heading off for a day at the National Gallery, where they would take an informed interest in winged altar pieces. They bid him a cheery 'Grüss Gott!'. He nodded to them and smiled, and crossed to the buffet to make his selection for breakfast. Salami, mangoes, little French cheeses wrapped in foil. Sugary cakes. High-fibre cereals. Hard-boiled eggs. Odd how unappetizing it was, heaped together like this, the catering manager's vision of plenty.

He drank two cups of coffee (too weak), ate half a grape-fruit (not bad), and returned to his room, where he brushed and flossed his teeth. He had been booked in for three nights, with an option to extend, though please God it would all be over before then. There was nothing to do now but wait, and he hated waiting. He lay back on the bed, massaging his chest and thinking of the hundred and one things that might go wrong. Then he buttoned his shirt, put on his blue Nino Danieli jacket, checked himself in the mirror, scowled, and fled into the streets.

Emil was right, of course: the place had not changed much in six years. There was more traffic, more of the brand names one would expect in Paris or New York. More bars and casinos and sex clubs (their neon boasts – 'Beautiful Nude Girls Inside!' – almost erased by the glare of the sun). More tourists too, gangs of them with floppy hats and brightly coloured knapsacks, peering at buildings, staring at menus, vying with each other, it seemed, to be most like a tourist. But on the broad pavements of Andrássy ut the young women still walked arm in arm with just the right degree of sexual boldness, and in the gloom of the street corners the men still smoked and gossiped like amiable shades in the vestibule of Dante's Inferno. The same air of indulgent melancholy, the wry humour. It was still Budapest.

He called at the Writer's Bookshop on Liszt Ferenc tér, drank an espresso at the café there, then turned towards the river, passed the new Bank Centre on Anany János ut with its slabbed marble hide, walked through Szabadság tér, and came out on to Steindl Imre utca, where immediately he felt some barometric shift in the atmosphere, as if the density of the known, the familiar, the *ingrained*, had subtly increased. Behind the new coats of paint and the rows of German and

American cars (not the latest models, of course, and it was not hard to find old Skodas and Trabants), this was the old neighbourhood where the past of fifty years ago loomed like a tinted print under tissue paper. And it was here, in '91, that a voice had called out his name and he had turned to see the face of his old school-friend, Sándor Dobi – Sándor the questioner! – and though that face had grown slack with time, darker, less nervously resolute, there had been no hesitation in László's response. They had embraced, and over lunch become as drunk as students, stumbling over their stories. Sándor had spent twenty years in America – the construction industry, then a small restaurant business – and had two daughters in Minneapolis, and two ex-wives with whom he was still on excellent terms. 'Fine times,' he said, as they broached a fresh bottle of Palika. 'But my dear Laci, in the end you have to come home. Nowhere in the world will fill your heart like the place you first saw the light.'

Was Sándor still alive? He had confessed to prostate trouble ('a year ago, my friend, I thought "prostate" was something you went to a lawyer for!'). Had he meant cancer? How many of them were there now, scattered like ashes over the widths of the Earth? Lives such as theirs had not been conducive to longevity.

At the end of the street he crossed a line from shadow into broad sunlight. Ahead of him were the Buda hills, Fishermen's Bastion, Matthias church, and away to the right, almost out of sight, the river split at the prow of Margarits island and poured its tons under the wings of the bridge. Cruise boats, the sleek and the frankly chaotic, were moored by both banks, and advertised trips to Visegrád or Esztergom, some of them promising lavish dinners, and even erotic shows, as if witnessing a Russian or Romanian teenager wiggle her hips to a tape of gypsy violins were the acme of old Hungarian romance.

On Szechenyi Rakpart, the apartment building had been given a new livery of pale green paint, though the effect was spoiled somewhat by a graffiti artist who had sprayed an illegible protest in red swirls along one side of the building. László approached the heavy double doors and read the names beside the bells: Binder, Serfleck, Kosztka, Dr Konig. In '91 there had been at least one name he thought he knew, but not now, though he could not quite rid himself of the sense that if he looked again, rubbed his eyes and stared, he would find 'LAZAR', and push the worn button and go up to the old apartment and see his father listening to the sport on the radio, his mother rolling the pulp of dumplings between her palms, János combing hairballs from Toto the dog; and Aunt Gabi – the majestically breasted Gabi – complaining of how the veins in her legs were wide as bootlaces, and András, listen, András, don't you have some kind of cream for it? Aren't you supposed to be a doctor?

In the midst of his daydream the door was opened, and from the dark of the hallway two Persephones emerged with their shopping baskets. They eyed him suspiciously – this pale, dapper little man – then crossed the road to catch the number 2 tram, which was arriving with a tap-tapping of the overhead wires, like a giant yellow grasshopper rubbing its steel legs together. The door swung shut and he turned away. He needed somewhere cool to sit, somewhere that didn't press upon him with the past, and retracing his steps he found a restaurant in the square south of the Basilica, with wooden booths and cotton tablecloths and not a tourist in sight.

He took a table by the window and ordered his old favourite – goose livers in sour cream with mashed potatoes and onion – and while he waited he flicked through an edition of the previous day's *Hirlap*, trying to take an interest in the antics of the government, though it was the same game of musical chairs he had grown so weary of everywhere. In the middle pages, however, two items caught his attention. The first was a short article about the Balkans, warning of a coming storm in Kosovo, where Serb abuses had become more outrageous. Milošević, argued the journalist, survived by the manufacture of crises, and was in need of another war. Any war, even a disastrous one, would serve him better than a peace in which his enemies would have time to organize. There was a photograph of the militia leader, 'Arkan', in beret and black fatigues, machine-pistol over his shoulder, chin jutting, a real people's hero. Looking at him, László found that the voices of doubt in his head were momentarily stilled. Arkan made questions of right and wrong, for and against, seem simple: one was instinctively opposed to such a man – no special virtue was required – and if the money in the bag hurried this gangster on the road to hell then so much the better. It was an end that justified a great deal.

The second article, ostensibly comic, concerned a minor scandal in one of the old bathhouses – a local government official caught *in flagrante delicto* at the Király on Fo utca, with one of those anonymous, hollow-eyed young men who go on the prowl in such places. It was a grubby story, somewhat sad, but reading the piece László was drawn irresistibly back to his own adventures in the bathhouses, those softly dripping worlds, relics of Ottoman times that survived into the heart of the People's Utopia like orchids in a commissar's lapel. And there he was again! A skinny boy hunched on the slatted bench of a steam room, surrounded by the old men with their sagging balls, their starbursts of purple veins, their damp newspapers . . .

He used to go with his father or Uncle Ernö, sometimes with Péter's family – a weekend treat – and it was in the bathhouse at the Gellart Hotel, the grandest of them all, that Péter had kissed him for the first time as they changed into their clothes at the end of the session, Péter's Uncle Miklós dressing in the next cubicle, whistling folk songs. It was a kiss that fell like a splash of rain from a clear sky, breaking on to the back of his shoulder, transfixing him.

Nothing was said. What could be said with Miklós half a metre away, climbing into his flannel suit? But at the apartment that night, while János slept and the moon crossed the window right to left, László had sat up, feverishly trying to pass the moment through the machinery of reason, for already, at sixteen, he was condemned to be an intellectual, possessor of a mind that stared at itself. What had happened to him? He could not think of the moment as sexual: his understanding of such things was too shallow, too schoolboyishly vulgar. The kiss, he decided, must have been an expression of that ideal friendship Comrade Biszku spoke off in the Pioneers, and this soothed him for a while, tamped him down. But his daydreams of intense conversations, of epic chess matches and cross-country bicycle tours, had given way, in flashes, then in long sustained reverie, to the blatantly erotic; to the need for skin and hard breathing and intimacies whose names he trawled for in the pages of his parents' medical textbooks, and later, more tantalizingly, in the cache of foreign novels they kept in a suitcase under the bed. Zola, Milosz, Thomas Mann . . .

And Miklós had had a further part to play, for it was in his apartment in District VII, more spacious than László's or Péter's, more private, that they at last lay down together, clumsy and furtive as a pair of apprentice house-breakers, unbuttoning each other on a bed with ruined springs and a coverlet of brown corded wool that smelled of the nineteenth century.

How much had old Miklós known? That bachelor and old-style liberal, with his card evenings, his tears at the first notes of Bartók's 'Rhapsody'. Did he spy on them? Was he excited by it? Well, he was long since dead, cutting the veins in his legs with a barber's blade and dying in a bath of rose-red water the winter that followed the uprising in Prague. His housekeeper, Magda, had discovered the body, and László's mother had telephoned László in Paris, and been surprised at his long silence, the weight of sorrow he could not keep quite secret from her.

After eating, he returned to the hotel.

'Any messages?' None. He went to his room, caught the news on TV1, and fell asleep over a book, his head pillowed on his arm, his face quite solemn in repose. Now and then there was an out-breath that seemed to contain the fragment of a word. Then he would frown, grow momentarily tense, and faint back into some more profound level of sleep.

When he woke the room was dim. The arm he had rested his head on was quite insensate. He had to move it with his other hand as though it were a piece of driftwood.

He looked over at the bulb on the telephone, wondering if he might have slept through a call, but there was no flashing light. Was something not ready? Had something gone wrong? Would they warn him? He wondered how many others there were, men and women in rooms like this one perhaps, half bored, half anxious, waiting for a signal, a note under the door, a tap on the shoulder.

He switched on a table light, pulled up his shirt and examined his chest in one of the room's several mirrors. He could not decide whether his mysterious 'complaint' was marginally better or slightly worse, though there was no particular discomfort now, nothing that required him to take a painkiller with his aperitif. All the same, he thought of shadows on the lungs, of emphysema, of gross impediments in the branching of his airways. When he got back to Paris he would see someone about getting an X-ray, and he sat on the end of the bed, recalling the names of all the doctors he knew.

13

The night of the visit to Granny Wilcox's house, Alec was woken by a noise he could not at first identify. He lay in bed, staring up through the not-quite-dark of the air, listening, but hearing only his heart, his breath, his brother's breath, and the faint mechanical basso of the water pumping station behind the Joys' house. Yet whatever it was that had woken him, it had thrust him out of sleep, startled him, so that he knew at some level he had been listening for it all night – for many nights perhaps – monitoring the audible world for a sound that could not be innocently explained.

He sat up and lifted a corner of the curtain. The storm that had broken over their heads on the drive home (striking the windscreen with waves of stone-coloured rain) had passed, leaving in its wake a coolness of clear, moonless air. It felt late – three, four a.m. – but the alarm clock on the table with its luminous hands was turned away from him towards the camp-bed.

'Larry?'

'Yeah,' said Larry, 'I thought I heard something too.'

'What?'

'No idea.' Larry fumbled for the rocker switch on the cord of the bedside lamp, put the lamp on, and unzipped the sleeping bag.

'You're going out?' asked Alec.

'I need to piss.' He yawned until his body shuddered, then pushed a hand through his hair and moved to the door. He was wearing a pair of Felix the Cat boxer shorts. 'I may be some time,' he said.

Alec heard him flick on the landing light. Then a pause of three, four seconds, and he was back, leaning into the room, brittle-faced. 'Mum', he said, and disappeared again.

Alec climbed from his bed. He felt small and powerless and utterly unprepared. He put on his glasses. There was really nowhere to hide. After a few moments he went out.

Alice was face down in the doorway of her bedroom, her nightdress caught up around her thighs, her panties in a tangle round her ankles. The backs of her legs were streaked with diarrhoea, and there were small black pools of it on the carpet. It was not hard to see what must have happened. The confusion. The floundering in the dark. A last panicky attempt not to foul herself. Had she called out to them? Was that what they had heard?

Larry was crouched beside her, his fingers feeling for the pulse at her throat. He looked up at Alec. 'Go downstairs and call Una. Tell her what's happened, but that it doesn't look like she's broken anything. And she's not unconscious. Tell her I'm going to get her back into bed . . .'

'Should she be moved?'

'I'm not going to leave her here. Not like this.'

'No,' said Alec. The stink was very real. A smell of rot. A stench like the smell of the sickness itself.

'Ask if there's anything else we should do. Anything we should give her. And when you come up bring all the cleaning stuff you can find. OK? Go!'

Alone with her, Larry spoke in a whisper, telling her he

would take care of her. He checked again for signs that she had damaged herself in the fall – he had once performed a similar procedure as Dr Barry, though on that occasion the patient had been a female lifeguard thrown from a moving limo by her jealous lover – then he stood, leaned, lifted her in the cradle of his arms, and carried her into the bedroom. Her legs were very cold. He thought: She's going to die on me. I came too late.

He laid her on the bed, covered her feet and went into the en-suite bathroom. In the mirror he caught glimpses of himself frantically snatching towels, sponges. There was a pink plastic bowl. He put a bar of soap in it and filled it with warm water.

When he came back into the bedroom Alice was stirring, tugging feebly at her nightdress. Her breathing was much louder now, though whether that was good or not Larry had no idea. He put the oxygen bottle on the bed, opened the valve and pressed the mask over her face. It seemed to frighten her at first, as though he were trying to stifle her, but as she took in the gas she grew calmer.

'Everything's all right,' he said. 'Everything's dandy.'

He pulled off the soiled panties and dropped them on to the floor by the bed. 'We've got to clean you up,' he said. 'Is that OK?'

He dipped the sponge into the bowl, squeezed it out, and began to wipe her legs. He worked methodically, wiping her with the sponge and dabbing her dry with the towel. He washed between her legs, wiped the pinched red skin of her backside, cleaning her as sometimes he had cleaned Ella. He was unaware of any emotion other than an irreducible tenderness that embraced them both. He was babbling, telling her things he had told to no one. Shameful moments. Low-life moments culled from his progress through the bars and motel rooms of America. Private, frightened moments in the last third of a bottle on nights when getting drunk would not do at all. He gave her names, acts, everything he could dredge up, including the deal with T. Bone and Ranch. The garage at San Fernando. The gorilla mask. 'And this is *me*,' he said, 'this is what I am now. The other's all gone. I fucked up. Do you see? I fucked up and I can't get back. I'm sorry, Mum. I'm very, very sorry.'

While he spoke he went on washing her, towelling the wasted muscles, the tissue-paper skin, the black-and-grey pubes that still seemed to grow strongly from her sex. When he thought she was clean he fetched a fresh nightdress, a good warm woollen one, from the chest of drawers. He was hurrying now. She was so cold. Her arms, thin as his wrists, had no force of their own. He had to guide them into the sleeves of the nightie, trying not to get her fingers tangled.

'Larry?'

It was Kirsty. She was standing by the open door in the long T-shirt she had been sleeping in. He wondered how he looked to her, his face glazed with tears, dried shit on his arms. What kind of madman.

She came closer, leaning over Alice from the other side of the bed.

'How is she?' she whispered.

He shook his head. 'I really don't know.'

'I spoke to Alec. Una's coming first thing. We have to call her again if, you know, we get worried.'

'Where's Alec now?'

She touched his cheek. 'He can't deal with any of this. You *know* that.'

He nodded. A tattoo of mulberry bruises was starting to show along the length of Alice's right forearm, but there were no marks on her head.

'You sit with her,' said Kirsty. 'I'll clean up outside.'

'Ella?' he asked.

'Asleep.'

'Good'

'You were talking to her,' said Kirsty. 'To Alice.'

'Yeah. Though I don't suppose she could hear any of it.'

'It's better to think that she can.'

'Yes.'

'Baby? Talk to me some time. Will you do that? Talk to me some time.'

She left him and went on to the landing. 'God, you frightened me,' she said. Alec was kneeling on the top step of the stairs, his hands in the pink rubber gloves Mrs Samson used, a scrubbing brush in one hand, a blue J-cloth in the other. He didn't have his glasses now and in the white light of the overhead bulb he looked about sixteen. He held up a brightly coloured plastic bottle of disinfectant spray that he had found under the sink in the kitchen and asked if she thought it was the right thing, or whether it would bleach the colour out of the carpet.

'I can do that,' she said, soothingly, but he ignored her, and after watching him work for a few moments, she shivered and slipped past him and went down the stairs.

14

On Monday afternoon, just as László was convincing himself of the mission's failure, that he would have to go back to Paris with the bag and find some way of returning it to Emil, they contacted him.

He was walking in the shade on Révay utca, a few metres from the entrance to the hotel on his way back from lunch, when a child – a boy of eight or nine – crossed from the sunlit side and held out an envelope.

'For me?' asked László.

The boy thrust it into his hand and sprinted away in the direction of the Basilica. László looked to the end of the street, and thought he saw a man step hurriedly out of sight, but the light there was too dazzling to see things clearly.

At the steps to the hotel the doorman asked: 'Did the kid want money?'

'No,' said László.

'They try it on with the foreigners sometimes.'

László read the note in his room, then used the box of complimentary matches to burn it in an ashtray. There were only two lines to remember: a place – Statue Park – and a time – 3 p.m., Tuesday. He had heard of the park but had never been there. He asked the woman at reception. She said that it was in the XXII district on the other side of the river. Did he want to go there? They would book a car for him.

'Tomorrow,' said László. 'And I'll need my bag. The black bag.'

'Of course,' she said. If he gave her the ticket now she would have it waiting for him. He gave her the ticket, though he didn't like to hand it over. There was nothing now, nothing material, to connect him to the money. What if she were not on duty tomorrow? What if he had somehow to *prove* the bag was his? But she was there the next afternoon, and the bag was waiting for him behind the desk.

'Heavier than it looks!' she said, passing it to him.

'You're right,' said László, and they wished each other a nice day, like a pair of Americans.

A taxi was parked by the steps of the hotel. The driver, in short-sleeved shirt and sunglasses, introduced himself as Tibor. László sat in the back of the car, the bag tight against his thigh.

They crossed the river, climbed into the hills, and reached the edge of the city. Dusty green verges. Twenty to three. A small golden cross swinging from the rear-view mirror as Tibor gunned the car on a blind bend past a lorry loaded with stone. (As a rule, László avoided taxis with religious trinkets in them after nearly dying in one in Spain that had an entire shrine on the dashboard. Recklessness was a trial of faith for these men.)

There wasn't much to announce the park, just a single billboard a hundred metres before the turn-off. They slowed – though only barely – and swung into an empty forecourt, pulling up in front of a raw-looking, red-brick, neoclassical façade. A kind of folly.

'Want me to wait?' asked Tibor.

'Come back in half an hour.'

'Want to leave the bag?'

'My cameras,' said László, climbing out of the car. 'I may take some shots in the park.'

'Maybe you'll see some pretty girls,' called Tibor, leaning from the window. László raised a hand, but didn't look back.

In the ticket booth a middle-aged woman was reading a magazine. She had taken off her shoes and was resting her stockinged feet on a stool. When she saw László she folded the magazine, swung down her feet with a grunt of effort, and flicked a switch on the CD player behind her head. A men's choir, in full voice, surged from the speakers at a volume that made László wince, and as she tore his ticket from the roll, he saw that the discs were for sale. *Soviet Anthems One. Soviet Anthems Two.* And there were various old communist badges and red stars and even identity books, like the one he had burned in Paris on the rue Cujas a few days after he arrived there. Who bought this stuff? Was it humour? Irony? He took his ticket and his guidebook and walked through the turnstile into the park. The music abruptly ceased. He was, as he had feared, the only person there.

Ahead of him was a space about the size of a soccer pitch. A large formal garden rather than a park, though without a single tree or flower. White sanded paths connected a pattern of grass rings, and around the edges of the rings the statues – those saved from the gleeful acetylene torches – were deployed in the sunshine like pieces of defunct weaponry.

Soldiers, political leaders, abstracts of ideal citizens cast in monumental bonze or sharp-edged steel or stone, their hands raised, their bodies straining forward to greet the future. Some he recognized. Others dated from after '56 and were new to him. But glowing in the mid-afternoon sunshine they were still impressive, still exercised some remnant of their old imperium, the light flashing from their massive shoulders, their bayonets, their metal chins. The strangeness was in seeing them all together, corralled in the park, walled in, as though they might break out and impose themselves again on the squares of the city. It had been wise of someone to insist on keeping them. There was even an element of humiliation to it, a sense that the monuments could be shamed, their failure kept in public view. And how utterly of the past they were! How soundly beaten! But moving among them, László began to feel a flutter of unease, like the survivor of a sea battle washed up among the bodies of his enemies, afraid that one might groan and stagger to his feet and be vengeful.

Their spell was broken (it was always thus) by laughter. A tour bus had arrived, and the park was cheerfully invaded by teenage students from some international summer school, who fanned into the park with worksheets and baseball caps, calling to each other in French and Italian and English, and taking each other's pictures in front of the statues. What did they care for all this scrap metal? Communism was something their fathers and grandfathers had known about, perhaps feared. Now it was the pelt of an old wolf, a shaggy old bear, moth-eaten and ready for the tip. Did they find it odd that people had been so easily duped in the past? That anyone could have been so foolish as to believe in the common ownership of the means of production, the abolition of class, the equal distribution of wealth? Their generation was more sophisticated, more knowing, and yet, thought László, also more childish than the one he had grown up in. He liked their irreverence – no looming fathers with black moustaches to keep *them* in line – but what would they do with this freedom? He worried for them. *Les Enfants du paradis.* A pair of them, necking behind the Heroes of the People's Power memorial ('Those loyal to the people and the Party will be forever remembered . . .') stared at him sharply, as though he were the litter man, or perhaps a pervert, and he moved quickly past them.

It was seven minutes after three. Using the bag as a seat, he squatted in the shadow of Lenin – the incarnation that used to greet the workers at the Manfred Weiss iron factory – and leaned his head against the hem of the dictator's overcoat. He was thirsty, light-headed, longing to be rid of the bag and riding the train home to Paris. Would Kurt forgive him? Excuse it all as menopausal adventuring? A somewhat delayed mid-life crisis? He gazed at the toes of his shoes, the sand in the suede. In this heat it was difficult to think things through, and he began to feel like a figure in the far background of a painting, two or three strokes of the brush, no real face at all, there simply for balance or colour, while in the foreground the emperor's army rode past on their magnificent horses.

It was twenty past before his contact appeared. A tall, darkly dressed figure ambling through the students, another of the famous black bags over his shoulder. It was strange never knowing who would come for you. This one, with his lank hair, his bristly chin, his easy and rather charming smile, looked as though he might play jazz piano in a nightclub.

'A friend of Françoise?' he asked, standing at the side of László, though not too close. László got to his feet.

'To me,' said the man, gazing up at Lenin, 'he always looks as if he's hailing a taxi. But he won't get one here. Not for a long time.'

'Where does it go now?' asked László, nodding to his bag.

'A little farther,' said the other. 'But your part is done. Any trouble?'

'I don't feel I've done anything at all.'

'That's how it should be.' He put his bag next to László's. 'You know, they could plant something here. Grow roses on him. Or is that a very romantic idea?'

'It's a good idea,' said László. 'But we'll have to put it to the committee.'

The man chuckled. 'Of course, Comrade. We must go through the proper channels.'

He reached down and swung László's bag on to his shoulder.

'It's heavy,' said László.

'Good. You have a car?'

'Yes.'

'You go first.'

'Do we shake hands?'

'It's quite optional,' said the man. He held out his hand. 'Until next time.'

*   *   *

In the carpark, Tibor was sharing a story with the driver of the tour bus. The only other vehicle was a small, slightly battered Toyota that presumably belonged to the contact.

'The heat bothering you?' asked Tibor, opening the rear door.

'A little,' said László. His shirt was stuck to his back, and from his chest he thought he could hear a distinctive wheezing, like those poor asthmatics he sometimes came across in the street or the Métro, fumbling in their pockets for an inhaler. More of them all the time, it seemed. A sly epidemic.

Tibor started the engine. The air-conditioning came on. 'Where to?' he asked. 'Back to the hotel?'

'No,' said László, after a pause. 'Drop me by the Gellért. I'll walk the rest of the way. It'll do me good.'

'You're the boss,' said Tibor, and he bounced the car on to the road, the rear wheels kicking up a cloud of dust that hung for several seconds in the air behind them.

By the terrace café outside the Gellért Spa, László settled his fare, then set off towards Petofi bridge, turned right on Lajos ut, and entered the grounds at the back of the Technical University, where students, relaxing in the sunshine, sat on wooden benches, or lounged in small groups on the grass, reading, talking, flirting.

It was here that Péter had studied in his first year of training to become an electrical engineer. László had often visited him, and had memories of tall green corridors, the smell of soldering irons, the whirr of the machinery in the demonstration rooms. Péter had even tried to persuade László to join him at the school, but László had had quite different ambitions. A sharp-looking, sharp-minded young man, vain and shy and talkative, he had harboured immoderate dreams of artistic glory. He thought he might be a great film director (he was a regular at the Corvin Film Palace), or some kind of Hungarian Picasso. He wanted to live freely, have a lakeside villa at Balaton, perhaps even work in Hollywood like Mihaly Kertesz. For that one summer of his life – before anything had been attempted, anything failed at – everything felt possible. Why not? He was seventeen, fired by love, and all around him, as though history were rooted in the excitements of his own heart, his country, frozen for so long like a kingdom in a fairytale, was beginning to thaw.

In July '56, First Secretary Rákosi, the arch-toad, the arch-Stalinist, was dismissed on the orders of the Moscow Politburo. In October, they exhumed László Rajk, hanged after a show trial in '49 (his old friend Kádár had persuaded him to 'confess'), and reburied him with state honours at the Kerepes cemetery. In Warsaw the Poles defied Krushchev, and across Budapest, as the weather turned crisp and hoar frost glittered on the trees along the Danube, the first mass meetings began. Here, at the Technical University, the evening of the 22nd, Jozsef Szilágyi and István Marián spoke of 'the sunrise of modern Hungarian history', and the next day a crowd of students and workers (many of the latter still in their overalls from the factory floors) marched to the statue of the Polish hero, General Bem, and crossed the bridge to Parliament Square. 'Now or never!' they chanted. 'Russians out! Nagy into government!'

From believing they could do nothing, the people were suddenly convinced of their power. Changing the world might, after all, require nothing more than the belief that change was possible. In the space of a few hours, thousands of minds blossomed with the same remarkable idea: freedom. On a rooftop by the square, László saw a young woman waving a Hungarian tricolour with the Soviet insignia torn from the middle. By nightfall the bronze Stalin at City Park had been toppled and the radio station was under siege. The government panicked; threatened crackdowns; appealed for calm; offered amnesties; but nobody was listening to them any more. Bookstores were raided and Russian books burned on bonfires on the streets. Councils were formed. Armouries looted. On the boulevards, Russian tanks, twitching on their own fuel slicks and belching clouds of diesel fumes, hunted their invisible enemy. Everywhere, rumours of fresh fighting, of massacres, of victory. And under the dust from shelled apartment blocks and burned-out shops, under the tangled tramlines and the red and golden leaves of shattered trees, corpses lay in postures exclusive to the dead, many of them Red Army conscripts no older than László, boys from Kharkov and Kiev, who must at the end have wondered how they had earned such hatred, why children were killing them.

László pushed the sweat from his eyes, and walked along the drive to where it was crossed by double rows of squat stone pillars that carried a passageway to one of the outbuildings. He put down the bag and squinted ahead: the drive curved towards a second gate, hidden from the pillars, then as now, by a line of trees. He could not quite believe he was back. Was there some buried fragment here – a scrap of cloth, a cartridge case – that would prove it? But this was it all right. *This* was where he had stood in the grey of a November afternoon, waiting for Péter and Zoli to return. They had taken the Skoda – the old black 'Spartak' – to the Szentkiralyi barracks to bring back ammunition. The rest of the gang – Feri, Joska, Karcsi and Anna – were in the college print room, running off another batch of proclamations and demands, to be fly posted around the city after dark. László was on guard duty (it was merely his turn), patrolling between the pillars in leather cap and belted jacket, his nose and ears ringing with the cold. He had been given the precious tommy-gun, and Feri, the old man of the group at twenty-two, the only one who had actually done any military training, had explained how to use it.

'Don't shoot like a gangster, Laci. Fire from the shoulder. Short bursts. You've got seventy-two bullets in the magazine. That's enough to hold off a battalion. And if it jams for Christ's sake don't look down the barrel or you'll blow your head off. Got it?'

Got it.

He had not expected to use it. Thus far he had avoided even handling a gun – there were always plenty of others who couldn't wait to get hold of one – keeping himself useful with driving and stretcher-bearing and running errands. But when he heard the car, and knew from the speed at which it was coming that something was wrong, he dragged the weapon from his shoulder, pushed the safety off, and thought himself ready. From the gates on Budafokí ut there came the smack of metal on metal, and seconds later the Skoda swung into view, Zoli at the wheel fighting to keep control but coming much too fast, swerving to avoid the trees but somehow bouncing off the side of one and toppling the car on to the driver's side, where it spun in a sheet of sparks before coming to a stop.

Almost immediately, Péter was hauling himself from the shattered passenger window. He saw László, shouted a warning, and pointed back up the drive, though there was no need. László had already seen the other car, a Russian military saloon pulling up twenty metres from the Skoda, three men inside (two in uniform, one in the back in plain clothes), who flung open their doors and began to shoot with pistols. Seeing it again, seeing the distances involved, it seemed extraordinary how even in the fading light they could have kept missing. Half in, half out of the car, Péter was a simple enough target, yet between them they must have fired a dozen times before they hit him. Then Péter had stopped struggling for a moment and became utterly still, as though the bullet were a thought, an idea, the most extraordinary he had ever had. The second caught him as he slithered down the blackened underside of the car. He cried out. A shocked, aggrieved sound. A sound of appalled protest at the realization of what was happening to him. The third dropped him on to his knees, though even then he didn't stop, but kept crawling towards the shelter of the pillars.

All this László saw through the loop of the tommy-gun's forward sights. He had raised the gun and pressed it to his shoulder, just as Feri had instructed him. He had drawn a line over Péter's head to the plainclothes man, the most dangerous of the three, the one who fired with the greatest deliberation. And so intent were they on murdering Péter, such an appetite, they had not even noticed László, braced in the shadows, dark beside the dark of the stone. But as his finger touched the steel kiss-curl of the trigger, he knew that he would never pull it. Whatever it was a man needed in his nature to destroy another, he simply did not possess it. The act was beyond him. He could not kill. Could not. And this he learned about himself at the very moment when the human being he adored most fervently of all was gunned down by men who *ought* to die, but whom he could not bring himself to harm.

How long did it last? As long, he thought, as it took to tell it. Long enough. Then the *crack! crack!* of a rifle from one of the ground-floor windows to the right, the plainclothes man slumping against the car, the uniforms bundling him on to the back seat, and the big car reversing at speed, swaying its plated flanks like some ungainly animal startled at a water hole. Feri sprinted from the double doors behind László, wrenched the gun from his grip, and set off in pursuit, shouting wildly and firing from the hip, gangster-style. At the wreck of the Skoda, Karcsi and Joska knocked in the windscreen with rifle butts and dragged out the unconscious Zoli. Anna, crying his name, ran to where Péter lay between the car and the pillars, his jacket torn open beneath his ribs, and so much blood, and such a smell of blood, one of the bullets must have burst his liver. She knelt beside him, pressed her cheek to his lips, then turned to László, gazing up at him with such mysterious intensity that he realized – sudden shock of embarrassment and gratitude – that she knew everything, knew exactly what Péter had been to him, and had guessed it long ago. Their secret! Had she also, then (this girl majestic in the presence of death), understood why he had not pulled the trigger? Why he had abandoned his friend to the killers?

When Feri came back they wrapped Péter in a tarpaulin and carried him, all five of them, into one of the classrooms, and laid him on the table. Nobody reproached László – if nothing else, the utter dumb misery on his face would have made accusations impossible – but he spent the night apart from them, curled in a ball under his coat, shivering, while in the distance scattered gunfire played out the last hours of the revolution. Nagy was gone; General Maléter a prisoner of the Russians; and though the radio continued to broadcast appeals, the world had its eyes elsewhere, and there would be no help for Hungary, no miraculous intervention. In the fighting by the Killian barracks the next evening, Feri was killed by a grenade blast. At the end of November, Joska and Anna were arrested, beaten for days, and sent to Tokol internment camp on charges of armed conspiracy. Zoli went into hiding. Karsci fled the country. Two hundred thousand that year, László among them, crossing the winter marshes with their suitcases, their parcels, their spoiled lives.

A girl with black hair and a little silver stud in her nose put her hand on his arm and asked if he was unwell.

'It's just the heat,' said László.

'Sit in the shade,' she said, leading him to a bench under the trees. 'I thought you were going to faint.'

'I just need to breathe,' he said. 'Really, I'm feeling much better already.'

'Shall I fetch you some water?'

'I'm fine now,' he said. 'You're very kind.'

'Sure?'

'Thank you.'

They smiled at each other, and she left him on the bench. For a last time he looked to where, beyond the pillars, a breeze was pooling the heads of the chestnut trees. It was done. He had come back and stood as a penitent. He had paid his dues of memory and love. He had done what was possible. And though he knew he could never entirely forgive himself for Péter Kosáry's death, and certainly could not put it right forty years after the fact, could not now pull the trigger, he wanted his freedom. One fatal moment had held him captive for two-thirds of his life, and it was time for that to stop.

He joined his hands like a Buddhist and bowed his head. The gesture somewhat surprised him. Had he seen Kurt do it during his yoga practice at the apartment? But the impulse was honest, and the occasion demanded its ritual. Then he stood, shouldered the bag, waved to the girl on the grass, and returned to the road, seeing, in the oracle of his imagination, the other bag, the heavy one, already being handed on (another meeting, another dry exchange), until it reached the men in the smoked-glass BMWs, the new kingmakers of the old Soviet empire, and a deal was struck, so that on some moonless night Emil Bexheti and his friends could come down from the mountains and cross the border in hushed columns. In this at least he had played his part. Who knew what else he might do? Strange how a little faith may strike a man so late in life, how bad beginnings can at last be overcome. László the Bold? It amused him to think he might now die an idealist, a man of action, and he crossed the Szabadság bridge to Pest, his shadow on the brown water striding behind a nexus of spars, unhindered.

15

All morning there were flowers, bouquets that arrived from Interflora or were dropped off by friends who said, 'I won't come in just now.' When Larry answered the door they reminded him of their names and said how nice it was to see him again, what a comfort it must be for Alice to have him home. 'Give her our love.'

'I will.'

'And tell her we're all thinking of her.'

'I promise.'

There weren't enough vases for so many flowers. They used buckets, saucepans. Even the washbasin in the downstairs toilet, a spray of lilies.

In the kitchen, Ella and Kirsty baked a cake. They wrote 'HAPPY BIRTHDAY GRANDMA' in pink icing, and dotted the 'i' with a candied lemon diamond. Mrs Samson arrived at midday. She put on an apron, rolled up her sleeves, and made watercress sandwiches and a batch of scones to be eaten with clotted cream and the last of last year's bramble jelly. When she worked she liked to have the radio on, a station with sing-along music and the local news. The weather forecast was for skies clear all day, temperatures in the mid-seventies, a small chance of rain after dark.

Alec and Larry carried the trestle table from the workroom

into the orchard. They set it in its usual place – the bulbs were still strung overhead, pointlessly – and spread it with darned white cloths, then brought out chairs from the dining room, the dark wood and dark leather a little strange and comical in the brightness of the garden, like the men in their frock-coats in *Déjeuner sur l'herbe*. Larry lit a cigarette and sat at the table. He had been drinking, but not heavily. Alec sat opposite him.

'The big day,' said Larry.

Alec nodded. He was dressed in black chinos with a dark collarless shirt. He had his glasses on with the sunshade attachment clipped to the front.

'Come to America,' said Larry.

'OK,' said Alec.

'I mean it.'

'OK.'

'Stick with family. You could learn to surf. Take yoga classes.' He chuckled. 'Ella would love it.'

'And what would I do there?'

'The same as here. I doubt you'd even need a green card. You should think about it.'

'OK.'

'Seriously.'

'What about you?' said Alec. 'What's to stop you coming here? You're not doing the show any more.'

Larry shook his head. 'I've got a couple of other projects cooking.'

'What sort of projects?'

'Anyway, I wouldn't fit in here.'

'You used to.'

'I remember.'

'You used to fit in perfectly.'

'A thousand years ago.'

'I thought things were difficult for you over there. I thought that was the point.'

Larry made a face. 'I've thought about it once or twice. But it's too late for all that. All that *coming back* shit. I've got a house out there. A family! And coming back now would be like saying I'd been wrong all along. That it had all been a mistake.' He flicked his cigarette away. 'America's the only big idea I've ever had. If I stop believing in it it's like I stop believing in happiness or adventure or fuck knows. Great cars, great sex. Love.' He leaned across the table. 'America's my optimistic heart. Do you see?'

Alec nodded, but Larry reckoned he had heard no more than one word in three. There were changes in his brother, certain unsettling alterations that dated from that fuss between them in the kitchen. It wasn't just the distractedness, the sense of him looking in all the time at some demanding secret; there was a new control, a self-discipline that seemed at times to verge upon the manic, but which was nonetheless somehow effective. The little-boy-lost look was gone, that air of helplessness and incipient panic that had been so obvious at Heathrow. What underlay these changes was hard to say, but the night before last, out under the stars for a smoke, trying to put his *own* thoughts in order, Larry had seen through the summerhouse window his brother in agitated debate – gesturing, grimacing, pressing his brow – all this despite his being utterly alone in there. A troubling sight (and a good deal more than he had wanted to see), for what question was it that needed such emphasis, such violent settlement?

He raised an arm and waved to Una, who was coming towards them in a dress the colour of the grass. 'Guess what?' said Larry. 'Alec's going to come and live in America.'

'Is that so?'

'He won't go without you,' said Larry.

She grinned, touched her hair. 'What time are your guests coming?' she asked.

'Around three,' said Alec. 'Though there won't be many.'

'Do you think Mum can stay down for long?' asked Larry.

'I'd say she'd be fine for an hour. I'm going to see her now. Will you bring her down when she's ready?'

'Call me,' said Larry.

In Alice's bedroom a bluebottle flew revolutions in the shaded air. Una opened the curtains and sat by the bed, then lifted one of Alice's hands from the covers and cradled it between her own. Though Alice had survived the fall, the shock of it had snapped something in her that would not show up on X-rays or CAT scans. A thread, or a delicate valve like the ones inside the old TV sets, something that could not be repaired and which had left her like this, struggling to live, struggling to die, waiting for the next fall, the next seizure, the next small-hours crisis.

The day after the accident, when at last she had been able to speak and make some sense, she had said, 'Death's taking me a piece at a time,' and she had wept so piteously Una had had to turn away, afraid of what the words moved in her, the sorrow that burned behind her own eyes. Here, with the

Valentines, she had strayed across the line. She had dropped her guard and in the end she would pay the price for it, grieving on her own without the comfort of a family around her. It was a failure they had been warned against in training. Inappropriate emotion. It was unprofessional, and it didn't really help anyone, didn't make her a better nurse. But how were you supposed to control it? You couldn't give the heart orders – thus far and no farther. It wasn't human.

She squeezed Alice's hand and folded down the sheets to check for signs of bedsores, discovering on her back – the coccyx – a patch of irritated skin, which she treated with the Granuflex. The whole puzzle of Alice's skeleton was visible now. The long bones jutting against her skin, her eyes sunk into the sockets of her skull. She had taken no solids since the fall, so her body scavenged on itself, eking out another week or month with scraps of protein, lipids, a last swirl of glucose. Life, which a child could dab out with the pressure of her thumb, was also mystifyingly persistent, the flesh outliving the will, all pleasure, all usefulness, going on and on in the grip of some biochemical imperative, something fashioned right at the start, before we had bigger brains or better hands. Sheer blind tenacity.

She tucked her hair behind her ears and watched the bluebottle crawl across the face of the mirror on the chest of drawers. Comfort was all that mattered now. To find among the vials and bottles something useful, something to match Alice's suffering without making her nauseous or terrifying her with hallucinations. What else? Light a candle for her? Say a prayer? She was out of practice. Hail Mary and all that. She hadn't prayed since she was a girl in Derry, when the whole family used to kneel in the front room at the sound of the angelus bell on the television, and her father would recite the rosary. That was all behind her now, like the sea light and the banter and the checkpoints. She had a Buddha at home, one of those hollow brass ones, part household god, part paperweight, and sometimes she put flowers next to it, though she didn't know much about Buddhism except it seemed a kind sort of religion, less bullying than most. What she did know about was nutrition, care planning, morbidity. Whatever it was you learned about the psychologies of grief and courage sitting through the last hours of forty, fifty people. But what it all actually *meant* (the slow destruction of a woman like Alice Valentine) she had no idea. She was twenty-seven, for Christ's sake. She lived on her own in a small rented flat she didn't much like, and two or three times a week she took Temazepam to stop the dead visiting her in her sleep.

Kirsty came up to help with the dressing (the young women liked each other and worked well together), and though there was very little from among her clothes that Alice could still wear, they found a summer frock of blue-and-white cotton, and a woollen shawl, cream-coloured, to wrap about her shoulders. As they dressed her, gently rolling her between their hands, Alice dozed and muttered, and on waking seemed surprised to find herself transformed, her hair brushed out, the big white trainers on her feet. Kirsty kissed her cheek and ran downstairs to call for Larry.

'You don't have to go out, Alice,' said Una. 'Not if you'd rather stay up here.'

'Out?' said Alice, her eyes widening. 'Where?'

'Into the garden. For the party.'

Alice nodded. 'Who's in charge?' she asked.

'Well. Would you like Alec and Larry to be in charge?'

'Write,' said Alice, holding out a hand.

Una took the felt-tip she used for her notes, tried it first on her own skin, and then wrote across Alice's palm: *Alec and Larry in charge*.

'How's that?' she asked.

Larry carried his mother down the stairs and settled her into the wheelchair at the bottom, lifting her feet on to the hinged rests, then steering her through the living room into the kitchen.

'Happy birthday, Mrs V!' said Mrs Samson, touching for a moment Alice's shoulder and leaving a faint row of flour prints on the blue of the dress.

Alice showed her hand.

'That's it,' agreed Mrs Samson. 'The boys are in charge all right.'

They manoeuvred her on to the terrace, but getting her up the bank on to the lawn was more difficult. Alec raised the small wheels at the front, tilting the chair backwards, while Larry leaned his weight from behind.

'I can help!' called Osbourne, hurrying towards them from the direction of the stile. 'Many happy returns,' he panted.

'Where's Stephen?' she asked.

'This side please, Dennis,' said Larry.

'Righto.'

They gathered around the chair, lifting it up the bank like Sicilian villagers struggling out of the sea with a seated Madonna in re-enactment of some half-remembered miracle. Ella watched from the top of the bank, a scarlet balloon in her hand.

In the orchard the tablecloths were patterned with the shadows of the leaves. Larry wheeled his mother to the head of the table. Una came out with a sunhat she had found in the hall, a large straw affair with a wide ribbon that tied under the chin. In the shade of the brim Alice's face was hardly visible. A butterfly settled for a moment on the stillness of her arm, then went on, drunkenly, across slabs of green light.

'Someone's here,' called Kirsty.

It was Judith and Christopher Joy, who had strolled from their cottage in matching linen jackets and panama hats. They carried gifts: a pot of luxurious hand cream from Jolly's in Bath and, from a beach in County Galway, a large pebble that Judith Joy had painted in healing colours. Next to arrive was Mrs Dzerzhinsky. Her present was an illustrated calf-bound edition of Gibran's *The Prophet*, and as she put it into Alice's hands Alec overheard her murmur words in a language that was not English, a blessing perhaps, or a piece of folk wisdom from the old country, wherever that was. He had noted this recently, how people needed to communicate to Alice something intense and private, to give voice to the seriousness she provoked in them, as if her affliction flushed out the trivial from their lives and made them all mystics and philosophers.

The last of the guests was the art teacher, Miss Lynne. She said it looked like a scene from one of those endlessly long but delicious Italian films. She tucked her head under the brim of Alice's hat to kiss her. She said she'd love to paint it all.

Mrs Samson brought out a tray with two large teapots on it. Larry carried the sandwiches and the scones. On Alice's right, Una sat with a box of tissues on her lap, wiping Alice's chin when the juice she sipped through a straw spilled from the slack of her mouth. Behind them, the oxygen bottle lay in the grass like an unexploded bomb.

When the scones had been eaten, Ella and Kirsty went to the kitchen and came out with the cake. Larry used his Zippo to light the candles – one for every ten years of Alice's life – and while the candles burned they stood up to sing 'Happy Birthday', finishing the song with a burst of applause. Ella blew out the candles. They clapped again and took their slices of cake, and after trying a few forkfuls of sugary sponge and praising it, the guests began to take their leave.

Mrs Dzerzhinsky blamed her tears on hay fever ('Worse every year!'). Miss Lynne knelt by the side of the wheelchair, then went, with a hurried wave, through the trees to her car. Christopher Joy, sweeping off his hat, kissed Alice's hand in a gesture that was genuinely gallant. Osbourne said he would volunteer for the clearing-up detail, and in the kitchen, his jacket dropped over the back of a chair, he tried to make himself useful by passing absorbent paper towels to Mrs Samson, who wept openly and noisily as she wrapped the leftover sandwiches in clingfilm.

Una moved Alice into the shade and untying the sunhat gave her a few minutes with the gas bottle. Alec, coming out for the last plates, stood unobserved under the trees, studying them as though one day he would be called on to recite the details. The wasps dancing around the cake crumbs. The silvery tracks of the wheelchair in the grass. The cat padding through a private corridor of air. And at the heart of the picture, his mother, her eyes shut above the plastic mouthpiece, her eyelids grey and flat and leaden. Would he have pitied her more if she had been a stranger? Some woman whose name he did not know and to whom he owed nothing but an ordinary debt of compassion? Then at least he would have felt something manageable, not this tangle of pity and fear; this childish revulsion like a weapon he did not know whether to turn against himself, or her. So why not leave like the party guests? Take the car. Get out. He had done it before, running from that gulag of a school he had taught in (thirty-five fourteen-year-olds, some almost savage); a week's fugue of which he could remember very little other than a noise in his head like the hissing of pylons, and an image, strangely beautiful, of the lights from the esplanade reflecting on the wet shingle he was walking on. No one would be surprised if it happened again. They would be expecting it.

'Who's there?' asked Una, shading her eyes.

'Just me,' he said. He came forward and started to stack the plates. She was squinting at him, smiling, and he saw that the sun had brought out a dozen freckles on her nose and cheeks, which made her look younger and somehow carefree.

He put the wicker tray on the table and quickly loaded the last of the crockery. He didn't want to disturb them – didn't think he should be there with them at all – but as he moved away Alice opened her eyes, tugged the mask from her face, and called out after him, a single garbled word of protest that froze him in mid-stride.

'Mum?'

But whatever it was she wouldn't repeat it. The effort had set her off and she needed her gas again, her oxygen. It was several minutes before Alec realized that the word had been '*menteur*', and that she had called him a liar.

At half past five, Una came to the summerhouse to say goodbye. Alice was back in bed, she said, resting. Alec thanked her for staying so long. He thought she would leave then (he could think of nothing else to say to her), but she stayed, looking round as if she had never been in the place before.

'I wouldn't mind a hideout myself,' she said. 'Somewhere like this.' She stepped up to where he was sitting and reached past his shoulder to open the manuscript on the desk.

'It's funny,' she said, turning over the pages, 'how this makes sense to you and none at all to me. What's this here? This bit?'

He twisted in the seat and looked to where her finger pointed. 'It says, *Who here is cruel enough to leave a brother behind? A father underground? A sweetheart in hell?*'

'You don't like me looking at it,' she said, standing back.

Alec pushed the manuscript to the edge of the desk. 'It just reminds me how much I still have to do. That's all.'

'You'll get it done.'

'I'll have to.'

'You will.'

'You've been very kind to us,' he said.

'I haven't done so much.'

'No.' He shook his head. 'Really kind.'

'It's my job,' she said.

'Even so.'

'May I?' She gently lifted his glasses from his face. 'I can't talk to you with these on. You look like a hit-man.'

'Sorry.' He took the glasses from her and unclipped the shade attachment. Una leaned against the whitewashed wall, watching him.

'I know it's an awful time for you all,' she said. 'And people sometimes think it goes on and on for ever. Always the same. But it doesn't.' She paused as if to gauge whether or not she was making any sense to him. 'People think they'll never be happy again.'

'Happy?'

'Yes,' she said, smiling broadly. 'Remember happy?'

'I've no idea what you think of me,' he said.

'What do you think I think?'

He shook his head.

'Well . . .' She paused. 'I think you're a good person.'

'Really?'

'A good son. Does that surprise you so much?'

'Perhaps.'

'It shouldn't.'

'Are *you* happy?' he asked.

'My father used to tell us that happiness and unhappiness are two dogs that follow each other around. When you saw one, the other wasn't far off. He didn't really believe in happiness. Not as something you spent your life trying to get.'

'What did he believe in?'

She shrugged. 'The Pope. Not getting into debt. Cleaning the heels of your shoes as well as the toes. I think he was saving

the family wisdom for the boys.' She fell silent, watching him.
'You're in a dream,' she said.

'Sorry.'

'You want me to ask Larry to do her medicine tonight?'

'It's easier for me,' he said.

'If you're sure.'

'I'm sure.'

He walked to the door of the summerhouse with her. A
breeze loaded with grass smells and soil smells and the warm
ozonous whiff of the air itself blew the fine ends of a dozen
hairs across her cheeks.

'You know how to get hold of me,' she said. 'You'll be all
right?'

When she had gone he lingered in the doorway a moment,
then went quickly to the table and opened *Oxygène* to the
last page (*Hammer blows, steel on rock . . .*), where a twist
of newspaper was Sellotaped to the inside of the card binding.
He unpicked the tape with his nail, unwrapped the capsule,
and rolled it into his palm. He heard Ella's voice, and looked
up to the window in time to see her go by, hand in hand with
Kirsty. They were a good thirty feet away, and he didn't think
they could have seen anything. What could they have seen?
They were probably planning to water the garden together,
now it was cooler.

He placed the manuscript back on to the shelf beside the
dictionaries and briefly laid his head against the spines of
the books, as if the mere touch of them were helpful in
some way. Consoling. Everything was in its place now. In

his hand he held the thread that ran through the labyrinth; he had only to follow it. There were no more decisions to make or to unmake; no more of the vile anticipation. He felt a calmness, a quietness on the far side of thinking, that was immensely restful. He looked at Lázár, who stared back from his winter's day in the Luxembourg. Would he understand all this? How nobody could be expected to be weak *all* the time. One day, thought Alec, he would confess it to him in some Paris bar or London hotel, then see how this man who had handled tommy-guns reacted.

Going into the house, he met his brother coming out.

'Seen Kirsty and Ella?'

'Bottom of the garden,' said Alec. He saw that Larry had put on a clean shirt, and carried, almost hidden behind his thigh, a posy of a half-dozen small blooms and herbs – honeysuckle, lavender, rosemary – the stems wrapped in a scrap of baking foil. He looked chastened, excited.

'Catch you later,' he said, grinning, and they crossed, one brother stepping out into the light of the terrace, the other going into the house, going up the stairs, and opening the door to his mother's room.

16

So what was left to be done? László had returned to find himself forgiven, understood, well loved, an Odysseus with bloodshot eyes and no rivals to scatter. Of his adventures he had told whatever could be safely told, and answered, honestly, the few questions Kurt had put to him. He began to think he might welcome a reproach. Such largesse, such big-heartedness, was slightly daunting. To be so trusted! Was he not escaping too lightly? But when he took the young man's face between his hands, searching out some reservation, something undeclared, he found there only the clear blue depths, the eye-part of a smile.

That first night László slept for thirteen hours and felt his life being rearranged in dreams. He was not quite familiar to himself. He was shedding a skin, discovering, in his fifty-ninth year, a self still supple with life.

The next night, a waning moon rose over a city in thrall to rhythm. It was the Fête de la Musique, and every bar, each café large and small – French, Brazilian, Arab, Russian, Vietnamese, even those little places on the side streets where a good night's business was half a dozen glasses of mint tea or screw-top *rouge* – were suddenly reckless with music and dancing. Brass bands, flamenco, crooning black-eyed chanteuses, every kind of drum imaginable. No need to *go* anywhere to dance; enough to find space in the road and start to sway. By ten o'clock many of the roads were impassable but no one complained. The police kept out of sight, parked up somewhere, smoking and teasing their dogs. It felt like the end of a war, but more democratic, more personal, as if everyone had won a war of their own, a private war against a private enemy, emerging – for a night at least – victorious from the long campaign.

For László, squeezing with Kurt through the throng on rue Oberkampf, only one difficulty remained, one last stone in his shoe. Laurence Wylie had called while he was away, had wanted him, had said she *needed* him, and then, finding he was unavailable, had become angry and rung off distraught. Several times since his return he had tried to call her back but had succeeded only in talking to the answerphone, where the sound of her voice delivering the speak-after-the-beep message had pierced him. It was intolerable that such a woman should go under, intolerable and unjust and wrong. In his last message, left that afternoon, he had told them both to wait in at the apartment. He would come to them. They would open a bottle together. Stay in, go out. Whatever they wished.

Privately, he was determined to share his new energy with them, his new faith. His new manliness! And if he could get them out tonight, surely they would find themselves stepping a waltz – they had loved to dance, had been the kind of couple other dancers stopped to admire – and then they would remember laughter and lightness and the times before, and their poor bruised hearts would begin to warm.

*　　*　　*

At rue St Maur, they pushed through the ranks of a small salsa orchestra and walked to the rue du Deguerry, where they knocked for several minutes at the door of the Wylies' apartment. László shrugged, but he was becoming agitated. Where the hell *were* they?

'We could try Le Robinet,' said Kurt. 'If they're out drinking they'll show up there sooner or later.'

So they went back to the music, to streets still snug with the heat of the day, and worked their way around to the boulevard Ménilmontant, where among the couscous restaurants and sweet-pastry shops, Le Robinet, ablaze with light like a small ship on fire, was the scene of yet another impromptu party. It was not, in truth, much of a bar at all: a dozen tables, a curved *comptoir* to the left of the door, a cramped steamy kitchen in the back, but what it lacked in size and facilities it made up for in character, and was generally considered (by the discerning bon vivants and barflies of the Eleventh) superior to all its rivals.

'László!'

It was Angela, the *patronne*, waving to him from the step beside the till, her command post. László fought his way through to her and they kissed.

'Have you seen Laurence? Or Franklin?'

'Not for a week,' she said. Then added: 'Someone else was looking for them.' She pointed towards the back of the bar. 'Isn't that Whatshisname?'

At a table by the kitchen hatch, Karol was holding court among a huddle of young men and women, devotees of culture, drawn by the flame of the old writer's promiscuous charm. He had one of the waitresses on his lap (all highly educated girls) but catching sight of László, he eased her off, stood up on stiff legs, and clasped the playwright in his arms.

'You look different,' he said, leaning back to scrutinize the other's appearance.

'Even at my age,' laughed László, 'I'm still growing a face.'

'*Your* age,' mocked Karol. 'A boy!' He turned to the group at the table. 'Now here is a real artist. Allow me to present Maître László Lázár, and his faithful companion, Herr Engelbrecht.'

They ordered a lot more wine. Space was made for László on the banquette, and he too was lionized with a warmth that made him wonder what it was these youngsters saw, or thought they saw. It turned his head a little. Even now, after so many years, he found it hard to make the connection between what he laboured over so privately in his study and the manner in which he was received on occasions like this. Were they *really* interested in him? What did they want? But it was too loud for any serious conversation, and Angela, a woman Ingres might have done justice to, ordered them on to their feet. 'Have you forgotten how to dance?' she cried. 'Or do you mean to talk each other to death!'

So they danced, fifty or more, crushed together in the heat and the smoke. László found himself nose to nose, hip to hip, with a woman of Middle Eastern looks, a real beauty with a thrillingly stern expression on her face. Karol swayed with the queenly Angela, while Kurt, moving with that sweet, politely sexy style of his, was much in demand with both sexes and all persuasions. There were two accordionists installed now, a pair László had seen before playing on the Métro; children of Ceaucescu or Hoxa, who spent their days scurrying from carriage to carriage with one eye open for the patrols, one ear cocked for a cry of 'Papers!'. They played some Piaf numbers – 'Johnny', 'La Foule', 'Sous le ciel de Paris' – then gypsy music. Tzigane! They knew what was wanted, and on a night like this any musician could sway a crowd to tears or to frenzy. It was exhausting, but no one wanted it to end. Why stop when there was still beer and wine and cane-liquor to drink? Why stop before the music stopped?

At five o'clock, Angela had had enough. She cleared the bar without much ceremony, though an inner circle of favourites was allowed to linger, drink coffee and regain their senses. László, Kurt and Karol were among the last to go, leaving only a serenely drunken Englishman who apparently lived in the bar, and clearly hoped the party might somehow be made to start again.

Outside, the three friends gathered under the trees that lined the central walkway of the boulevard, and breathed in air cool as tap water. László tilted back his head, sore eyes looking into the great scooped pearl of the morning sky.

'The floating happiness?' asked Karol.

'The floating happiness,' agreed László, feeling foolish at having to wipe the tears from his cheeks.

'Once upon a time,' said Karol, 'I could simply miss out a night's sleep. A "white night" hardly troubled me at all, but now . . .'

They made their slow goodbyes. The shutter at Le Robinet rattled down. Kurt and László seemed like the last people abroad.

'Home?' asked Kurt. Then seeing László's hesitation, he said: 'Let's go back, have something to eat, relax a little, and phone them in a few hours. If they were out last night they won't want us calling on them now.'

The Citroën – László's prized maroon-and-silver DS23 'Pallas' – was parked outside a charcuterie on boulevard Voltaire, and with László at the wheel they headed south, passing the July column and crossing the river where the last of the night lingered in bruise-coloured shadows under the bridges.

At the apartment they drank fresh coffee and made each other laugh, wondering – in ever-wider loops of absurdity – how the Garbargs had spent the night. Then László stripped off in the bedroom, put on his bathrobe (he favoured a Japanese yukata for the summer), and went to take a shower. He had just worked up a good lather of shampoo on his head when Kurt leaned into the room. László shook the foam from his ears and turned off the shower. 'What?'

'Laurence. On the machine. I think you'd better hear it.'

Wrapped in a towel, László hurried to the study and stood dripping on the parquet as Kurt rewound the tape. The message was halting and mostly unintelligible, but there was no mistaking the desperation in her voice. It sounded as if some ferocious undertow was pulling her away even as she spoke. Something had happened, or was perhaps about to happen (it wasn't clear which). Something very bad indeed.

'When did she call?'

Kurt checked the Minitel screen on the front of the phone, then looked at his watch. 'Just over an hour ago. What do you want to do?'

'You try to call. I'll put some clothes on.'

In the bathroom he rinsed off the shampoo, then dressed

in the same smoky clothes he'd been wearing in Le Robinet. He was back in the study in five minutes.

'Anything?'

'Nothing. They've even switched off the answerphone.'

'OK. Let's go.'

They took the stairs rather than wait upon the stately descent of the elevator, then drove in silence through the littered streets, the car's long bonnet slicing the air, the needle of the speedometer flickering at sixty as they motored on to an almost traffic-less Beaumarchais. How tender the city looked! The first of the early risers carrying a newspaper or walking a dog. The street cleaners in their green overalls hosing the pavements and opening the sluices; fresh water running in slack silver ropes around the wheels of the parked cars. Impossible to think any crisis could occur at such an hour, and when, pulling up at rue du Deguerry, there was no police van or Samu ambulance, László began to wonder whether he was overreacting, whether the call had been nothing but the sequel to another fight, and the pair of them were upstairs now, sleeping it off and snoring like ogres.

He left the car by the church, crossed the road to the street door and tapped in the code. Inside, the courtyard was scrubbed and chilly. The gardienne would not be in for another hour or two. A neat little 'fermé' sign hung from a nail on the door of her office.

They found Laurence in the gloom of the third-floor landing. Two female neighbours were in attendance, sombre, grey-haired women in slippers and bed-jackets. László vaguely recognized one of them. Madame Bassoul. Blumen. Some such.

'Where have you *been*?' asked Laurence. She slapped him, hard, then put her arms around his neck.

'Is Franklin upstairs?' he asked.

'He has a gun, monsieur,' said the woman László recognized. 'Like so . . .' She indicated with her hands the dimensions of the weapon. 'We wanted to call the police, but Madame has expressly forbidden it.'

'He pointed it at *me*,' said Laurence, shuddering at the memory. 'I had to run out of the door. He's crazy now. Completely crazy.'

She looked very close to collapse. László stroked her hair. 'You know he wouldn't have used it.'

She pushed him away. 'You think I'm inventing this?' Her voice broke in a sob. 'He'll use it on himself, László. I've been waiting for the noise. I can't stand it.'

The women came forward to support her, but as they gathered her between them, those sturdy attendants, she looked at László, a sudden sharp glance that made the hairs prickle on his neck, for it was precisely the look of the woman in the painting, the bride in the dress of rose blooms. 'I still love him,' she whispered.

'We all love him,' said László. 'I'll go up and make him see sense.' He turned to go, but Kurt caught hold of his arm. Gently, László freed himself. 'I won't do anything dangerous,' he said. 'But really, who else is there?'

He went up the broad bare wooden stairs, acutely aware of them watching his back. He felt slightly ridiculous, like George Orwell on his way to shoot an elephant, but he could hardly turn around and say he had changed his mind. He would have to trust himself. He was not tired. And if he stayed with the others and Franklin blew out his brains? No. That was not an option. He would have to go on. Go in.

The door of the apartment was half open, and he hesitated,

listening for a minute, wondering whether he should call out. He put his head around the door. The hall light was still burning, and he noticed on the tiles Laurence's suede jacket where she must have dropped it in her flight. On soft feet he went past the empty kitchen (the old clock ticking in the silence) and along the passageway to the door of the studio, where he leaned his ear to the wood. At first, despite the intensity of his focus, he could discern nothing except the ebbing and flowing of his own body, and certain stray effects from the street. But then, from near by – close! close! – he heard the hushed complaint of a floorboard, and had a vision, shockingly clear, of Franklin Wylie at arm's length from him on the other side of the door, wild-eyed, the little snub pistol in his fist, waiting for the moment when the door would be opened.

László swallowed. It would be sensible now to be afraid, but what he *felt* was excitement, the need not to let the moment be squandered. He raised his fingers to the brass of the handle, and as he touched it there came, like a message flung from out of the remoteness of his boyhood, the name of the English soccer captain in the match at Wembley. Billy Wright! He almost laughed aloud at such inconsequence, but it heartened him, and he grinned fiercely at his shade in the varnish of the door panel. Three breaths, he thought. Just three more breaths. Then I'll go in and save my friend.

ACKNOWLEDGEMENTS

I owe a debt of gratitude to the following people, each of whom contributed in some way to the writing of this book. Katie Collins, who was my first encourager. Debbie Moggach, who introduced me to her Hungarian friends, in particular Sandor and Betty Reisner. Rachael Jarrett, together with Alison and Sam Guglani, whose expertise in the field of cancer care was invaluable. Adam Bohr who guided me in Budapest. Misha Glenny (courtesy of Kirsty Lang) who answered my Balkan questions. Ali 'the cat' Miller and Marcie 'po-meister' Katz in Paris. Sparkle Hayter in New York. Raina Chamberlain in San Francisco. Laurence Laluyaux in London. My parents and step-parents, who recalled on demand the Britain of the 1950s. My sister Emma, loyal to a fault. My editor, Carole Welch, who made this a better book than it could possibly have been without her. And Simon Trewin, my agent: always a good man to have in your corner. Any factual errors are, of course, the sole responsibility of the author.

Andrew Miller, London 2001